RAGNARÖK RISING

THE OMEGA PROPHECY I

NORA ASH

Illustrated by
NATASHA SNOW DESIGNS

Edited by
RJ CRAMER

ABOUT THE AUTHOR

Nora Ash writes thrilling romance and sexy paranormal fantasy.

Visit her website to learn more about her upcoming books.

WWW.NORA-ASH.COM

To Coyote. For your brilliant mind.
To Randie. For your unwavering patience
To Margarita. For your hunt for justice

1

ANNABEL

"Annabel Turner?"

I looked up from where my suitcase's wheel had managed to lodge itself in a grate just outside Keflavík International Airport. My name, as plain and American as you could get, had never sounded so sonorous before, so exotic rolling off another person's tongue. The echo of it snatched all the crisp Icelandic air right out of my lungs.

As did the man who'd spoken it. He was leaning against a trolley sign, appraising me the way a jeweler might assess the value of a rare gem. Even from a distance, I caught the silvery flash of his eyes and the way they took me apart piece by piece, twin scalpels cutting away at my clothes to better imagine my body underneath.

I'd expected to work on my thesis, delving into certain aspects of Viking history during my vacation in

Iceland—I hadn't expected to see one in the flesh. The man currently sizing me up as if he were a wolf and I his dinner was most definitely a descendent of the old Norse warriors known to inhabit this region.

I swallowed so hard I almost choked. His thick, muscular arms and the way he folded them over his wide chest, the span of his shoulders and looming height; the way his nostrils flared as he took stock of me, pupils dilated; he was most definitely an alpha.

He was also *scenting* me.

As my parents' insistence I take a vacation at their old family friends' farm in Iceland echoed at the back of my mind, I narrowed my eyes. Since the day I'd turned eighteen, they'd suggested I visit, growing more and more adamant during the past decade until they'd finally *insisted*. I'd thought they just worried about how hard I was working on my thesis, but the sight of this alpha's flared nostrils made me suspect there was an ulterior motive at play.

Such as getting their spinster daughter married off.

In past times an alpha in such peak physical condition as this man would already have an obedient omega wife by his side, and possibly a couple of kids. That was the order of things; alphas married omegas, whose sole responsibility it was to bear him offspring, while beta women—such as myself—got to pursue careers in whichever field we pleased and marry a beta of our own choosing. But that was before fertility rates plummeted some thirty years ago, and the birth of omegas became exceedingly rare. These days most alphas were all too happy to claim betas for their wives, stupidly expecting the same servitude from her as they did an omega.

And judging by this Nordic giant's wry smirk, as he looked me up and down, *someone* might have suggested I was in the market for a husband.

Dammit, Mom.

I gritted my teeth as I forced my cheeks into a polite smile. If there was one thing I had no interest in, or time for, it was overbearing alpha males. I was on track for a doctorate degree in history, despite her fervent wish that I find a husband. A wish she'd voiced since the *day* I came of age.

Apparently, she'd finally decided to make the leap from insistent nagging to international matchmaking.

"That's me," I said, forcing myself to lift my chin and hold his gaze. *Sexy Viking here may as well know from the get-go that I'm not the kind of girl to submit to alpha dominance.* "You're one of Arni and Magga's sons, I take it?" I hadn't seen any pictures, but I knew my parents' friends had three sons. And right about now I wished someone would have told me one of them was an alpha.

His lips curved from the insufferable smirk into a devious smile that made my cheeks burn. "Sure am, sweetling. They asked me to pick you up...."

He pushed off the sign he'd been resting against and stalked toward me, muscles coiling beneath his sweater. A distant primal instinct wormed its way to the surface of my brain, an animal warning that straightened my spine. This man—this *alpha*—cast a shadow tall and wide enough to engulf me that just his presence threatened to devour.

But then he stopped, offering his hand in greeting. "I'm Saga Lokisson."

"Oh. Right," I murmured, lowering my hackles as I reached out in return. Maybe I'd misjudged him. Maybe alphas in Iceland knew how to behave themselves. "Nice to meet y—"

Saga grabbed my hand and tugged me into him, plunging my face into his chest, our bodies flush. I took in a lungful of hay and wool from his sweater, pine and smoky black oud, and... something else. Something wilder, headier, that lit me up from the inside out.

As he closed his arms around me to complete our very sudden and very unnecessary hug, I shut my eyes for just a moment, trying to identify the fragrance dripping off him like spiced tupelo honey. With each new breath, the rest of my senses dulled, the din of the airport fading away until I was awash in the tide of his scent, lost to the undertow.

His chest rumbled under my cheek. At first I thought it was laughter, a chuckle at my expense, but as it rattled against his sternum, it felt more... *exciting*. My pulse quickened and my blood sang in harmony, until a throb low in my belly made me open my eyes again as reality came crashing down on me all at once.

Saga smelled like alpha, but much more potent than I'd ever encountered before. That was what had me enraptured—the sheer scent of *him* burning its way through all the others, beckoning me to remain in his arms.

Was he that in touch with his nature out here, surrounded by clean arctic air and unspoiled wilderness?

And why the hell did I care what he smelled like?

Jerking back, I stared straight up at him, a half-formed excuse for my behavior withering on my tongue when his smile widened, a little wrinkle forming above his nose. Just like that, I was back at ease, realizing that while Saga was definitely a tall, powerful alpha, he also couldn't have been much older than I was. He might have been a big Viking hunk, and apparently I hadn't gotten laid in way too long if my reaction to him was any indicator, but that didn't mean I was about to turn into a shrinking violet.

"I... like your sweater," I said lamely, stepping away from him at last. Immediately, the wind bit into my nape. I hadn't realized how warm he was keeping me.

"Uh-huh," he replied around a knowing smirk. *No,* I firmly corrected myself, *not knowing—insufferable.* As was that damn lilt in his accent.

Christ, Anna. Get a hold of yourself.

Saga eyed my luggage still stuck in the grate. "Do you need help with that?"

"I can get it," I began, loath to let him do anything that even remotely resembled saving me. But apparently, I'd mistaken his statement for a question.

With an effortless yank, he freed my bag and grabbed the other one too, lifting them as though I hadn't stuffed both to the brim with everything I'd needed for my trip. Despite my sigh, or maybe even because of it, he looked quite pleased with himself.

Awesome.

As he slung one bag his shoulder, the contents clattered and he raised a golden brow at me. "Shoes?"

I shot him a look as I smoothed out my clothes, but no matter what I did, the scent of alpha still clung to them—and now to my hands, of course. "Books, actually."

Saga chuffed through his nose, starting off ahead of me toward the parking lot. "I thought you were on vacation."

"Well—yeah," I said, struggling to keep up with his long strides, even though I wasn't the one weighted down by about a hundred pounds of luggage. "That's *half* the reason I'm here. My parents didn't tell you I'm a historian? My thesis is on the Viking settlement of Iceland, actually, so I'm planning on getting a lot of research done while I'm here."

He shrugged. "They told us you were coming. Finally. We expected you ten years ago, you know."

I snorted at his huffy tone. "You can't *seriously* be holding a grudge about that. I got accepted into an Ivy League school right out of high school! I *wanted* to backpack around Europe and meet my parents' old friends, but I had to put my education first."

Saga grunted, either unimpressed with my explanation or not paying attention. A stitch pinched my side.

"You could slow down," I suggested. "Not all of us are built like a giraffe."

"This is how I walk, sweetling," he replied as we crossed into the parking lot ahead. "Keep up, or get carried."

I scowled up at him, squinting against the sun casting a halo around his stupid blond head. "I think I'll manage."

His eyes sparkled. "Suit yourself."

True to his word, Saga didn't slow down for an instant, maintaining his "leisurely" pace all the way across the lot to where he'd parked his truck.

His *truck*. Not a car, as he'd said. Throwing my bags unceremoniously into the bed, he left me staring at the back tires. They were almost as tall as I was.

"Need a boost?" Saga asked, using his key fob to unlock the solid black behemoth he expected me to climb into the belly of. When I glared, he grinned. "There's also a step."

Coming around to the passenger's side did, in fact, reveal a step—one that was about level with the tops of my knees.

Fuck.

I opened the door, scanning the interior for a handle to help me hoist myself up, but it too was beyond my reach. "The hell is this, a car for giants?" I muttered, planting my palms on the leather seat instead.

I'd just gotten a knee up onto the step when Saga's shadow fell over me from behind.

"I gotcha," he said, and, not waiting for my response, clamped two dinner-plate sized hands tight around my hips.

I yelped when he dug his fingers into my hips and pushed me up, tossing me into the passenger seat just as nonchalantly as he had disposed of my luggage. I whipped around to stare at him, only to find myself at eye level. Good Christ, he was tall.

He wet his lips before speaking, and I absolutely hated it—that slow slide of his tongue like he was tasting my breath on his face. "Should I buckle you in too, sweetling?"

"Are you always like this?" I hissed, furious at how at ease he seemed, at how his exquisite scent thickened in the air between us when I had nowhere to hide from it. His arms blocked my exit, his body an obstacle I could never hope to surmount. God, how I hated alphas.

Another low, insistent pulse rippled through me, all the way into my tailbone this time. The muscles in my hips tightened like a cramp, only I wasn't due for my period. When I grimaced, Saga smirked.

"No," he purred. "You bring it out of me."

He shut my door and I flinched, so quickly cut off from his scent it made me dizzy. Or maybe it was the weird way my muscles were spasming. It crept into my lower back now, a sensation of stretching and thinning that made sitting like this uncomfortable, so much so that when Saga slid easily into the driver's seat, started the engine, and turned on the seat warmers, I was forced to be grateful.

"Thank you," I mumbled as he closed his door.

"Anything you want, just ask," he purred, the rasp in his throat shooting pangs through my abdomen. *Damned alpha.* But he could bait me as much as he wanted—it wouldn't get him anywhere.

I was completely in control.

2

———

ANNABEL

I stared up at the complex of buildings before me, jaw sagging and eyes wide. "You told me this was a farm."

"It *is* a farm," Saga said, parking his truck inside of a detached carport with a turf roof. "We have animals."

"You have a compound!" I replied, laughing in disbelief. "There must be... what, six, seven buildings here?"

"Eight," he corrected, then shrugged. "It's a big farm. Come. We will take your things inside."

He killed the engine and the seat warmers suffered a slow death with it. I missed them immediately, but as they waned, I found the ache in my pelvis and back had passed, and I breathed a sigh of relief. Maybe something I'd eaten on the plane hadn't agreed with me. In-flight meals weren't exactly known for their quality. Or it could have been all that time I spent sitting there.

First-class seating was pretty comfortable, but it definitely wasn't ergonomic.

Whatever the case, I got out of Saga's truck feeling way more at ease than I had when I'd climbed into it. The drive out here had taken a while, around two hours and forty-five minutes, but it was pretty pleasant in that the scenery was gorgeous and Saga didn't talk much. He was *way* less annoying when words weren't coming out of his mouth and his hands were occupied on the wheel. He was nice to look at, though, and admittedly I'd spent a good portion of our ride committing his features to memory. Maybe I'd write about him in my dissertation. Just... leaving out all the aggravating parts.

That wouldn't leave me with much material, though.

"Do you know much about your genealogy?" I asked him as I walked around the back of the truck. He was unloading my bags, the wind tearing locks of his blond hair free from his ponytail.

"Less than some, more than others." He hopped down from the bed and shut the tailgate. "Why?"

I shrugged, looking out over the hill we'd driven up to get here. The Lokissons' farm was insanely isolated, even more so than I would have expected for the Icelandic countryside. Besides grassy plains interrupted by the occasional hill or knoll, there wasn't much out this way. The landscape was breathtaking, though.

"I know a lot of Norsemen came here originally. I

was curious if your family was related to any of them. If you had some kind of history here on the island."

One corner of his mouth twitched into a lopsided smirk. "And here I thought you were interested in my pedigree. That you might want tall, blond babies someday."

I sighed, rolling my eyes as I followed him up the stone walk toward the main house. "I'll just ask Magga or Arni. Or your brothers, if any of them know."

As we rounded a bend, the earth gave way into a man-made pond. The portion of the property I'd thought was built on stilts actually sat atop an entire story comprised of floor-to-ceiling windows. Much of them sat below the level of the water, offering what must have been one hell of a view of the pond's contents.

"You have fish here?" I asked him, momentarily distracted.

"Yes," Saga answered. "But Magga and Arni are not."

I snapped my head around to stare at him. "What? Why?"

He paused, glancing at the pond, then at me. "It's heated. So they don't get cold and die."

"Not the fish!" I huffed. "Your *parents*. Where are they? I thought...."

"You thought they'd be here to guard your virtue from their big, bad alpha sons?" he teased.

Great. So they were all alphas.

This was not the first time I'd glared at him since we

met, but every time I did, it only amused him. His nostrils flared as he blew a laugh through his nose. "They'll be back. You have nothing to fear."

Something panged again—this time in my gut rather than abdomen. A whisper of a warning. Or, more likely, a warning whisper from the scrambled eggs I'd consumed on the flight a few hours ago. I forced myself to stop gnawing on my bottom lip and asked, "When?"

"Soon, Annabel," he answered, and for the second time, the way my name left his lips, so sweet and syrupy, stopped me in my tracks. "But for now, I would like to introduce you to my brothers."

"Okay. Are they as..." *Insufferable*. "...uh, *charismatic* as you?"

"They are alphas too, if that's what you're asking," he said, flinty eyes turned almost jade by the sunlight. "Don't worry—we don't bite. Much."

There were a million things I wanted to say next, many of them scathing, some of them involving only four letters. But none would come. I opened and closed my mouth several times, intending to say them all, but all I could manage was an indignant squeaking sound as heat prickled in my cheeks.

Saga regarded me for a time, an expectant eyebrow raised, but when no tirade came, he just chuckled and swaggered off toward the door. "I guess I should warn you—Bjarni is gentle with women, but if you think I'm bad, wait until you meet Grim."

Well, then.

I trudged along after him, finally muttering, "Who even names their child *Grim*?"

As he set my bags near the door to fish out his keys, Saga said, "He has had a surly disposition since he was an infant, and that has not changed."

"Awesome," I deadpanned.

He opened the door and held it for me to enter before him, the first genuinely polite thing he'd done all day. I murmured my thanks as I passed him, then immediately regretted it. He was staring at my ass so intently I could *feel* it.

My attention was diverted the moment I took in the interior of his house.

I'd seen people try to make minimalism work before. Mostly it came off as boring or sterile—white rooms with white decor and furniture and art that cost tens of thousands of dollars, but to me it usually looked like little more than a blank canvas. It was off-putting, like stepping into a spaceship or a hospital where everything good and interesting goes to die.

Saga's home was not like that at all.

Everything in the space was necessary and functional, but cast in neutrals—café latté beiges and warm grays. Much of the furniture was crafted from wood, and the enormous fireplace at the far end of the living area was made from stones that looked like they could've been plucked from the yard or a nearby riverbed. Exposed beams kept the ceilings from feeling too tall, the space too vacuous, and yet the way the shadows played near the peaks still made them feel colossal.

They had an enormous sectional near the fireplace, above which they'd mounted a TV. Even if they didn't have a private room for me here, which they clearly did, I was certain I would've been able to sleep on one of their couches just fine. They looked plush enough to swallow me whole.

"Holy crap," I said, marveling at the sheer size of it all. "It's big enough to be a bed and breakfast."

Saga smirked. "I suppose I could arrange for some room service...."

Before I could put him in his place, he stepped into the living room and gestured to the east end of the house. "That's the kitchen." He took me by the shoulders and aimed me toward the west. "There're the bedrooms and baths." Then he turned me north again, facing the enormous sliding glass doors. "And out there's the rest of the farm, and likely my brothers. Do you like sheep?"

"Sure," I said, though it must not have been with much enthusiasm, because Saga followed up with, "What about horses?"

I looked back at him. "I fucking *love* horses."

"Do you know how to ride?"

"Yeah. Will I get to?"

Saga shrugged. "We'll see what mood they're in today. Grim's the one who handles them. They're temperamental beasts, just like him."

I couldn't hold back a laugh. "You're *really* not selling me on your brother."

He led me out the sliding glass doors toward the back of the property. The earth rolled in great, heaping mounds dotted with four-legged clouds grazing or playing with one another across the verdant fields. Some of them had been recently sheared, their coats cropped so close the pink of their skin shone through. Others were way more woolly. One in particular looked like a thunderhead on the horizon, standing atop one of the hills its compatriots were ignoring. I never knew a sheep could look that angry.

"That's Slagathor," Saga said, jutting his chin at the beast. "She's a bad sheep. Won't come in for her shearing. Bjarni's been chasing after her for ages, but she gets down in the woods and he worries about chasing her too far out. Could be a fox would get her, or a wolf."

"I didn't think there were any more wolves in Iceland," I said, squinting as a shadow fell over Slagathor from behind.

"Well, there weren't for a long time," he answered, cocking his head as he noticed, too. "But they're on their way back, it would seem...."

The shadow darkened, congealing into the shape of a man. I let out a startled cry, spooking Slagathor, who tried to make a break for it down the side of the hill.

She was too late.

The man was upon her, framing Slagathor's Brillo-pad body between his huge biceps. She bleated, not in terror, but in *rage*, still attempting to mount a valiant escape with only the use of her front hooves.

"Oh, no you don't!" the man crowed, wrapping himself around her like a soldier might throw himself on a grenade. "And don't you bite me, or I'll bite you back this time, I swear it!"

Slagathor bucked, the effort tossing them both sideways. They slid down the hill together, grass and dirt bursting in the air, until finally at the foot of it, he grasped both sets of her legs in one hand each and draped her across his shoulders.

"Settle down, girl," he urged her, his booming laughter echoing across the field as he stood. "You fought well, old friend. One day, there will be a place for you in Valhalla."

I stared at the blond giant. He had the same fair hair and eyes as Saga, his ruggedly handsome features finalizing any question of their blood relations before I could ask. But somehow, he was even bigger than the man by my side, if that were even possible. Wider, at least, if not taller, and from the way he moved with the sheep draped across his massive shoulders, it was clear that every inch of him was made of pure muscle. The scruffy but soft-looking beard covering his jaw completed the image of a bear in human form.

"Bjarni," Saga said with an eyeroll, "and his girlfriend."

"I heard that," the giant called, an easy grin spreading across his face as he headed toward us,

Slagathor still securely clasped in his grip. His eyes darted first down and then up my body as he approached, but when he stopped in front of us he didn't level me with a smirk like the one Saga seemed to wear permanently.

"Annabel, I take it," he rumbled. "You're even lovelier than we imagined."

Despite his obvious flirting, his eyes held a glimmer of warmth—and just a touch of blue amid the gray, offering a softer contrast to Saga's unyielding steel.

"So you *do* know how to appreciate a female not sporting four hooves and a wooly coat?" Saga said, raising his eyebrows in mock surprise.

Slagathor shot Saga a withering look beneath the wool that had accumulated over her face. Bjarni only laughed. It seemed to come rushing up out of somewhere deep inside him, a joyful roar as golden as his hair.

"I would shake your hand, but then Slagathor would kick me," he said to me, offering me a wink. "Though I'm almost willing to let her, if it means having your hand in mine."

My heart stutter-stepped, another blush overtaking my face. I'd been flirted with before, but Saga had already knocked me off-kilter, making it harder to steel myself against Bjarni's flattery. *Damn alphas.* "Oh. Well, I...."

"She wanted to see the horses," Saga cut in, returning his hands to my shoulders in what I tried to tell myself wasn't as possessive a gesture as it felt. "Where is Grim?"

"In the stables, I think," Bjarni said, though he never looked away from my face. "Let's check, shall we?"

One thing he definitely had in common with his brother was that he didn't give me the opportunity to answer. Immediately he whistled, but it was unlike anything I'd ever heard before. It was almost like a songbird, but amplified, echoing between the buildings and over the terrain. There was something deliberate about it, a rise and fall in pitch and in the length of the notes. My stomach fluttered along with it as I watched the undulations of his throat.

At length, he paused. Silence draped over us, save for Slagathor's annoyed grunts. One of her ears twitched, and a moment later, I heard it—a sharp, melodious reply.

"That's... beautiful," I said once it faded on the wind. "What is it?"

"A language," Bjarni said. "A very old one. Used by herders and hunters to communicate over long distances."

I'd heard of a few countries where small groups of people used similar methods to relay information. In some parts of West Africa, certain people like the Yoruba whistled whole conversations. But I'd never heard of it being used in Iceland before.

It made me even more curious about the Lokisson genealogy. If this was isolated to people in their family, maybe they had a connection to a different group of settlers. Maybe I could even link it back to the Vikings as a previously unknown form of communication in their society.

A new thrill rushed through me. I might have just hit the dissertation jackpot.

"To the stables, then," Saga declared, only this time when he guided me, he placed his hand on the small of my back.

I was too excited to care. Also—there would be *horses*.

Ignoring the slight twinge crawling up my spine, I hurried to keep pace with the two alphas as they led me to the stables. To my disappointment, they were all empty—or so I thought.

As we got closer, a soft huff shattered the illusion. A stallion nearly as dark as the shadows around it tossed his mane and was answered by a low, smooth voice cooing in a whiskey rasp.

> "Sofðu, unga ástin mín
> úti regnið grætur
> Mamma geymir gullin þín
> gamla leggi og völuskrín
> Við skulum ekki vaka um dimmar
> 　　nætur...."

I stopped so hard and fast my bones rattled. I'd heard this lullaby before, but never... never like *this*. It stirred an ache in my heart, each word more mournful than the next and leaving the singer's mouth like notes plucked on a funeral harp. Clouds that hadn't been there before shrouded the sun.

> "Það er margt sem myrkrið veit
> minn er hugur þungur
> Oft ég svarta sandinn leit
> svíða grænan engireit
> Í jöklinum hljóða dauðadjúpar
> sprungur...."

Bjarni stopped too, turning to scrutinize me. "What? You don't want to see the horses?"

"It's not that," I choked, doing my best to clear the knot of emotion from my throat. "It's that song... Is that your brother singing like that? It's...."

Saga rolled his eyes. Three times, he pounded on the gate. "Grim! Stop singing about dead babies!"

The horse whinnied, followed by a curse, both of which were soon drowned in the tide of Bjarni's laughter. And just like that, the sun returned, chasing away the dismal gray that had threatened to envelop me.

"I am tending Draugr's shoes," Grim snapped, his accent thicker than that of his brothers. "The least you could do is not incite him to kick."

Saga opened the gate to let me through. "It's not our fault he's a terrible beast. The horses are your responsibility. Could have trained him better."

He tried to come through after me, but Bjarni strode in instead, coming to stand right behind me as I peeked into the stall.

The horse, Draugr, was magnificent. As the sunlight slipped in through the slats in the roof, it brought out the decadent chocolate hue of his coat, turning charcoal as it slipped into shadow. For an Icelandic horse he was surprisingly tall, cutting a strikingly handsome figure.

When he turned his head, I noticed his asymmetry for the first time. The poor thing only had one eye. The top of his mane had been styled so as to obscure it, but with each defiant toss of his head, he revealed the hollow socket.

"Jesus," I whispered, only for my view to be interrupted by a sudden opening of the door.

I stumbled backward into Bjarni, the breath knocked from my lungs by the rock wall of his chest. Instinctively, he wrapped an arm around my waist to catch me, and for a moment, the ache in my heart migrated south.

It was only my pulse pounding, and nothing more than that. Spurred by the slick slide of adrenaline through my veins, my muscles tightened, but the worst of it subsided away when Bjarni let go to grab hold of Slagathor again, who'd begun kicking fiercely.

All the Lokisson men cast formidable shadows. But the one *this* brother cast was impenetrable, and damn near terrifying. As it passed over me, I felt that same dark undertow I had back when I'd first heard him singing. For a moment, it was like his very presence blotted out all the light in the world.

Where Bjarni and Saga's hair shone like spun gold, the only thing that glimmered about Grim was the steel hoof rasp in his hand. His hair, shorn close on the sides with a little length on top, fell over his forehead on one side like a vial of spilled ink. Immediately, I thought of Draugr and his missing eye, but Grim had both—one a pale, frozen blue, the other a dim, smoldering amber.

I understood that undertow better—the sense that I was being pulled toward him, into some realm both alien and bleak—now that I'd seen those eyes. It wasn't the first time they'd held me fast in both captivation and horror. And it wasn't the first time I'd heard that song, either.

"You," I whispered over the blood crashing in my ears. "You're *real.*"

3

ANNABEL

Grim only blinked mildly at me. "Yes. I hear most people are."

I gaped. He looked so much like the man I'd been seeing in my dreams, the ones my mom referred to as my "daymares." I'd chalked it all up to stress over school, whether I'd get my doctorate, whether the university would offer me a position. But now, staring at Grim, I couldn't help but think....

What? That you're psychic? Please.

Grim looked over my head and beyond Bjarni. "They didn't say anything about her being dim."

"Says the man who spends all his free time with horses," Saga snorted, moving to push past Bjarni. "Is there one she can ride? We want her to have a pleasant stay, *remember*?" The way he emphasized the last word, I got the distinct impression there'd been some conversation about my arrival—and that perhaps Grim hadn't been fully pleased.

Bjarni interrupted the tense moment by turning abruptly, swinging Slagathor down off his shoulders and onto Saga's. "Here, hold this."

Slagathor bleated sharply, thrashing to escape. Saga had no choice but to grab onto her, or risk getting his skull kicked in.

"Ah, yes," Grim murmured as his gaze drifted over me. Compared to his brothers', there was a distinct lack of interest in his mismatched eyes. "We wouldn't want Miss Turner to be unhappy."

I cocked a brow. His rudeness had managed to cool my shock at seeing one of my daymares made flesh, reminding me that déjà vu happened to everybody. It didn't mean anything. "Unhappy?"

This time when Bjarni took me by the waist, it was with both hands. "What my brother is trying to say is that we've been looking forward to your visit and want to make sure you have a good time."

A good time my ass. Bjarni might be somewhat better at manners than both his brothers, but it was blatantly obvious what kind of "good time" he was thinking about as he pulled my back tight against his front. He was even discreetly *scenting* me, his breath hot on my scalp despite the chill in the air. Something stiff grew rapidly against the swell of my ass, poking me in the lower back.

I squirmed away, fighting back the prickle of sensation spreading all across my skin.

"Is Draugr your horse?" I asked. Grim might be rude and kind of scary, but at least he didn't seem to want any part in whatever fucked-up game his brothers had going. I was getting the unpleasant thought that they had some sort of wager going for who could bed the American girl—and I wasn't interested.

Even if they looked like Norse gods.

Not one bit.

"He is." Grim shot Bjarni a look over my shoulder, then returned his unsmiling focus to me. "You can't ride him."

"Oh, okay." I managed a light tone, despite his unfriendly demeanor. Did he have to be such a prick about it?

Saga muttered something in Icelandic, and from the tone it sounded like he was scolding Grim.

"We have so many horses, surely you can find one for the girl to ride," Bjarni said, his hand clasping lightly around my shoulder. I considered squirming away again, but that would bring me into Grim's personal space—a place I had no desire to invade.

"Ideally one that won't break her neck," Saga added.

Grim turned away from us to face the horse again. "Draugr is getting shoed. I have to finish before you can harass him."

"I would never...," I began, but Saga cut in.

"Let her pat the horse, Grim." He sighed, shifting the peeved-looking sheep still wrapped over his broad shoulders. "You should be happy she doesn't mind ugly beasts."

"He's not ugly!" I snapped, glaring at Saga for insulting the gorgeous horse.

"Maybe not *ugly,* per se," Saga said, that damned smirk pulling up one corner of his mouth. "But that sour disposition doesn't usually help him with the ladies."

Too late, I realized who he was talking about and it wasn't the horse.

"I meant Draugr," I muttered, turning my glare at the chuckling Bjarni.

"*Fine.* Hold his head still while I shoe his hind hooves then," Grim said. Despite his obvious lack of enthusiasm at my presence as he disappeared into the stall, I was thankful he didn't join in with his brothers' teasing. "You two, get that bleating ball of wool out of my stables. Draugr hates it."

I turned my back on Saga and Bjarni just as Saga lifted Slagathor off his shoulders and slung her across Bjarni's. "Go shear her before she manages to kick anyone's ribs loose. I'll make sure Grim doesn't scare our pretty guest off in the meantime."

Bjarni muttered something that sounded an awful lot like a curse, but his heavy footfall disappeared out the stables, followed by Slagathor's furious bleating.

I ignored them both, and the goosebumps spreading down my back when Saga's stare returned to my ass, and instead focused my attention on Draugr.

"Hello, pretty boy," I cooed, grabbing his harness with one hand so I still had one free to pet his muzzle. I hadn't been around horses much since I started my postgrad, my academic schedule not leaving much time to a life outside the university. Once upon a time I'd been an eager rider, and the beautiful Icelandic horses were not a small part of why I'd been looking forward to visiting.

I inhaled deeply, savoring the fresh smell of horse and hay—but wrinkled my nose when the scent of alpha hit. No matter how hard I tried to ignore them, it was impossible to escape the Lokisson sons' presence permeating every inch of the compound.

"There," Grim said, lowering Draugr's hind hoof. "He is ready to return to his friends now."

"I can lead him," I said when he reached for the reins. Too late, I realized that Grim was reaching for them too, and our fingertips brushed against each other.

His skin was so cold it chilled my skin, a sharp contrast to his brothers' alpha heat. Icy tendrils traveled up my arm, making my heart stutter in my chest.

He stared at me, capturing me with those mismatched eyes as effectively as a snake charmer.

Once when I was much younger, I'd fallen through

some thin ice. The water took my breath away, slicing through me, into my bones like a thousand knives. For a moment, my heart had stopped beating altogether. My dad was quick to pull me out, but I was sure I'd never be warm again.

Touching Grim, and the way he looked at me when I did, made me feel exactly the same—as if I were being suffocated by my body's inability to draw in breath from the shock of cold seizing it.

A distant image echoed through my mind, a glimmer from the dream I'd had of him. He'd stood over me, face twisted in rage. Hatred burning in his gaze.

I gasped and stumbled back a step, but Grim didn't stare at me with violent rage in the real world, just silent disapproval as if my mere presence were an affront to him in some way.

Grim narrowed his eyes slightly at me. "Draugr is not for you to handle. He will only follow me."

He took the reins without another word, shoulder-checking Saga on his way out the gate.

"Don't take it personally," Saga said lightly, as if he hadn't noticed the tension in the stables. "He's always a bit of a prick, especially when it comes to his precious horses. Come, let's see if he'll be able to get his head out of his ass long enough to find you a gentle one to ride."

We followed Grim out to the pen where the other horses were. It was an open, massive space, save for the fencing around the perimeter, and teeming with fine examples of the Icelandic horse breeds. They'd shed their winter coats and were all the sleeker for it, meandering about in a kaleidoscope of gray, blond, white, and russet shades.

I came right up to the fence, standing on its lowest cross section as Grim slipped Draugr free of his harness and lead. Then he opened the gate and ushered him in, locking it up once he was finished.

Draugr trotted out to meet his friends, shaking his mane and pawing at the dirt to test his new shoes. A pale mare and her dapple-gray foal glanced up at him, ears twitching. It struck me that every horse in here was much bigger than typical for the breed.

Just like Saga's truck. And their house.

"What do you use them for?" I said as Grim returned from the gate. There were so many, clearly they weren't just work horses for the farm.

"We sell them to others, mostly." He was winding the leather lead around his palm and between his fingers. "For competition riding or leisure. Sheep herding, of course. We would have used one to fetch Slagathor, if Bjarni hadn't insisted it impugned his honor."

Saga arched a sardonic brow. "Aren't you going to tell her the other reason, brother?"

Grim shrugged. "You told me not to upset her."

I climbed down off the fence, a sinking feeling settling in my gut. "It's not for glue, is it?"

"No," Saga said. "It's for eating. Horse meat is

considered a delicacy. Though the leftovers do end up at the glue factory."

I winced. It wasn't like I was so soft I couldn't handle knowing, but the thought still hurt my heart, especially as I watched the little foal trot over to the water trough with its mother. Neither of them were likely to be on the chopping block; the mare was still in her prime, and since they'd bred her, the foal had to belong to a buyer. And surely that buyer would purchase an adult horse to butcher, not a baby.

Right?

"Um... could we take some out? To ride?" I asked, wanting desperately to take my mind off the grim reality of farm life.

Grim sighed and headed back to the pen. When he returned, he was leading a docile-looking chestnut mare. She had gentle eyes underneath a thick forelock and nickered softly as he tied her to the fence.

"I can groom her," I offered, some of my gloom already disappearing at the prospect of running my fingers through her heavy mane.

"No." Grim didn't so much as look at me as he turned around and disappeared back into the stables.

"Is he always like this?" I muttered.

Saga chuckled. "More or less. Don't worry, sweet-ling. *I* am very happy you're here. And I'll keep my brother in check."

I drew in a deep breath when he slipped an arm

around me. He was pleasantly warm against my stiff body, a sharp contrast to both Grim and the Arctic air, but the intimacy of the gesture unsettled me nearly as much as his brother's mismatched eyes. The lungful of alpha scent I got when I breathed in didn't help ease the churn in my abdomen, either.

I squirmed out of his grip, and he let me, though when I shot him a glare for—yet again—grabbing me like we were in any way intimate, the amused challenge in his eyes had trepidation rising in my throat. Clearly, he wasn't planning on relenting with this little game anytime soon.

A touch of relief flickering through my chest when Grim returned, grooming tools, bridle, and saddle in arms. As much as the dark-haired brother unsettled me, I vastly preferred his presence rather than being alone with Saga for any stretch of time.

I looked away from the two brothers, studying the landscape as Grim began grooming the chestnut mare. It was so beautiful here, even if the rugged nature of the terrain had a haunting quality. The dark clouds gathering behind the hills surrounding the farm were eerie in their majesty.

Movement on a nearby ridge caught my eye, and I frowned when I saw a hunched-down figure. At first, I thought it might be Bjarni, but then the wind picked up, tossing the man's fire-red hair into the open.

I looked over my shoulder at the two Lokisson

brothers. "Do you have any farmhands around?" It would make sense, considering the size of the farm, but I hadn't seen anyone but the three brothers so far.

"No, why?" Saga raised his eyebrows in question at me, and I turned back to the ridge to point out the man watching us. But he was gone.

In his place, a dark shadow stretched along the grass, creeping down the hill toward the Lokisson farm. It was so dark and menacing every hair on my body rose at the sight, and it took me a moment to realize it was just the cloud casting its shadow on the ground as it rolled over landscape.

"That doesn't look good," Saga said, and despite his light tone I noticed the serious note in his voice. "I think we best get inside."

A few of the horses whinnied, gathering in clumps near the gate. A cool wind cut through the air, hitting my cheeks like a slap, and over its howl Grim said, "It's starting. You go—I'll settle the horses."

"What's starting?" I asked, frowning at the clouds as the wind picked up, penetrating my clothes like knives made of ice. Without meaning to, I stepped back toward Saga, seeking out his warmth to combat the chill already sinking into my bones.

"The storm," Saga said, easing his arm around my midriff again. This time I let it stay there. It felt good— like a warm anchor ensuring I wouldn't be torn to shreds by the freezing winds now tumbling off the hills.

"Come—it's going to snow any second. Trust me, you don't want to be outside when it starts."

I followed when he tugged on me to get me to follow him, away from the horse pen and Grim toward the safety of the house. "You guys get bad blizzards this late in the spring?"

"Not usually," he admitted at a rumble, "though stranger things have happened."

It was such a clear day. "Where did these clouds come from?" I said, grimacing as an unexpected cramp pulled at my abdomen. *Not this again.* I did not want to get sick in the middle of a blizzard, this far from civilization and the nearest doctor.

But it eased when Saga pressed a hand firmly against my lower stomach, engulfing it in warmth. "Precipitation. What do they teach you in American schools?"

My gratitude died somewhat at his mocking, and I shot him a glare for good measure. He didn't look down at me so he didn't notice, but that insufferable smirk was back on his lips.

Even if my random cramps turned out to be nothing more than the early onset of my period, I still didn't look forward to the risk of getting snowed in on the farm with three alphas.

Hopefully their parents would make it back before the conditions became too dangerous for travel.

The wind nipped at my nape, and I glanced over my shoulder at the ridge one last time. The redheaded figure was back. He was watching us as we neared the pond by the main house.

I blinked, trying to clear my eyes to get a better view of him, but when I opened them again he was gone, leaving only the stinging kiss of the wind on my cheek.

4

—

ANNABEL

"Father called," Saga said on his way back from the kitchen where the Lokissons kept their landline. "They won't be able to make it back while the storm's raging."

I glanced up at him from where I'd curled up on the couch after dinner, a thick woolen blanket around me. Bjarni, surprisingly an avid home cook, had produced enough food to feed an army and insisted I finish two full plates before he let me leave the table. I'd been digesting for the past two and a half hours.

"I didn't hear the phone ring," I said, the weirdly formal way Saga talked about his dad pulling me somewhat out of my food coma. That, and the prospect of being all alone with the three brothers overnight. A sliver of unease made its way past my sleepy contentment. The snow must have been several inches deep outside by now, the fierce mountain wind tapping on the sliding glass doors like an unwelcome friend seeking entry. Bjarni had lit the fireplace some time ago, but the howl of the storm made me shiver despite the warmth of the flames and the thick blanket cocooning me.

Saga didn't answer, and the sense of unease tingling at the base of my spine built.

"How long does this sort of weather usually last?" I asked as he sat down at the other end of the sofa, cool gray eyes locked on me as I fidgeted under the blanket.

"*Usually* we don't have snowstorms this late in the spring." The non-answer didn't come from Saga, and I jolted when I realized Grim was in the room. I twisted around to see he was standing by the big windows overlooking the fish pond. He had his back turned to the nook where I was curled up, seemingly lost in thought as he watched the snow tumbling down. His arms were folded across the wide expanse of his chest. The muscles beneath were so tightly wound I was worried the cords in his neck would snap.

"*Usually* it takes a couple of days tops, if it's a bad one," Saga offered, flashing me an easy smile. "Don't mind him—we're far enough north that the weather's always a bit unpredictable. You're perfectly safe, sweetling."

A couple of days. Alone, with the Lokissons. I rubbed my hands along my thighs underneath the blanket, trying to ease the tingle of awareness in my skin.

"Are you feeling all right, Annabel? You look flushed." For once, Saga didn't smirk at me, but his darkened gaze unsettled me. His pupils seemed larger than normal, something about the way he tried to suppress rolling his shoulder as he looked at me setting me on edge.

"I'm fine," I rasped, coughing to clear my throat as I fidgeted under his stare. "Just jetlagged."

Bjarni chose that moment to push open the door from the kitchen. He was like a breath of fresh air, dispersing the beginning tension in the room with his broad smile and a waft of chocolate following him. He had two large mugs of hot cocoa in his hands.

"Nothing like storm cocoa, hmm, sweetie?" His frosty eyes sparkling as he offered me a steaming mug, handle first. "Careful, it's hot."

"Thank you." I forced a smile when he sat down right next to me, not in the least worried about such concepts as personal space.

"No cocoa for me, brother?" Saga's tone was sardonic as he watched Bjarni slip underneath my blanket as if I'd invited him and casually slung an arm over the back of the sofa behind me.

"You know where the kitchen is," Bjarni rumbled, without bothering to look in his direction.

I stiffened at the alpha's uninvited closeness, but the bear of a man didn't try to touch me this time. He just leaned back by my side, stretching his long legs out on the wide chaise longue and blew into his mug.

I guess so long as he didn't start sniffing me again... I shot him a cautious side-glance before I looked into my own mug. At least two dozen tiny marshmallows bobbed on the surface of the sea of hot cocoa.

My forced smile softened.

Out of the three alphas, Bjarni made me feel the most at ease. Though earlier he'd practically mauled me in the stables, his demeanor was neither mocking like Saga's nor cold and scary like Grim's. His powerful build and the masculine scent that clung to him was all alpha, but there was an affability to him, an irreverence, as well as a consideration that bordered on tenderness.

"Thank you," I said again.

He winked at me over the rim of his mug with a smile that made the heat from the mug warming my hands travel to my abdomen, easing the tension there just a little.

We sat in comfortable quietude for a while, the roar of the storm as it beat against the windows and howled down through the chimney.

I sipped my cocoa and, at first, relished the warmth it spread through my body. But soon, the heat from it, as well as the fire and my woolen blanket became too much. I kicked off the blanket and rubbed the back of a hand over my forehead. It felt warm and damp against my dry hands.

"Is the temperature heating up again?" I asked, casting a look out the dark windows where Grim was still standing like a sentinel with his back turned.

Despite the darkness outside it was impossible to miss the flurries of snow beating against the large panes of glass.

"It won't be warm again for a very long time," Grim said, voice dark and solemn. Despite my rising body temperature, a chill traveled up my spine at the sound of it. The third Lokisson affected me in ways I didn't understand. It wasn't in the same way as his two brothers, though he was certainly every bit the rugged alpha they were. He didn't set me on edge because I thought he might get too handsy if I didn't stay on guard—far from it. No, it was that every time I was in his presence, that persistent sense of déjà vu set in, coupled with a dark sense of foreboding. A coldness, gripping my gut in a tight squeeze.

"You all right?" Bjarni asked, an eyebrow cocked as he looked at me.

I touched my mug-free hand to my face, finding it scalding to the touch. But my mind wasn't hazed or feverish, If anything, I felt... alert.

I was definitely coming down with something. "I... think I need some water," I mumbled, pushing out from our shared blanket to set the mug down.

The three of them looked at me then, even Grim, and there was a matching darkness in all their gazes I didn't understand.

They watched me stumble toward the kitchen in silence. I pushed through the door and headed for the sink. The moment I reached it, the room spun. I grimaced and closed my eyes to stop it. When I opened them again, Bjarne and Saga were on each side of me. I hadn't even heard them move.

"You need to lie down, Annabel," Saga said, the words rough on his soft lips.

"Let us take you to your room," Bjarni agreed. Even his deep voice was pitched lower than normal. He wrapped a strong hand gently but firmly around my upper arm, anchoring me like a tether made of cast iron.

"No, that's fine, I can make it there on my own," I said, swallowing thickly as my pulse sped up. Something about their presence, from the rumble in their voices to their flared nostrils and their invasion of my personal space set me on edge. But despite that, and the nagging discomfort of instincts stirred from the close proximity of two alphas, part of me... wanted them to move in closer. My abdomen cramped, ligaments pulling tightly.

I bit down on a pained groan and shook Bjarni off so I could reach for a glass. I filled it with shaking hands and downed its content in three deep gulps.

When I turned back around from the sink, both Bjarni and Saga had taut expressions on their faces, hackles raised as though they planned to move in, to force me back until I hit the refrigerator. For the briefest moment, I imagined what a rough alpha like Saga would do to me if I let myself get caught in a vulnerable position. I could almost feel the cool nip of the fridge door cracking open at his behest, only for him to slam it shut again, my hair caught in the jamb to ensure I couldn't move—that my throat was bared to him as he leaned down close to my ear and snarled.

This time, the pang from my abdomen almost doubled me over. This had to be a stomach thing, some virus I'd picked up on the way over. Didn't they say planes were basically flying cesspools?

"Let her get some rest." I hadn't noticed Grim slipping into the kitchen, but suddenly he was there, a cold darkness filling the room and calming the smolder in my blood. "She's not well."

Saga let out a frustrated snarl as the two blond men turned to their brother, finally taking their focus off me. Breathing seemed easier all of a sudden.

"We only want to help her—*remember?*" Saga said, barely containing a low growl to his chest.

"She will let you know when she needs our help," Grim said, folding his arms across his wide chest as he stared his brother down. "Let her go to bed."

Saga narrowed his eyes, but Bjarni breathed deeply through his nose and stepped away from me. "He's right. Go rest, Annabel."

I glanced from Bjarni to Saga and back to Grim, the tension between them spreading goosebumps along my skin. I wasn't entirely sure what was going on, but I got the distinct impression Grim had saved me from... something. Something I wasn't entirely sure I wanted to be saved from, yet the creeping fear up along my spine was impossible to ignore.

"Now." Grim's voice was quiet, but the ring of command was unmistakable.

"O-okay. Goodnight," I croaked. Feeling light-headed yet like lead was weighing down my abdomen, I turned and stumbled out of the kitchen, past the three tense alphas and down the hallway to my bedroom.

I'd barely made it to the door before the cramping returned with a vengeance, my muscles seizing all the way to my spine.

"Fuck," I muttered as I pushed open the door into my darkened room. Fumbling for the light switch with one hand, I managed to scramble inside and then closed the door and leaned bodily against it. Whatever the hell was wrong with me, it seemed I'd only earned a brief reprieve. Still, I was thankful for it. Better to be sick in my room than in the truck on the way here, or at the stables.

I tried to distract myself by surveying the room. I hadn't had much of a chance as I dropped off my luggage after visiting the stables, but it was kept in the same luxuriously sparse style as the rest of the Lokisson farm. Warm wood covered floors and ceiling, and the pretty lamps on the walls cast a cozy glow around the room. The dominant piece of furniture was a king sized bed with a gray sheepskin sprawled over fluffy pillow and comforters, while two doors led to the small walk-in closet and a spacious en suite.

At this time, I was mostly interested in the bed—namely how damn comfortable it looked. With a groan, I threw myself upon it, sprawling on top of the sheepskin to stare at the ceiling fan spinning cotton candy shadows onto the ceiling. Why they'd turned it on when the snowstorm was shrieking outside I didn't know, but I was grateful nonetheless.

Even with it on, it was still *hot*. It had to be the fireplace. The brothers had probably kicked on the central heating too. But it seemed to be working a little too well; my hair was sticking to my nape, errant strands of it now stiff with salt.

"Gross," I muttered, sitting up to unpack a few of my things. The moment I did, the world tilted much too fast. I laid back down as swiftly and carefully as I could. Fine, no pajamas. I'd sleep in the nude. It was too damn hot for flannel.

I tugged off my jeans, instantly soothed by the lack of thick denim clinging to my skin. My sweater came next, and then my bra, and finally my panties. I had to peel them loose; as much as I would have liked to have chalked it up to sweat, there was another layer of slickness between my thighs. An unmistakable one.

Dammit. As much as my brain hated the stunts these assholes were pulling, my body was on a different wavelength. Objectively speaking, they were an attractive bunch—Bjarni and Saga were the epitome of tall, blond, and Scandinavian, while Grim was tantalizingly... *not*. And that polarity was just as sexy as the similarities between the other two.

Not that the blond brothers weren't different. Bjarni was thicker in muscle and frame, a bear of a man with an easy grin and shockingly gentle hands. Saga was leaner, but a little taller too, with a wanting look that made me wonder if he'd ever been satisfied. If anyone could ever fit that bill.

His hands were so rough. Unlike Bjarni, nothing about Saga was gradual or accommodating. When he saw what he wanted, he took it, just like when he'd grabbed my hips as I tried to get into his truck at the airport. They'd fit so easily in his palms, and his grip had been so sure, like he was meant to hold my body, like he was meant not to fit into me, but to mold me to fit him.

I snorted at myself. Wasn't that typical of alphas? They were no give and all take, men who imagined themselves as conquerors on the lookout for new lands to plunder. In the Lokissons' case, I supposed that was even more accurate. If they truly descended from Vikings, then that was exactly how they'd ended up in Iceland—through colonization.

My fingers still lingered on my nether lips. I hadn't even realized until two of them began to play of their own accord, lightly parting and exploring the wet valley between. When I skirted my clit, I just barely stifled a gasp. It was so swollen, so sensitive, so eager to be touched.

But was that even a good idea? I'd just been feeling flushed and dizzy, and I was still so uncomfortably hot. I probably wouldn't be able to sleep, especially with the keening cries of the wind still prowling around the house. Not unless I had something to relax me.

I closed my eyes, and to my shame, the first thought that popped into my head as I dipped my fingers into my entrance was what would happen if one of them opened that door. As I dragged my fingers back up to my clit, glazing it with a little more of my silky wetness, Saga's eyes flashed in my mind. Namely, the way his pupils had blown wide when he was looking at me in the kitchen.

Oh, this was wrong. But what good fantasy wasn't? And why did it have to mean anything more than a not-so-innocent reverie about three hot guys tending to my growing desire?

I imagined the backs of my thighs over the tops of Bjarni's wide shoulders, the sensation of his grin against my pussy as he lapped at the very spot I was rubbing now in earnest. I thought of his low growl, his rippling muscles, and the warmth of his hands as he held me down with one and groped my breast with the other, thumb flicking my nipple to rapt attention.

Saga would ready me differently. He'd have me on my stomach, two of his fingers digging into my channel from the start, my cunt spread so he could watch me stretch around his knuckles. With his other hand, he'd pinch my nipple stiff and sore, tugging it relentlessly as he found the spot inside me that made me squeal into the pillows.

And Grim... what would he do? He was still such a mystery to me, cold not just to the touch, but in manner too. Maybe he wouldn't ready me at all. Maybe he'd just pull me to the edge of the bed, my hips canted at a steep angle, and open his trousers just enough to get his cock out to fuck me. Maybe the first time he touched me, it would be from the inside.

Fuck. They were huge men; their cocks had to be just as big. How would I be able to fit them? I was sure I'd never been so filled as I would be writhing on one of their shafts, mewling as they gave me every throbbing inch... and then the *knot.* I'd never taken one before, but right then... God, I wanted to know what it felt like.

Bjarni's mouth on my tits while Saga swelled to bursting inside me, lodged so deep he couldn't pull back out....

Grim watching, thick cock in his hand, stoicism broken at the sight of me taking his brother's load....

Bjarni next, his thrusts deep and almost frantic, his knot threatening to split me in two even though his entry had been eased by Saga's cum....

Grim in my mouth, throbbing and twitching, his hips giving involuntary bucks as he fucked my throat with all the violence he wished he could lavish on my pussy.

"Oh, shit!" I whined, covering my mouth with my free hand as the first clench of my muscles overtook me.

This time, it was bliss. Technicolor stars birthed and died before my closed eyes, my spine wracked with tremors as I squirmed against the frenetic ministrations of my hand. In my mind, Grim had pulled out to ram himself inside me, to let my orgasm take him the last mile to forcing his knot past my threshold and spilling against my cervix, knowing I'd be too enraptured to struggle, to try to escape.

I never had thoughts like this. Not this dark, this... twisted.

Then again, I'd never come this hard, either. I was fucking my own fingers, the bed softly creaking as I rubbed myself until the last of the climactic spasms fluttered into nothingness once more. Into a strange sort of *emptiness* I'd never experienced either.

I should have been satisfied. I should have been able to dash all thoughts of the alpha brothers out of my mind.

And yet, besides the mere suggestion of relief, what I felt was... hollow.

But for the most part, it worked. I was still hot, still sticky, still wildly uncomfortable, but my limbs were leaden and the rush of endorphins, coupled with exhaustion from my flight and all that had come after it, had lulled me closer to slumber than a few shots of whiskey could've.

Things would be better when I woke. All I needed was rest. My body was going haywire from the difference in climate, in time zone, in culture and scenery.

Plus I'd eaten more than I was used to, and different food. Bjarni's proud smile as I'd finished my second plate of dinner flickered for my mind's eye.

No. No more about the brothers tonight. Not when I was in this half-addled state. A fantasy was one thing—genuine desire another. I couldn't afford to confuse the two, because I had no doubt that the second I let my guard down the tension that'd been between us in the kitchen tonight would snap, and I probably wouldn't like what came next. Even if my still-buzzing libido currently suggested otherwise.

Hopefully, everything would calm down as soon as their parents returned to keep them in line.

I reached for the chain on the ceiling fan, forcing myself to sit up just enough to tug it. The light snuffed, and my head hit the pillow.

I woke up to the creak of my bedroom door being pushed open.

My brain kicked into high alert, even as my body was still halfway lost in sleep, I forced my eyelids open a millimeter. The only light in the room came spilling in from the crack of the door, so it had to still be night.

One of the brothers was trying to gain entry to my bedroom while I was sleeping.

I kept my breathing calm and even despite the fear sparking along my spine—and the rush of heat gathering between my thighs. I had little hope of winning a confrontation, but hopefully whoever it was, he'd have enough decency to not molest a sleeping woman. Even if hazy images of being held down and penetrated in the dark made my pulse throb heavily at the apex of my sex. *For fuck's sake, Anna, what the hell?*

"She's sleeping." The low rumble belonged to Bjarni—I could pick out his deep timbre anywhere.

"Then we talk to him now," Saga whispered from somewhere in the hallway. "She won't last much longer after she wakes up again, and Grim's still being a twat about it. If we don't all do it tomorrow, we have to wait, what, a month until the conditions are right again? He needs to get on board *now*."

"Shouldn't be too hard," Bjarni murmured. He said something else, too, but the low whisper got cut short when the door closed again, sealing me inside. Unmolested, but not at all calm.

What exactly were they planning on doing tomorrow that Grim wasn't fully on board with? That had them sneaking into my bedroom to check that I was asleep?

Despite the lingering heat between my thighs, no good images danced for my mind's eye.

You're being ridiculous, I told myself as I stared into the once-again pitch-black room. *They're family friends. They'd never hurt you.*

But they could.

I was alone with them, trapped on a remote farm in the middle of a blizzard, and their parents were God knows where.

Quietly, I slid out of bed and fumbled for my phone.

If I could talk to my parents, maybe they'd be able to calm me down. Or, if needed, get in touch with their friends so they could rein in their sons.

But even though my phone lit up brightly in my room, the dead signal quelled my plan before I could set it into motion. I wouldn't be calling anybody—not even 112, Iceland's version of 911, should I need to.

I drew in a deep breath, trying to calm my rampant imagination as chills that had nothing to do with the temperature traveled up my spine and set the hairs at my nape on end. There was no reason the three brothers would hurt me in any way. No reason at all.

But that didn't change that they'd been creeping on me while I slept, or the ominous comments about tomorrow.

Moving as quietly as I could, using only my phone's display for light, I pulled on my clothes from the day before and—ensuring the hallway was quiet—opened the door.

The hallway was dark now, the house quiet except for the storm making parts of the timber creak now and then. I took a moment to orient myself, then followed the low, flickering light from where the great room was located.

I snuck on my tiptoes, holding back my breath to not warn the brothers of my arrival, but it was for naught. No one was there, only the dying embers from the fireplace showed any sign of life.

Had they gone to bed?

Did I imagine the whole thing?

I rubbed my forehead—still hot to the touch. Even if I didn't feel sick, I was clearly running a fever. Maybe I hallucinated it?

But no matter how much I hoped for that to be the case, I knew it wasn't true. I had full use of my mind. They'd been there. They'd said those things.

Just then, a flicker of light from outside caught the corner of my eye. I turned to stare into the darkness, trying to spot where it had come from.

There! Another flicker of light, almost muted out by the thick swathes of snow still falling from the darkened sky. It seemed to come from one of the big barns by the stables. The wind tore at my hair and ripped at my face and hands as I snuck across the courtyard, doing my best not to slip and fall. My heart pounded in my throat, adrenaline souring on my tongue as I inched closer to the building still casting a soft glow of light from the cracked-open door.

Probably just Grim checking on the horses. Though if that was the case, why was he in the barn and not the stables?

When I made it to the barn, I peeked through the crack and saw stacks of hay bales but no alphas. A wave of relief swept through me—someone just left the lights on in the barn. They weren't out here, plotting….

A low murmur made my heart jump back into my throat. I bit my lip until I tasted blood, then quickly slipped in through the crack in the door and immediately sank into a low crouch.

I crawled around the bales of hay, toward the murmur of voices and the source of the light, making sure to stay out of view. Only when I could hear them clearly did I still, peeking out through a space between two bales.

All three brothers were there, gathered with an old-fashioned oil lamp in a clearing between the stacked hay, but that wasn't what had my heart drop to the pit of my stomach.

No, the knot of dread gathering in my belly was thanks to the maybe eight-feet-tall contraption the alphas were facing. It looked to be made of branches and animal bones, tied together in such a way that it vaguely resembled a creature with two arms and two legs underneath a cranium sprouting two abnormally large horns curling up above it. Red smears on the white skull looked an awful lot like someone had swiped a finger dipped in blood between its horns in what I recognized as a runic symbol.

It was an effigy.

I hadn't studied Norse mythology as diligently as I had the northern countries' early history, but I'd seen similar drawings depicted in a book before. I remembered it vividly, because it'd given me goosebumps just from the old black and white photograph.

No one had been able to prove a thesis on what such a contraption had been used for, but the book's author had theorized such effigies representing Jotunn magic, the dark counterpart to the Norse gods.

I didn't believe in black magic—of course I didn't, not even as the storm howled outside the barn, the flickering from the oil lamp casting leaping shadows that danced around the barn, seemingly bringing the effigy alive before my eyes. I was a woman of academia.

But the text that'd accompanied that picture played in my head so loudly it drowned out even the pounding of my pulse: *Assumed used for rituals based on human sacrifice.*

"There has to be another way," Grim growled as he glared up at the monstrous contraption.

"You know there isn't." Saga sighed, clearly irritated with his brother's unwillingness to go through with whatever the hell they had planned. "We've been over this again and again. She's finally here, at the last possible fucking moment. We don't have time for your bullshit."

"Then why don't you two do it? Leave me the Hel out," Grim asked, lip curled up in anger. It was mirrored in his mismatched eyes, lending his pale face an even starker appearance than usual.

"Because there's no guarantee the magic will include you, brother." This time Bjarni was the one to speak, and his tone was kinder than either one of his brothers'. "We only share blood on one side of the tree, and we're not prepared to risk your life, you stubborn mule."

"So get the fuck over yourself and focus," Saga growled. "Because we need our pretty little house guest to pop, and the Fimbulwinter is already here. This ritual for her heat has to be completed *tonight,* or we might not get another chance to claim her tomorrow."

"She has a human life back home," Grim said, turning to stare up at the effigy. "And we're about to take that away from her. For good."

"There is no other way," Bjarni said softly, clasping a large hand to his brother's shoulder.

"I know," Grim murmured. His shoulders slumped for a moment before he drew in a deep breath and straightened his spine. "Fine. Let's get on with it."

I didn't wait to watch their sick ritual, however much the historian in me would have loved to see such an ancient practice handed down through generations. I'd been right that the Lokisson genealogy had histor-ical treasures buried in their bloodline, but my acad-emic interest had vanished completely in the face of my imminent death.

They were planning to *sacrifice* me.

I had to get out of there—now. Blizzard or not, if I stayed, I'd be dead. Grim had said as much. I shook off the strange notion that he, out of all of them, had been the one reluctant to end my life, and slipped out of the barn. There wasn't time to ponder how the cold and, frankly, scary alpha had been the only one seemingly concerned with taking my life.

But as I stared wildly across the dark courtyard, I

knew I'd die if I ran into the snow-covered wilderness without any preparation. The snow was already too deep for even Saga's truck to make it through, and even if it hadn't been, it'd be easy for them to track me on the sparse roads.

Not to mention, they would hear me the second the engine kicked in.

No, I had until the morning. I needed to wrap up warm, and then I needed to plan my escape so I wouldn't die in the wilderness, or get captured and dragged back to play the unwilling sacrifice in the brothers' little horror show.

5
—

ANNABEL

The snow beat against my heated forehead despite my best efforts to hide in Draugr's thick mane, and my teeth hadn't stopped clattering since I'd passed the ridge that protected the Lokisson farm from the worst of the grueling winds howling down from the frozen glaciers.

I'd packed warmer than I'd normally dress back home—because Iceland—but I hadn't expected a full-blown snowstorm. Even my rapidly increasing fever couldn't hold off the ice from settling deep in my bones as I drove Draugr forward in a rapid trot.

The dark horse wasn't keen on our little excursion, and I had to dig my knees into his sides to ensure he didn't turn around and run straight back to the warm stable.

Back to the Lokisson brothers.

The psychopaths had *planned* this. For ten long

years they'd waited for me to finally make it to Iceland. Wherever their parents were, they had to be in on it, too. They'd tricked me, tricked my parents.

A debilitating cramp made me cuss and press a hand to my midsection, but there wasn't time to stop. Whatever illness plagued me, I had to wait to deal with it until I was safe.

I'd snuck out of the house at the crack of dawn and made my way to the stables with the small pack of food and water I'd gotten ready as soon as I'd returned from the barn last night. I'd picked Draugr despite Grim's warnings that he was a fiery mount, because I knew I needed a horse strong-willed enough to plough through the storm.

Just then, Draugr dug his hooves in, coming to an abrupt stop that tossed me forward in the saddle.

"Come on," I whimpered, but he just tossed his head with an angry whinny and pulled hard on the reins, nearly succeeding in taking control from me. Grim hadn't lied when he said Draugr wasn't an easy horse to ride. He might be a psychopathic murderer, but he wasn't a liar. *Great.*

"If you don't stop this right goddamn now, they'll catch up to us, and then I'm dead. Do you understand?" Of course he didn't understand—he was just a horse, after all. But right then, he was the only living being within a sixty-mile radius of this white-out hell I had even the smallest amount of faith in, and so I pleaded with him as if he could understand me as I drove him on.

Finally, moments before I burst into panicked tears, he took another hesitant step forward. And another. Slowly, he carried me away from the insane brothers, and I drew in a shuddering breath of relief and rubbed my knuckles gently against his neck. "Thank you."

Draugr snorted, and in my fevered mind it sounded irritated.

"I'm sorry," I mumbled, burying my face back in his mane. "I promise, if I make it out of this alive, I'll make sure you get so much prime quality hay, you'll be at risk of exploding. I—*Holy SHIT!*" My promises of gratitude died on a shriek when the blanket of white broke before my eyes, and I finally saw why Draugr had been so hesitant.

Immediately to our left was a tall cliff wall, shielding off the worst of the howling wind and whirling snow. Ahead was the narrowest of rocky paths, and to the right a sharp fall into a ravine filled with snow-clad rocks deep below. It had to be at least fifty yards down —also known as *guaranteed-broken-neck* distance.

"Omigod, oh fuck!" I pulled hard on Draugr's reins, forcing him to a full stop. It was a miracle we hadn't both fallen to our deaths. Panic souring in my throat, I cast a desperate look over my shoulder to see if there was any way we could trace our steps back, but the path was far too narrow to turn on. Draugr would have to back without being able to see where he set his hooves. It was guaranteed death.

"Fuck, fuck, *fuck!*" I tried to force my breathing to calm so I could focus, but now we were out of the icy wind, my fever was making itself known again, fogging up my thoughts. I clutched my shaking hands around Draugr's reins, not wanting my panic to transfer to my mount.

The path ahead looked even worse than the one behind us, with far more broken parts making the icy rock treacherous for any who'd dare set their feet—or hooves—there. There wasn't even enough room for me to dismount and try to lead Draugr, if I'd even be able to trust my quaking body. I looked behind me again, wondering if there was any way I could guide Draugr from his back.

"You look like you're in trouble?"

A jovial shout made me jerk and snap my head forward again. Across the ravine, on the other side where the treacherous path connected with steady ground stood a redheaded man. His lower face was shielded from the weather in a thick scruff, and his long hair danced in the wind despite the cliff shielding us from the worst of it. To me, he looked like a rugged angel.

Wild hope soared in my chest, and without meaning to, I burst into tears. I'd never been much for the damsel in distress act, but right then, there was nothing I could do to contain my relief.

"Y-yes! We're stuck!" I managed between sobs. "Please, can you help us?"

"Yeah. Just stay put. I got you, pet." He cocked his head as he took in my predicament and then climbed onto the path with easy, agile movements. Whoever he was, he was clearly very familiar with the terrain.

Despite the jagged rocks and slippery ice, he reached us within moments, and grabbed Draugr's reins.

But the horse seemed less thrilled about our rescue than I was. He tossed his head with an angry whinny, ears pointed flat backward as he snapped his teeth at the stranger.

"Whoa, fuzzy," the man rumbled, pulling back his fingers before they got chomped on. "You better behave yourself, or I'm only bringing your lady friend back to safety."

Draugr tossed his head again and stomped, making loose rocks clatter down the cliff to the ravine far below.

I yelped and clung on to his mane, but despite his less-than-friendly demeanor, I wasn't keen on leaving him behind. He'd gotten me this far, despite the blizzard, and it was my fault we were stuck out here. "Come on, Draugr. You need to let him lead you. Please be good—I don't want to die here, and neither do you."

He snorted angrily in response, making another lunge at the redhead with his teeth, but it was half-hearted. The temperamental horse seemed to understand that he was our best hope off the cliff, even if he had some weird, horsey dislike toward him.

"That's better," the man rumbled, though he kept a wary eye on Draugr as he grabbed his reins from me and pulled him over his head. "Nice and easy, now."

Slowly, feeling his way with his feet, the stranger walked backward, reins in hand, mumbling words of encouragement as Draugr reluctantly followed him. Somehow, he knew exactly where to put his feet, and how to guide the horse around the slippery traps that littered the path, but it wasn't until we got to the other side and he climbed up the short, dirt-covered ledge there that my heart finally stopped thumping uneasily in my chest.

Draugr scrambled up the ledge after him, bringing us to the top of a flat plateau. Immediately, the icy wind we'd been shielded from on the path hit against me, so powerful and dense with snow it was like being hit with a bucket of ice water.

"We need to get to shelter!" the redhead said. He had to shout to be heard over the roar of the storm.

I nodded, more than happy to let him take charge, and huddled against Draugr's mane as the stranger led us farther into the white wilderness.

I don't know how long he plowed through the mounting piles of snow, and I only looked up from Draugr's warmth when the wind abruptly stopped tearing at my flesh.

I blinked in surprise at our surroundings as he led

us past a tall cliff wall shielding what looked to be a cave opening from the storm. So he wasn't taking me to his house, then.

"It's too dangerous to stay out in the open while the storm's still raging," the man said, as if he read my thoughts. He looked at me over his shoulder. "I've got some food and firewood stashed here. We'll be safe until the weather calms."

I nodded. It wasn't exactly like I was going to be picky with accommodations if it meant not dying at the bottom of a ravine, or in the middle of the frozen wilderness. "Thank you. Thank you so much. I don't know what would have happened if you didn't show up."

He grunted, dismissing my gratitude with a shrug of one shoulder as he stopped Draugr so I could dismount. "What are you doing out here, alone in the middle of a storm? You're the Lokisson's guest, right? I'm surprised they let you out of their sight in such dangerous conditions."

Another shudder passed through me, this one not summoned by the cold. "They... I had to escape. They were planning... I think they were planning to murder me."

I knew how insane it sounded, but the redhead only pinched his lips together in a grim expression. Without commenting, he reached out and grabbed me by the hips, lifting me off the horse. The ease with which he lifted me was startling, and for the first time I looked properly at him.

He was very tall and very broad in the shoulders, about the same size of Saga, and from the width of his jaw and sharpness in his crystal green eyes, I realized that he too was an alpha. He was ruggedly handsome in that outdoorsy Scandinavian way, but I also got the distinct impression that he was as cunning and ruthless as the Lokisson brothers and most other alphas.

But so long as he wasn't a psychopathic murderer, too, I'd take my chances with him.

He seemed to be studying me, emerald eyes sliding across my features as if he was searching for something. And that's when I realized I'd seen him before.

"You were at the farm!" I blurted. "You were... watching us?"

His soft lips curved up ever so slightly at the corners. "I was."

"Why?"

He sighed and turned to the cave, resting a hand on my lower back to guide me over the rocks littering the floor in front. "Because word got around that they were bringing a lone omega to their farm. I was... concerned. They are not what you would call honorable men."

I blinked again. "An omega? But I'm a beta."

He looked at me out the corner of his eye. "A beta?"

"Yeah. Guess the rumor mill got that wrong. I hope you're not regretting risking your ass to save me now." It was meant as a joke to ease the mood, but just then another cramp hit my abdomen, and I faltered, curling in on myself with a moan.

"What's the matter?" he asked, grasping onto my shoulder to steady me.

"I'm sick," I groaned. "F-fever and cramps."

"Hmm," he said, rubbing my lower back with surprisingly nimble fingers for his size. It eased the horrid pull in my uterus and ligaments, and I sighed gratefully. "Let's get you inside."

I didn't protest when he swung me into his arms and carried me the rest of the way to the cave. The jagged opening broadened into what looked like a sixty square foot rounded cave. It was too dark to make out much other than that, but when the redhead set me down, it was onto a soft surface. I patted my hands and felt supple leather and fur under them.

He went a few steps away and knelt down, and seconds later sparks erupted in front of him, and then a flickers of orange flames illuminated his outline and made his red hair gleam. Seemed he'd thought ahead and brought a fire starter.

I looked around the cave and noticed a small pile of firewood by the far wall, and a rucksack made from what looked to be leather next to the nest of furs I was sitting on. It appeared this cave was indeed a pretty well stocked emergency shelter, if a bit rustic.

The alpha turned back around to me, an honest-to-god waterskin in one hand. Like they had in ye olden days.

Maybe he was eco-minded. A rugged Icelandic alpha who had shelters dotted around the wilderness probably cared way too much for the environment to leave plastic bottles scattered around.

"Drink," he said, holding the skin to my lips. "It will make you feel a bit better."

I hesitantly obeyed, not exactly used to having someone else hold my bottle for me. The water inside was cold and crisp, making me aware of my fever's return. It felt refreshing rather than too cold, and I drank greedily until it was nearly empty.

"Are you hungry?" he asked, a weird hoarseness to his voice that made my abdomen contract sharply.

I groaned in pain but managed to shake my head as I clutched my stomach with both hands. Just the thought of food had bile rising in my throat.

Cool hands touched first my forehead and then my chin, nudging my head up so he could catch my eyes. "Don't be afraid, Annabel. I'll take good care of you. Just let nature take its course."

I nodded mutely, finding comfort in his self-assuredness. He wasn't alarmed at my symptoms in the least, and in my vulnerable state I found myself slipping into an instinctive urge to trust the alpha with my care and protection.

He helped me ease down on my back in the furs, cool hands petting my hair and clammy skin, easing some of my discomfort.

"You know my name, but I don't know yours," I murmured groggily.

"I am Magni," he said, the roughness still evident in his voice. My abdomen panged again, but it didn't hurt this time. Not exactly. Warmth spread down low, trickling into my thighs and softening my muscles.

"Magni," I repeated, testing the foreign name as it rolled over my tongue like rich wine. That reminded me of something, and I frowned up into the cave's uneven ceiling. "You spoke English when you saw me. Not Icelandic."

"I recognized you, pet," he said. "No point speaking to a panicked female in a tongue she doesn't understand."

"But…." Something nagged at me. Something just outside the grasp of my hazed mind. Memories flickered like fever fantasies in front of my eyes. Of the Lokisson brothers talking to me. Laughing. Touching. "You don't have an accent."

"I only recently returned to this island. Not yet stayed long enough to pick up the accent."

"Oh." He looked so much like a Viking, I hadn't even considered he might not have lived here his entire life. Another pang down low stopped me from asking where he'd been living before.

Magni's hand on my forehead stilled as I groaned, his nostrils flaring.

"It won't be much longer now," he murmured, eyes roaming over my twitching body.

"What won't?" I panted, the glean in those green eyes making me twist uncomfortably as my fever seemed to move down through my body, settling like molten lava in my abdomen. He looked... hungry.

"Your heat is close," he said, soft lips curving up in smile that looked dangerous in the flickering shadows cast by the dancing flames. "And as soon as it breaks, I will make you feel all better, little omega."

6

ANNABEL

"W-what did you say?" It wasn't that I hadn't heard him—it was that his words made no sense. I'd told him I was a beta, not an omega.

His nostrils flared again as he scented me, a rough hum of pleasure at what he smelled rumbling from his throat. "You're going into heat, pet. Your first?"

The calm I'd felt at his presence evaporated into thin air as I stared at the alpha. The alpha who had me all alone in the wilderness. "I'm not an omega, Magni. I think I'd know! And this is not a heat, for Chrissake. I'm sick!"

His unnerving smile hiked a little higher as he took in my mounting panic. "So many omegas have been lost under the presumption that a lack of Presenting in puberty meant you were nothing more than betas. But I know what *you* are, Annabel. Even if you grew up never knowing your true nature. And I will not let you suffer through your first heat without an alpha to care for your needs."

I stared at him, nausea clenching my esophagus tight. Why did I keep getting stuck with insane alphas in this country? Granted, this one wasn't planning to sacrifice me to some heathen god, but Magni's intentions weren't any more comforting.

"If you rape me, you'll regret it," I said, my tight throat making it come out in a raspy whisper. I knew I didn't have a chance against him. I was woozy from my fever, and he was physically so much stronger than me. There was nowhere to escape to. If he forced himself on me, I wouldn't be able to stop him. But I would make him pay. Somehow.

Magni laughed, a rough sound that made my pelvis clench, but there was no malice in his verdant gaze when he looked at me again. "I like your fire, pet. But it is unnecessary. I won't harm you—I swear it. You have no need to fear me."

"I'm not afraid!" I lied through gritted teeth. Sweat beaded on my forehead and pulsed through my veins in languid flows, making me wish I were alone so I could strip out of my clothes. Except... I didn't want him to leave. *Something* inside of me found comfort in his presence, even though his words and obvious intentions terrified me.

Angrily, I scrubbed at my forehead with both hands,

trying to focus my scattered mind. "Why do you call me an omega, when I've told you I'm not?"

"Because you *are*, pet. Because I can smell your heat approaching." He stood in a fluid motion, rolling his shoulders as if to ease the tension in them. But all I could do was stare at the huge bulge in his pants in my line of sight. I couldn't tear my eyes from it, and the heat in my body rushed south, gathering down low in a molten ball of fire. My pulse drummed hard in every tissue in my body.

"It's why the Lokissons lured you to their farm. They knew their presence and foul magic would trigger your body to finally Present." He looked at me, and the dark seriousness on his face made me swallow thickly when the conversation I'd overheard back at the farm came back to me. What they'd said... it wasn't murder they'd planned.

"I... I heard them talking. That's why I left. I thought they were going to kill me."

Magni chuffed through his nose. "No, pet. No alpha in his right mind would end your life when you smell so sweetly. But they would have taken you, one after the other, until you were too weak to fight them."

I shuddered, even as my clit panged with the thoughts Magni's words conjured. To be taken by three brutal alphas, held down and forced to submit again and again... The hazy fantasy I'd shamefully brought myself off to the night before came back to me in vivid detail, and I shook my head angrily to get rid of it. "I don't... I don't understand what's happening to me."

"I know, Annabel." There was kindness in Magni's voice, and I clung to it like a drowning man would a lifeboat. "I know you're scared. I know you didn't expect this, that you don't know what will happen next. But I promise you, you are safe with me. All I want to do, all I *can* do, is make you feel better. Stop fighting against your body and start listening to it. It'll tell you what you need."

"It doesn't make any sense!" My protest came out as a whimper, because just then the molten lava in my abdomen melted into a liquid that drenched my panties and trickled down my thighs, soaking through my pants.

Magni's nostrils flared wide, the unmistakable hunger in his eyes intensifying.

I stared at the pool of liquid on the furs below me. Thick and clear and slick. Like the lubrication an omega produced for her alpha to ease their coupling.

"How is this possible?" I whispered, touching the soaked pelt. I didn't want to believe him, but it was getting harder and harder to refute what my body was so adamantly trying to prove to be true. *"How?"*

"The 'how' doesn't matter." Magni flexed his hands and knelt back down in front of me again. He reached for my face, and instead of flinching away, I pressed my cheek into his wonderfully cool palm. My body thrummed at the contact, and I became hyperaware of the way my tight nipples pushed against my shirt and the wet fabric pressing delicately against my swollen clit. It was too much stimulation, and at the same time not enough.

Magni drew me to him then, cradling my face against the side of his neck. I sucked in greedy lungfuls of his mouthwatering scent, and groaned when my sex expelled more of the clear liquid it wasn't supposed to be able to produce. He smelled like the wilderness, like the sky during a thunderstorm, and wild, earthy musk. He smelled like life. I pressed my nose against the side of his neck and sniffed him, shuddering for every breath.

The alpha groaned and clutched me tighter. "That's it," he rasped. "Smell me. Know me."

I needed him.

The confusion of what was happening to me, the horror and denial of knowing that I was suddenly something other than I'd thought my whole life melted away in Magni's arms, until all that was left was the bone deep knowledge that I *needed* him. My body thrummed, like a too-tightly strung violin, and I could no longer deny it. I wasn't sick. This wasn't a fever.

I was in heat.

And the only thing that would cure me, the only thing that would relieve the ache in my very blood, and return some semblance of normality to my life, was the alpha holding me so wonderfully tight against his strong body.

"Help me," I croaked against his neck. "Please. Help me."

Magni buried his face in my hair, a deep, rich growl rumbling from his throat in response. He nipped at my neck, sending tremors through my body as his hands moved down. He unzipped my coat and pushed it off my shoulders with ease, not pausing before he pulled my top off as well.

I sighed with relief at losing the constricting fabric, basking in the relative coolness of the air against my naked skin. But when Magni followed suit, shrugging out of his sweater and tunic, my focus quickly shifted.

He was broad in the chest and shoulders and narrow in the hips, but what had me staring was the definition of his brawn. He looked like a freaking *god,* all hard planes and row upon row of bulging muscles.

I whimpered without meaning to, and his soft lips quirked up in a knowing smirk. Then, he raised up and pushed down his pants, leaving his entire body bare in two smooth moves.

I stared.

His cock was flushed and veiny, with a blunt, purple head and thick rim. Precum leaked from the tip, and the musky scent of it had my tongue darting out to wet my suddenly dry lips without my conscious knowledge. But the *size* of it....

I swallowed thickly, the rational part of my mind screeching in horror even as my sex softened and my clit thrummed. "I... I don't think that'll fit."

Magni laughed again, a rich rumble that did nothing to easy my blood's heated throbbing.

"You're an omega, pet," he said, leaning in to kiss my jaw. His bulging body mercifully blocked the view of his terrifying cock, and the stab of fear I'd felt at the sight of it disappeared in the rush of excitement his lips sparked. "You were born to fuck."

I groaned unintelligibly as he pushed me down on my back, still kissing and nibbling at my jawline. Huge hands easily unsnapped my bra, and I pushed up against his touch as he cupped my breasts. My nipples scratched against his rough palms, sending shocks of pleasure to my clit.

"More!" I didn't mean to snap, but it came out like an angry growl.

Magni chuckled against my jaw and pushed his hands farther down. When he reached the button of my pants his lips moved to my left nipple. I groaned as he sucked it into the hot cavern of his mouth, and again when he undid my trousers and shoved a hand between my legs. Without preamble, he found my tight clit and rubbed it just right—and I *melted*.

Slick gushed from my pussy in hot rivulets as electric zings of pleasure danced up my spine and down my thighs.

I whimpered and moaned and bucked underneath him, mindless that my writhing made his ministrations harder. Everything from my hazed mind to my pulsing body *sang* with pure, unadulterated pleasure, but all it did was make the ache between my legs grow to a roaring hunger.

"Magni, more! Give me fucking *more!*" I snarled and tore at his shoulders with my nails, tried to force from him what I instinctively knew he was withholding, even if I didn't fully understand *what* it was. I just knew that I needed *more*—more of him, more of his body, until the burning ache was finally quelled. I was dying. I was fucking *dying*, and he was the only cure.

"*Now!*"

Magni growled, pinching my clit harshly until my snarling died to a pathetic whimper. But as much as it hurt, it eased my body's desperation just a little.

"I'm your first alpha," he said, voice rough with his own blatant desire. "I have to prepare you, or it'll hurt."

"I don't care!" I hissed. "God, make it fucking hurt! Just make it stop! Please, make it stop!"

He stared down at me for a moment, lip curled up in a silent snarl, and for the first time I realized what it'd taken for him to hold back so far. His face was drawn with tension, eyes wild with dark lust, and his broad shoulders trembled with restrain. He wanted this as badly as I did, needed it just as much, and yet he'd held himself back to ensure my readiness.

I felt a pang of gratitude somewhere deep in the fog of my mind, then instincts swarmed my brain, blotting out everything but bone-deep need for relief. I bared my teeth at him and dug my nails into his shoulders, deep enough to draw blood. "*Fuck. Me!*"

The alpha snarled, fury flashing in his green eyes. He grabbed me by the hips and flipped me over rough enough that I didn't have time to brace. Hands yanked at my trousers and panties, pulling them down my thighs to pool around my knees.

I struggled against the sudden aggression, fighting him even as my legs spread as wide as my trousers would allow, pushing my ass up and out in invitation.

Magni growled, yanking hard on my hips again until I was facedown ass-up in front of him.

Electric currents ricocheted through my blood, my heart hammering in my chest as my pussy softened and gushed in instinctive response to the submissive position. *Yes,* this was right, this was how it was meant to be—

Hard flesh pressed against my weeping opening, and I gasped hard at the feel of his blunt cockhead catching in the mouth of my pussy. He was so thick, my entrance resisted the intrusion despite how wet and open I was, but I *needed* him! I gritted my teeth and pushed back against him.

The tips of his cock shoved through my resistance, kissing my pink inners, but my relieved moan died on a shriek as hot pain bloomed from my overstretched flesh.

"*Ow!* Fuck! Wait!" I slapped my hands against the pelt beneath me, caught between wanting to escape the brutal stretch and knowing I needed him all the way inside to ever quell the desperate yearning.

Magni made the decision for me.

Large hands clamped around my hips, stopping my tormented bucking. And then he drove home.

I *screamed,* unable to form words as my pussy was wrenched open much too wide and all the way to my very core. His heavy balls slapped against my wide-splayed lips and forcefully bared clit before he stilled, mercifully allowing my body a moment to adjust.

I was no virgin, but nothing and no one had ever made me feel like *this*—so completely conquered, so *invaded.* It hurt so goddamn much I struggled to breathe, but at the same time, this was exactly what my body needed. My blood sang with relief even as my poor sex spasmed and drooled in its futile attempt at expelling the brutal cock lodged all the way up to my womb. For every shuddering breath I felt his thick cockhead kiss my pulsing cervix, an unyielding reminder of what lay ahead.

Magni moaned brokenly behind me, his ragged breath panting against the back of my neck as he leaned in over my shaking body, encapsulating me from the inside out. I could *feel* his pleasure as a physical manifestation, could hear it in his strained voice. There was no pain for him.

White-hot fury at the injustice of it penetrated my hazy mind.

Snarling like a wild beast I turned to rake my nails at whatever exposed skin I could get to, but Magni was faster. He clamped a hand around the back of my neck and forced my head back down into the furs. He let out a furious growl, an alpha's anger at being challenged, and then he showed me exactly who was in charge.

The first thrust through my painfully dilated pussy made me screech, hands flailing back to press against his rock-hard abs in a desperate attempt to ease the brutal penetration. I may as well have tried to resist a mountain.

He barreled into me with all his might, filling me to the brim in rough, fast thrusts over and over and over again. It hurt so much, white dots danced for my vision every time my pussy was forced open all the way up, but the wet, lewd squelches when he bottomed out in me betrayed the *other* part. Because even through my wails of agony and the stream of tears wetting my cheeks, there was no denying the mind-numbing pleasure rocking through my pelvis as he fucked me with everything he had. In his size and in his ruthlessness, even in the forced position of submission he had me in with his hand clamped around the back of my neck, something deep in the very core of my being found exactly what I'd needed for so long.

I was born for this—born to take every inch this brutal alpha, until the burning *need* that'd taken over my very being would finally be quelled. Mind-numbing pleasure mixed with pain for every thrust, until I could no longer tell them apart. My world consisted of nothing but the deepest of burns pulsing through the bones of my pelvis, driving me closer and closer toward a peak I didn't know if my mind could take without shattering.

Magni didn't give me any choice. He drove me toward that cliff with relentless brutality, pushing me closer and closer to the edge of insanity as he fucked me so hard and fast I could no longer tell where I ended and he began. I clawed at the furs underneath us to free myself from the brutal fucking, begging and pleading for mercy even as every muscle in my body ached for the release my instincts told me was coming. He didn't listen, his own groans of pleasure a constant rumble underlining my pained wails and the wet *thwacks* his hips drummed against my upturned ass, his hand keeping me pinned beneath him with no way to escape.

And then, it happened.

Without warning, every muscle in my body locked up tight, and I *came*.

I tumbled over the cliff and into a black void of madness as my pussy pulsed and quivered on his hard length, ecstasy stabbing through my pelvis, up my spine and down my thighs in hard, rhythmic jolts. I lost all sense of time, all understanding of reality as pleasure so intense stole my senses away ravaged my body and broke my mind.

But he was there with me. He pulled me up against him, molding my fitfully spasming body against his as he wrapped his arms around my waist and clutched me to him. Fucked me through the torment and bliss, and held me so tight I knew he would never, ever let me go. I came and I sobbed and I rode his unyielding cock through it all, until finally, several eternities later, my climax ebbed.

I sagged in Magni's arms, still sobbing and heaving for breath. Raw to the very depths of my soul. But I'd forgotten what came next—what it meant to submit to an alpha.

A hard stretch at my already gaping opening made me whimper and look down to where we were still connected, and the sight made a stab of panic snake its way through my numbed-out bliss.

The bottom of his cock was swelling fast, its expanding girth forcing my tormented flesh to stretch as he tried to force it into my swollen sex.

His knot. He was going to *knot* me!

"No! No, no, *no-oow! Fuck!*" I wailed in agony as he finally pushed through my body's desperate resistance, the thick knot popping inside of me, forcing my pelvis to yawn open as he seated it smoothly behind my pelvic bone.

Blinding pain pulsed through my sex for every frantic beat of my heart as I thrashed and fought to escape, but he was having none of it. With a growl that rattled my bones he clamped his teeth down where my right shoulder met my neck. Teeth pierced my skin, and hot pain lanced through the fresh wound, drowning out the agony from my gaping pussy.

I mewled, every muscle in my body going lax despite my brain screaming at me to get away.

But it was too late.

Magni moaned against my shoulder, hot spurts of his seeds coating my cervix as he bit down viciously on my shoulder, ensuring his Mate Claim would forever be carved into my flesh.

7

SAGA

They say hell hath no fury like a woman scorned, but I begged to differ—Hel hath no fury like an alpha forced to chase down an uppity little omega in the middle of a snowstorm.

And not just any snowstorm, either. This was the beginning of the Fimbulwinter, a herald of Ragnarök. I hadn't planned on seeing it come to pass—the way Arni and Magga had told it, the girl would be a sure thing from the start—but I should have known better, really. Modern women were pains in the ass. How long had it taken *madam* to get her sweet behind to Iceland? Oh, just a fucking decade!

Her parents had hemmed and hawed, unwilling to send their daughter to us even though the goddamn contract was binding. A thousand years it'd been since Arni and Magga secured an oath from the family fore-seen to produce an omega who would secure the survival of the bloodline who claimed her. A thousand years, and with Ragnarök—the *literal* end of the goddamn world—finally on our doorstep, the key to our very existence was too fucking busy *getting an education* and *discovering herself* to get on a plane and do her duty.

It was only when the signs of the end were finally indisputable that they caved and sent her to us. And what was the result of this long wait? Oh, just a stubborn and willful woman who didn't even realize she was an omega.

It was another sign of Ragnarök's coming—the lack of Presenting omegas. Normally, an omega would Present shortly after hitting puberty, but the shift in the fabric of the world had dampened the strength of most human alphas. With less powerful pheromones surrounding the young females, few had the biological push their bodies needed to Present. And so, they lived their lives in ignorance of their true nature, believing themselves to be betas.

Until they met an alpha strong enough to awaken them.

Despite the cold and my sizzling anger, my cock gave an achy spasm at the memory of Annabel's beautiful scent. She'd blossomed the moment we touched, like a flower eagerly stretching toward its first meeting with the sun. And she hadn't known.

It'd been perfect. The plan had been to isolate her on the farm, inducing her first heat as swiftly as possible so we could all claim her and secure our bloodline before Ragnarök truly gripped the world. Had she come to us ten years ago we could have eased her into it, but now there was no time. We'd even resorted to planting a fertility idol under her bed to hurry things along, and she'd found it.

I didn't know what she thought it was, knew she hadn't been raised with the knowledge of magic existing, but it'd apparently been enough to scare her into the wilderness. Into the grips of the fucking Fimbulwinter.

"You should've just been upfront with her," Grim said as we followed her tracks through the forest. "I told you as much, but you insisted it'd be easier if we trick her. Does this seem easier, brother?"

"I didn't say that," I snapped, stepping over a massive tree root half-concealed in snow. "And it beats Bjarni's idea by a country mile."

Bjarni shrugged. "I still think you should've said something to her in the car on the way over."

I snorted. "Like *what*, pray tell? That she's destined for our dicks? That we're the outcast spawn of Loki himself? Oh, and that by the way, the Norse myths are true—gods *do* exist. Welcome to Iceland! Or should I just have stopped with offering her a front-row seat to Armageddon?"

"There was no easy way to break it to her," Grim muttered. I side-eyed him; we so rarely agreed. "Still,

I'm sure we can agree chasing her through a snowstorm isn't the *best*—"

A wail carried on the back of the wind sliced through me to the bone. Grim halted, head cocked, listening. Bjarni sniffed, then glanced at me.

I waited. It could have been another bluster from the mountains, but it had sounded so... human. Like a woman in pain.

Like *our* woman.

It came again, a high-pitched keening that had me bursting through the foliage without waiting for further confirmation. That was Annabel. I knew it, could feel it in my bones. And regardless of what a problem she was turning out to be, I couldn't let any harm come to her. We *needed* her.

Not far ahead, partially obscured by half-frozen trees, a cave mouth came into view. A million possibilities came to mind—that the girl had pissed off a stray polar bear, or perhaps she'd fallen and broken an ankle.....

"That's Draugr," Grim breathed, indicating the black horse shaking snow from its mane near the entrance.

Another shriek, and I crossed the distance to the cave, prepared to take on anything, save for what I actually saw.

Oh, Annabel was there, all right. Naked, and hardly alone. In fact, she was on her hands and knees beneath a demi-god, that redheaded bastard Magni. Thor's illegitimate son.

The only sign of an injury on Annabel was the fierce bite mark marring one side of her nape. Heat flared in my chest, rising into my throat and face. Not only had Magni been fucking our omega, but he'd put a goddamn *claiming mark* on her as well.

"For fuck's sakes," Bjarni murmured beside me.

Magni glanced up, cocking a russet brow. His bloody lips tilted in an insufferable grin. "A bit late, aren't you? Then again, you lot were always slow on the uptake."

"What did you *do?*" Annabel wailed before I could wring his neck. She touched her nape, winced, and stared at the blood on her fingers. The speed with which she whipped around to face him almost gave me secondhand whiplash. "How could you?"

"I claimed you," Magni said coolly. Though he'd clearly filled her with his seed already, he rocked his hips, grinding his knot against her g-spot in a move I knew far too well. "Don't look at me like that. These assholes were going to do the same thing, only now I've ensured you'll bear the children of proper gods and not these..." A vague gesture in our direction. "...trolls."

"Trolls?" Bjarni growled, at the same time as Annabel snarled, "*Gods?* How full of yourself are you?"

"And this from the bastard offspring of a Jotunn whore and a god too dumb to drown the miserable result at birth," Grim said, suddenly appearing behind me. Though he'd barely shown an interest in the girl, both shades of his eyes had darkened in instinctive fury. "If we are *trolls*, does that make your father a troll-fucker?"

Despite the anger sparking in Magni's green eyes at Grim's taunt, he flashed his teeth in a grin. "Doesn't matter, does it? Jotunn-fucker or not, thanks to me his bloodline will survive. Not Loki's. The omega belongs to me now, and there's nothing you can do to—"

His voice was drowned out by a loud *thud* when Annabel kicked back, hitting him across the knee.

"I don't belong to anyone, you sick bastard! Get the fuck off me!" she hissed, trying to scramble away from him. Only she was still stuck on his knot, so all she managed to do was hurt herself as the thick swelling pulled savagely on her flushed opening. She stilled with a cry, legs shaking. "Get off me!" It was more of a whimper this time.

Magni worked his jaw, rubbing the flushed part of his face where she'd smacked him. From the flush of his skin, she got him good. Anger flashed in his eyes again, and I tensed, ready to stop him if he tried to retaliate. But when he grabbed her hips, it was with surprising gentleness.

"Stop struggling—you'll hurt yourself," he growled. "We're alphas. And you're an omega. We were *meant* to breed. I'm guessing those imbeciles didn't tell you *why* they were planning on gangbanging you, but the Fimbulwinter is here. And after that, Ragnarök will be upon us. And you—you're the only way I can save my bloodline. They were gonna keep you for themselves, they were gonna let every god *die,* save their cursed father. This is your destiny, Annabel. *I* am your destiny. I will fill your sweet little cunt with my seed, and you will bear me sons who will see us prevail."

"You're insane!" Annabel sobbed. She was shaking underneath him, and it took everything I had not to launch myself at that redheaded twat who thought he could claim *our* woman and fill her head with lies. But he was still stuck inside her, and if we attacked while they were tied, she would get hurt, too.

I clenched my fists as I glared at our rival. "She was never meant to be yours, mongrel. Her family has sworn her to us, a millennium ago, when the Norns first foresaw her birth. If your precious fucking dad had half a brain he'd have gotten in on her before Loki did, but he didn't. And she belongs to *us.* So get your cock out of *our* omega and prepare to pay for your trespassing!"

"Fucking finally," Bjarni muttered by my side, cracking his knuckles as he stared at Magni. He'd never been one for talk when a fight could solve an issue.

Magni's lip pulled up in a silent snarl at the threat. He might be a superior asshole thanks to his ill-gotten pedigree, but he'd inherited his father's infamous temper and zest for battle all the same. He reached down between himself and Annabel, wrapped his hand around the part of his cock and knot still sticking out of her, and squeezed. It only took a moment for his knot to shrink sufficiently, possibly in thanks to the presence of three enemies.

He pulled his still-swollen but visibly softer knot from Annabel's straining lips, ripping a hoarse cry from her throat as his glistening wet cock slid out of her gaping pussy. She was flushed and swollen, and a stream of white semen trickled out of her puffy entrance.

The sight of a rival alpha's seed in my omega made a red haze of fury cloud my vision. He'd not only claimed her—he'd done his best to *breed* her.

"You are going to die for this, son of Thor," Grim hissed.

Bjarni was the first in, colliding with the redheaded bastard just as he got to his feet.

Annabel squealed and scrambled away just as Grim and I joined the fray.

Magni put up a good fight, his fists, elbows, knees, and feet falling like hammers. But, Thor's son or not, he was outnumbered. This wasn't going to end well for him—I'd make sure of it. Too long we'd been shunned by the other gods, living as outcasts, banished to the human world for accusations leveled against our father. And now this half-breed came to *our* territory, to claim *our* omega? Oh, he was going to regret the day he slid from his mother's cunt.

Bjarni grabbed Magni's face, using it to turn the bastard around and away from Annabel. Magni snarled and swung at my brother, but Grim blocked his attack and kicked him in the gut, sending him flying out the cave opening.

I was just about to follow my brothers after him, when movement out the corner of my eye grabbed my attention. Annabel was huddled up in a corner of the cave, her trembling hands pressed against her abdomen. A wave of worry cooled my battle lust, and I turned fully toward her.

"Annabel—" My question died on my tongue when she groaned hoarsely, pretty face scrunching up as if she were in pain. But I recognized that groan on an instinctive level, and it had little to do with hurt.

My entire focus shifted toward the little omega huddled and naked in the corner, the sounds of fighting muting to nothing as my senses bloomed for her and her alone. Every small whimper she made, every gasped breath panged down my spine and straight to my cock. She was still in heat.

Magni may have knotted and seeded her, even claimed her, but she wasn't sated yet. She still needed an alpha to care for her.

She needed *me*.

"Annabel," I cooed, crossing the floor so I could crouch down in front of her and push the strands of hair clinging to her sweaty forehead away. "It's all right, sweetling. I'll take care of you now."

"Back the fuck off!" she hissed, flashing her teeth at me.

I arched an eyebrow at her combativeness. She

smelled as ripe as a peach, even the scent of Magni's seed dripping from her swollen opening not potent enough to dampen the ache in my cock every breath caused me. But Annabel wasn't the gentlest of women at the best of times—and right now she was undoubtedly confused, angry, and scared at what'd happened to her. What *we'd* let happen to her. Fucking Grim—if he hadn't told us to wait, we'd have fucked her when the first signs of her heat showed, instead of sending her off to bed to suffer alone until it broke fully. If we'd taken her then, despite her protests, none of this would have happened, and she'd have been home safe on the farm where she belonged. Without Magni's cursed mark brandished on her slender neck. But I could save this— she was still in heat, which meant I had a shot at claiming her.

"You don't want me to back off," I purred, unable to fight back a smirk when her eyelids fluttered at the sound and a wanton moan escaped her pink lips. "You want my cock inside you—and I'm gonna give it to you."

"No," she whispered, but she leaned toward me when I dipped my mouth to hover just above hers. "Saga, please... I don't...."

I swallowed her protest in a searing kiss, groaning with her as our tongues danced. She pawed at my shoulders, maybe to push me away at first, but when I deepened our kiss she clutched at my clothes. Surrendering like the perfect little omega I'd known her to be since our first meeting, despite all the independent beta facade she'd been hiding behind.

She was everything I'd thought she'd be, and so much more. I'd fucked omegas before, rare as they may be, but the scent of Annabel's heat, her desperate whimpers as I forced her on her back—nothing I'd experienced could ever compare. She *sang* to me, her very essence calling to the core of my being, bringing out every alpha instinct as if she were playing me like a fiddle.

I kissed her fervently, biting her throat, her shoulder, her breasts as I made my way down her body. For every brush of my lips over her molten skin, for every breathy moan she gasped into the cool air surrounding us, I lost more and more of myself to the rut.

When I finally reached her pussy and flicked my tongue over her clit, we groaned together. I shuddered in an eager breath, scenting my omega deeply. And was hit with the potent smell of my enemy's seed still dripping from her swollen opening.

Fiery rage flicked a switch in my brain and rushed through my veins, fueling my need for her to heights I hadn't known possible. He'd been in her, he'd taken what was *mine*.

My omega, the girl who'd been promised to my father's lineage for a thousand years, taken and soiled by Thor's bastard son.

I pulled back far enough to undo my pants and pull

out my achingly hard cock, blind with yearning to replace his markings with my own.

Annabel sucked in a sharp breath underneath me when I pressed the head of my cock up through her sodden folds, no doubt sore from her first mating, but I was far too deep in my rut to care. She'd welcomed my enemy into her body—she'd welcome me as well.

I thrust in deep, her still-gaping cunt and Magni's seed easing the slide all the way to her womb.

My omega *shrieked,* her worn pussy clutching me tight as she clawed desperately at my chest, trying to get away even as her heat made her cant her hips up for more. "Saga! Fuck, y-you're too big! *Ow*—Oh, my *God!*"

The fuck I was too big. "You were built to take me," I hissed, giving her a hard thrust as punishment when she tried to push me away. "So *take* me!"

That delicious little cunt of hers fluttered and clamped down hard, trying to simultaneously stop my assault on her most sacred depths and suck me in deeper.

"*Fuck!*" she cried again, when my thick cock stretched her all the way to her cervix in another punishing thrust. Fury mixed with the pain and ecstasy already playing across her pretty features, and she raked her nails at my face, trying to get at my eyes.

I snarled a warning to submit, but it was my own fucking fault—reluctant omegas got rutted on all fours for a reason. Hormones made them combative as fuck, and Annabel was already a feisty little thing. But I'd wanted to see her face when she took me, needed the visual of her inevitable submission more than I needed air. She'd let Magni rut her through the first part of her heat because we hadn't been here to take care of her—but she belonged to *us*. And when I was done with her, she'd never question it again.

Annabel swiped at me again, and I yanked her hips toward me, pulling her all the way down on my thick cock before I slung her legs over my arms and leaned forward, trapping her underneath me.

She howled at the brutal penetration and struggled to simultaneously scratch at my arms through my clothes in retaliation and save her sweet little pussy from the painful stretch. But I had her exactly where I wanted her now—helpless on her back underneath me, and there was nothing she could do to stop me from staking my claim.

"Fuck yes, take it just like that," I groaned, when my cock barreled in to the hilt once more, and her tight, slick inners gripped me. Her walls fluttered around me, sucking me in deep in rhythmic pulses. *She* might not want me inside her, but her body did.

"You fucking bastard," she hissed, but the animosity was draining from her hoarse voice as desperate need took over. "Don't—don't stop!"

As if any force in the universe was great enough to stop me now, even if I'd wanted to.

I put all my weight into the next thrust, and Annabel keened shrilly in response. But instead of fighting me, she tossed her head back in the furs, her dark hair fanning out like a matted crown around her. Displaying her vulnerable neck to me as she finally surrendered.

Electric ecstasy crackled up my spine and down my thighs, my mind going blank as every last thought disappeared into nothingness. There was nothing but *her*, the omega I was going to *take* until her tight cunt had milked every last drop of semen from my balls.

I fucked her with everything I had, pounding her squelching pussy rough, deep, and fast while she wailed and thrashed and *came*. She felt like nothing I'd ever experienced before, clamping down on my dick like a vise as she rode her climax out, shaking with the intensity of it.

I never wanted to stop fucking her, wanting to feel her milk me until the day I drew my last breath, but the pleasure of her tight heat was too much to withstand.

Before she came down from her climax, my knot grew hard and fast.

I gritted out a curse and pushed my hips forward, the swelling on my cock already too thick to enter her easily.

Annabel's beautiful eyes popped wide open, her face twisting from intense pleasure to agony. "Saga—! No! No, no, *no!*" Her whine of denial rose to a high-pitched shriek when I forced her all the way down on my cock. My already hard knot popped through her straining lips, and I seated it behind her pelvic bone with a groan of bone-shattering relief.

The first thunderclap of ecstasy rolled through me with brilliant, blinding violence. I'd never come so hard or so much in all my life. I could just barely move my hips; she was stuck on me, and no amount of her thrashing now would matter as I pumped everything I had into her waiting channel. She scratched at my chest, dug her nails into my coat, howling with equal amounts pain and pleasure as my thick knot wrung another orgasm from her trembling body.

I let her claw me, because the bite of her nails through my clothes only underscored how completely her little pussy belonged to me now.

And so would the rest of her.

I picked her up, sitting back on my heels and hauling her onto the tops of my thighs. She squealed at the sudden change in position, but my knot held her fast as I shoved her hair away from the unmarked side of her neck, grasping a fistful by the roots to make her bare more of her flesh to me.

A single world rippled through my throat in a growl beside her ear. *"Mine."*

And then I sank my teeth into her, curled around her to place my mark opposite Magni's.

Annabel let out a hollow sob, her nails finally stilling against my chest as I bit down on her neck. From the gasps against my skin and her pussy's tight spasms on my knot I knew she was coming again, driven over the edge by my claim. The self-assured beta historian I'd picked up at the airport finally transformed to the knot-drunk little omega I'd known she was all along.

"Goddamn you," she moaned, panting through her climax. "Goddamn you, you bastard...."

I chuckled, meaning to pull away and relish the look of reluctant acceptance I knew was painted all over her face, to revel in my triumph over her empty protests and Magni's attempt to claim our future as his own. But all I could do, all I *wanted* to do, was hold her tight against my chest and breathe in the scent of our union and the blood trickling from her new claiming mark. *My* claiming mark.

A rumble in my chest made me blink, the sound unbidden, the soothing effect it had on Annabel even more unexpected than its appearance. And yet as I held her in my arms, purring for her, clutching her tiny body against mine, I couldn't stop making it. All I could think about was how perfectly she slotted into all the empty spaces of me, like a missing puzzle piece.

How I never wanted to let her go.

8

MAGNI

My face was definitely not a fan of Bjarni's fist. Loki may not have been a god of war, but the biggest of his sons sure had hands like one.

And the Jotunn fucks had me at a disadvantage, what with me being buck naked and still weak at the knees from the hardest release I'd ever had. Fucking an omega was always a treat, but I hadn't been prepared for how completely Annabel's sweet cunt had drained me with its fluttering squeezes on my knot. It was almost like her pretty little pussy had sucked part of my life essence right out of my dick, leaving me dazed as I fought the idiot alphas who'd tried and failed to claim her for their own lineage.

Annabel might not understand the full picture, but that didn't matter. I hadn't claimed her for her sake, though she should be grateful she'd be carrying mine and my brother's offspring rather than theirs. I'd claimed her because I needed her. Because my family needed her.

I knew why Loki's sons were fighting so fiercely—without her they were doomed. Too bad I didn't give a flying fuck about them or their treacherous father.

"Give up, you've fucking lost!" I snarled, as Bjarni planted a fist in my shoulder. It would have been my jaw, but I managed to twist my body just in time to avoid losing a few teeth. My growls died on a hiss as Grim's fist jabbed into my kidney, rocking me off balance. Where Bjarni was brute strength, Grim was agile, darting in to occupy all the spaces Bjarni didn't, clever gaze always seeking out weaknesses, quick jabs or knees to soft places working to exploit them, often for Bjarni's benefit. Every time Grim knocked me off balance, his bear of a brother would go in for the kill. It was fucking infuriating.

And that smug bastard, Saga—

Wait... where *was* Saga?

I grabbed Bjarni's fist on his next punch, crushing his knuckles in my grasp before shoving him aside to get a look past him. Annabel was close to where I'd left her, still coming to terms with having been mated... but Saga was there with her, holding her, her face buried in his golden locks.

She was naked. His trousers were partway down.

And he was still seated inside her.

The dazed feeling in my body and brain washed away, replaced by a white-hot tendril of electric rage. My veins illuminated with its power, sparks dancing in front of my eyes as I strode toward them. Grim lunged, but a sizzling shock to his chest sent him on his ass, stunned and gasping.

Bjarni came next, barreling at me from behind, but stealth wasn't his strong suit. Thunder rattled my bones, followed by a streak of lightning that shot from my fingertips and ricocheted of the cave wall back into him. It took him off his feet, launching him into the shadows. I'd never been able to channel my magic quite like this before—but then, I'd never been this fucking furious in my entire existence.

Annabel looked up from where she was panting into Saga's shoulder, her eyes wide. She struggled to scramble off and away from me, but she couldn't disengage; the other alpha was buried deep, his knot stretching her wide. A fresh bite mark marred the opposite side where I'd placed mine.

He'd claimed her. Of-fucking-course he had. I could feel him now where once I'd only felt her, could feel the ache of his heart as it opened to her for the very first time.

I had no patience for it. Or mercy.

Saga turned just as Annabel yelped. I clamped my electrified fingers around the back of his neck and he seized, curving back so hard I thought his spine would break. His knot disappeared instantly, letting the girl clamber off him as though burned.

"Jesus *Christ*," she hissed, quaking with literal aftershocks. "What... what *are* you?"

"I am the god Magni," I said. "Son of Thor and Járnsaxa, brother to Módi the Brave. My name means Great. And I am your *alpha*."

"You're a great fucking liar," Bjarni snarled from the ground as he tried to claw his way toward us. "You're only half a god, same as the rest of us."

Annabel's eyes widened. "The... the rest of you?"

"Yes." I sneered, stepping past Saga's twitching body. "They're filthy spawn of Loki. Not all gods are worthy of the sacred halls of Valhalla."

She gaped at me, shaking her head. "No, that's not...." Then she set her jaw more firmly. Defiantly. "That's *not* possible."

I had no time for her existential crisis. Modern humans had long forgotten the Nordic gods, had forgotten about magic and the glory of Asgard. They lived their pitiful lives in ignorance, and not a single one of them understood that their end as a species was drawing near. That Ragnarök was coming.

Annabel would have plenty of time to learn the old ways when I brought her to Asgard.

I grabbed her arm, hauling her to her feet in front of me. "Look, I'm only going to say this once because we're sort of on a time limit here: Ragnarök is coming. In fact, it's already here. These storms? They're the Fimbulwinter, the unyielding blizzard that will turn brother against brother and cover your world in eternal ice. The idiots you see behind me are three of Loki's many, *many* illegitimate sons and not the kind of pedigree you want to attach yourself to."

Bjarni snorted. He'd gotten to his feet and was helping Grim do the same. "Please, like Sif's so glad to have Thor's bastard around."

I narrowed my eyes. My stepmother would be more than happy with me, once I brought home Annabel. "I was raised in Asgard, a boon to my father's lineage and embraced by the gods. Can you say the same?"

"This is insane," Annabel muttered, trying to pull away from me. "Let me go. I don't want any part of this!"

"I care little for what you want," I told her, grabbing her by both arms now. "Did you not hear me? The world is *ending.* You come with me, or you die like the rest of your kind. And I need you, little omega, so I'm afraid I can't let you commit suicide just yet."

"You-you *need* me?" she asked, voice pitched high with obvious disbelief. "For what?"

"You'll find out soon enough." I yanked Annabel's body flush with mine so she couldn't kick me. "There's no more time for talk—I'm taking you to Asgard."

"Asgard? Realm of the gods-Asgard?" she squeaked, as if that was the part that disturbed her the most. As if any mortal shouldn't count themselves blessed beyond imagination to be brought there. Even if not by their own choice.

"We'll follow you there," Saga promised, pushing up onto his feet. His mouth was bloody from where he'd bitten his tongue. Electrocution was a bitch. "I swear it. The omega is *ours*."

Annabel clenched her hands into fists. "I'm not *anybody's*. Leave me alone!"

I smirked. "The marks on your neck beg to differ, pet. But don't worry—once we're in Asgard, we'll see about getting the illegitimate one removed."

She shook her head at me again, struggling against my grasp in a way that was almost comical. Valiant, sure, but futile all the same. I swept her off her feet, throwing her over my shoulder with a yelp, her perfect, plump rear close enough for me to bite as I wrapped my arm tight around the backs of her knees.

"You'll understand when we get there," I told her, running my fingers over the weave of reality around us, searching for the root of the mighty world tree Yggdrasil that had brought me here. When I found the place in the fabric of reality where the threads had grown thin, I spread them apart as delicately as possible. I didn't want to cause a tear that would let the brothers run in after us. The gold bracelet around my wrist glowed hotly against my skin as magic as ancient as the the world tree flashed within the cave.

All three Jotunns came charging toward me then, spurred by the sight of the portal I'd opened to take us to the gods' realm. With a flick of my wrist, I summoned a chain of lightning that passed between them, scattering them in different directions.

Then, holding my prize high and doing my best to ignore her enraged screams, I stepped through the portal before they could regroup.

What in the actual *fuck*?

Everything had gone sideways in the last few minutes in ways I couldn't even hope to fully describe, but my brain was sure as hell trying to quantify them anyway. I liked lists. They made me feel comfortable. I took great pride in being organized. In the midst of chaos, my subconscious was apparently desperate to order things.

1. I'd gone into heat. A real, actual heat.
2. Which meant that I was an omega, not the beta female I'd thought I was—the woman I'd been raised to be.
3. I'd fucked two guys in... what, under an hour? First I'd opened my legs for a total stranger, let him *mate* me, then begged for the cock of a man I just *barely* knew better

while the first guy's cum was still dripping out of me.

4. And now I had two *mates*. Something that shouldn't have been possible for me, because I was *supposed* to be a goddamn *beta*.

5. But I wasn't. Somehow, the two alphas who'd claimed me like a piece of land had brought out a truth from my body I'd never known existed. And now... now everything I was and had believed to be, was gone.

6. My life was over. I'd never be anything but a broodmare. That's what happened to omegas—they were nothing but walking wombs to the alphas of the world. And my two brand new mates seemed quite determined to stick with that tradition.

7. Also they were gods. Or at least half-gods.

8. Gods were apparently real, and I was staring at four at them.

9. Magic. Real, visual magic existed.

10. What the fuck.

11. And while four demi-gods were squabbling over who got to own me, like I was some piece of meat, the actual, *literal* end of the world was happening right outside the cave, while *inside* the cave, I'd been thrown over Magni's shoulder while he shot lightning from his fingertips and opened a... a portal.

I stared at it. Magni had turned to address the brothers by electrocuting them all again. The air was pungent with burning ozone, sharp and overwhelming, even drowning out the musky fragrance of moss, earth, and sex.

Each lightning strike made my small hairs stand on end, muscles tensing in anticipation of a clap of thunder that never came. And yet that mind-boggling reality I was expected to just accept, according to Magni, paled in comparison to the *rift in time and space* he'd so easily manifested out of nothing.

He treated it like pressing the button on a key fob, or pushing aside a rug to reveal a trap door he'd always known was there. But just looking at it made my skin crawl and my brain go numb trying to get a handle on the physics of it. Everything about it felt alien. Wrong. Like I wasn't even supposed to be looking at it.

Yet Magni intended to carry me through this impossible gap into a world that didn't exist. *Shouldn't* exist.

In times of great stress, especially psychological, humans could fixate on the weirdest things. Odd details were able to jump out at us, which was our psyche's way of trying to protect itself by focusing on the one thing in the whole equation that does made sense. The goal to redirect our attention there giving the rest of our minds time to catch up and cope with the rest of the bullshit it was being forced to parse.

Maybe that was why the first real thought that came

to me as I stared into *an other-fucking-worldly portal to a new dimension* was....

"Shouldn't Asgard be... prettier?"

I wasn't an expert on Norse religions, or any religions for that matter. I'd taken the requisite courses to get a handle on the basics, sure, but my specialty was fact, not fiction.

Still, I'd watched the Marvel movies. Magni claimed what lay on the other side of the rift was the land of the gods, and yet all I saw were rocks and the faint silhouette of distant ruins.

He wasn't listening, though. He was turning away from the brothers he'd just lain out, strewn like ragdolls along the cave floor. One of them was my other mate.

Real, harrowing fear so intense it made my stomach lurch gripped me as I stared into Saga's blue eyes, the moment of realization hitting both of us in the same instant. Once Magni brought me through this portal, we would be separated. Possibly forever.

It made no logical sense. I hated Saga for what he'd done, just as much as I hated my would-be kidnapper. And yet I knew, into the marrow of my bones, that if we passed through this portal without him, the very essence of who I was would be rendered in two.

When he claimed me as his mate, he tied us together in ways I hadn't known were possible. That, judging from the wide-eyed expression of pure terror on Saga's face, he also hadn't understood before now.

"Stop. Stop, you idiot!" I pounded my fists against

Magni's broad back, trying desperately to stop him from wrenching my soul apart. "You can't!"

Just as I dug my nails in, trying to break his flesh, he crossed the threshold between realities and wrenched a gasp from all the way down in my chest.

That was where my bond to Saga lay. And with one small step, Magni had forced it to stretch through the vast gulf separating our worlds.

I'd suffered heartbreak before, but it had been nothing like this. This pain, sharp and breath-stealing, spread through my limbs like a poison. My throat clenched around a sob and some distant, half-forgotten organ in my guts yawned to birth a black hole.

It devoured all the light inside of me. All the joy. Left in its place was a cold rush of adrenaline. I had to get back to Saga, had to break away from Magni before the portal closed.

"Stop!" I shrieked again, straining with all my might to penetrate his skin. I clawed and raked until I was sure at least one of my fingernails would pop off, until my cuticles bled and my jaws ached from biting at his shoulders, but it was no use. Nothing could deter him. Nothing could rend him the way he was rending me.

As a last resort, I reached out, stretching as far as my body would allow—and to my utter shock, Saga grabbed my hand. Warm relief flooded me, a welcome reprieve from the chill of wherever Magni had brought us.

Saga leapt through the tear in reality just as it

closed. Magni whirled, ripping me away from Saga again. "Are you fucking kidding me?"

"That's my *mate* you're dragging off," the other god replied, teeth bared. "Put her down. *Now*."

Magni snorted. "Why, so she can run? So you can grab her and take off?" He tightened his grasp on my body. "Not a chance."

Being naked was bad enough, but having my ass and still-weeping pussy on display, thrust up into the air over Magni's massive shoulder, was an indignity I couldn't bear. The wind slapped at me ruthlessly, pins and needles flaring in my rear, my vulva, and the backs of my thighs.

"Magni, please. I'm cold."

"That's because this moron took you to Jotunheim," Saga said. Though I couldn't see him, I could hear the smirk in his tone. "Land of the Jotunns. The very people he turned his back on while he was busy playing the role of Thor's long-lost son. Good news for me, bad news for him."

Magni paused, frowning as he looked around. "Jotunheim? How the Hel did this happen?" A moment later, he slid me down the front of his body until my feet touched the ground. The blood rushing away from my head left me dizzy, the chill traveling up my soles and numbing my toes.

"Guess the rumors are true—you can't call on Bifrost to take you to Asgard, much as you claim to be a *god,*" Saga said. "You have to use treacherous dwarf magic to cross through the realms."

Magni turned to him, lip curling up in a silent snarl at the taunt. But I was having none of it—out of the three of us, *I* was the injured party here. Whatever quarrel they thought they had could wait.

I folded my arms around me, trying to shield my naked body from the cold as I rounded on the redheaded alpha. "I can't believe you did this. You just... *abducted* me!"

Magni looked down at me, distracted from whatever he was about to say to Saga. He drifted his knuckles down my side, then wrapped me closer to his strong body. Despite the temperature, his skin was pleasantly hot. "I've *saved* you, pet. You have no idea how brutal Loki's children are...."

Saga lunged then, shoving him away from me, and I stumbled back away from them. "Neither do you," he hissed, "but touch my mate again, and you will."

"*Your* mate?" Magni laughed, breaking Saga's hold on him. "Have you forgotten who claimed her first?"

"Can we not?" I shouted, my voice coming out higher and more desperate than I'd intended. "For fucks' sakes, what's wrong with you two? Look at where we are! It's...." I struggled for a word big enough to encompass it. "It's a *nightmare.*"

Saga turned to me, leveling me with a hard stare. "It's *home.*"

I was so not in the mood to be chastised about my

choice of words for where he apparently grew up. "It's freezing, is what it is. I'm so cold, and if you two keep this up I'm also going to be dead from hypothermia before we find a way out of here."

"Mortals," Saga said, eying my quivering form. He sighed and unzipped his thick coat, and then shrugged out of his woolen sweater, leaving him in a white T-shirt that hugged his sculpted torso. "Come."

I stumbled toward him, the cold ground numbing my feet too much for a more graceful approach, but Magni stopped me by grabbing my shoulder with one freakishly strong hand.

"You want to wrap *my* mate in *your* scent," the redhead snarled, glaring at Saga.

"I want to ensure *my* mate doesn't perish from the cold before we can get her to shelter," Saga said, raising an eyebrow in challenge. "Or has it been so long since you were around mortals that you forget how delicate they are?"

I wasn't thrilled with being called "delicate," but right then my teeth where chattering too loudly to argue the point.

"Magni, please," I said, shuddering as another gust of icy wind beat against my naked skin.

He growled again, green eyes gliding over my body as he took stock of my condition. With an irritated huff, he clearly came to the conclusion that I was, indeed, going to die without clothes. And since he was as naked as I, he finally relented and released my shoulder.

Saga helped me get into first the sweater and then his coat, zipping it up around me as if I were a child. Honestly, I felt like one in his oversized clothes. The coat came all the way down past my knees. But it also enveloped me in glorious warmth, residue heat from Saga's body still lingering in the fabric.

"My shoes won't fit you," he said, a frown drawing in his eyebrows as he looked at my feet. "Come, sweetling. I'll carry you."

He held out his arms like one might when trying to coax a cat into an embrace, and just as I opened my mouth to shoot him down, a steel band closed around my midriff from behind, hoisting me into the air.

"If my mate must be swathed in your stench, *I* will be carrying her," Magni said from behind me, before he maneuvered me over his shoulder in a fireman carry.

"If you try to take off with her again," Saga said, voice low with warning, "even the walls of Asgard won't be able to protect you."

"And what would you suggest we do, then? Stay in Jotunheim and wait for one of them to notice my mark on her neck? Go back to the human world and wait for fucking Ragnarök?" Magni huffed, shifting again so his shoulder dug into my gut. I grunted with discomfort— getting lugged around like a piece of timber was starting to get real old real fast.

"Our farm is safe," Saga gritted. "Once she's mated with all of us, the prophecy says—"

"The prophecy doesn't say dick about Midgard

being safe, not for her and not for any other human," Magni countered.

"And what makes you believe Asgard will be? If we're going to go with ye old legends, Ragnarök isn't just destroying the human world. *Remember?*" Saga said, tone pointed. "Which I'm guessing is why you kidnapped her to begin with."

"What prophecy?" I asked, pushing against Magni's naked back to try and get somewhat upright, in an attempt at regaining just a smidgen of dignity. "And excuse me, but maybe instead of trying to figure out how to hide from this Ragnarök business, you could try to figure out how to stop it? You're gods! Isn't your job to protect us humans? It doesn't matter where you take me, if everyone's dead. If... if my parents die."

In the middle of it all, the confusion and shock of everything that'd happened in the past few hours—and especially since I'd just gotten taken through a portal into another world by a *god*—panic that had nothing to do with being near-naked in an alien wasteland set in.

My parents. My home—my *world!* If what they were saying was true, it was the *literal* end of the world. Everything I'd loved, everything I'd known, was at the brink of extinction. And here these two idiotic immortals with powers I'd never even known existed were bickering about where to *hide* with me?

"There's no stopping Ragnarök, pet," Magni said, and for the first time he sounded truly sorry. "Everyone you've ever known will die, and there's nothing I or anyone else can do to stop it. But you will live, Annabel. And because of you, so will many of the gods."

"That's bullshit!" I snarled. "I don't care what your plans are—I'm not going anywhere with either of you without my parents! If you think I can just leave them behind and go be a meek little broodmare, you're insane!"

"You want to save the people who sold you to us in the first place?" Saga said, one blond eyebrow arced.

"W-what?" The anger and panic churning in my gut fizzled to embers at the look of complete sincerity on his rugged face.

"Your beloved family—they gave you to us in exchange for gold. A thousand years ago, my father made a trade with your ancestors. They received jewels and gold, enough to last them several generations, and in return they promised the first omega daughter to be born from their bloodline to us." Saga's silvery eyes flashed as he stared at me, forcing me to hear every word.

"You parents didn't send you on vacation, Annabel. They sent you to us to honor your family's debt. And in return, we gave them enough riches that they could live out the final days until Ragnarök in wealth and comfort. You owe them nothing. *We* are your family now. Me and my brothers."

It was like a punch to the gut. I hung limply from Magni's shoulder as every interaction concerning my parents' "'family friends from Iceland'" played for my mind's eye. They'd urged me to go ever since I came of age, and this time, when I finally went, they'd seemed… panicked, almost. And so relieved when I decided to go.

He was speaking the truth. How my parents had known I was an omega, and kept it from me, I didn't know. But knowing what I did now… it was obvious that they'd pushed me to Iceland knowing full well I wouldn't be coming back.

"You owe your ancestors nothing, if they made a deal with the trickster god for your life," Magni said, turning to stare at the bleak skies above us. Everything around us was bleak. The sky was ashen, low clouds stretching between every horizon, threatening snow or rain. Cliffs jutted in the distance like jagged teeth, like the maw of some great beast cleaved open and waiting for the chance to snap shut. When the wind swept between those teeth, it didn't just howl, it keened. It was a dark lament that reminded me of the storm that had come to the Lokissons' farm my first night in Iceland.

The redheaded god's gaze stopped at the tallest cliff in the distance. It was as black as jet against the unruly skies. "Sonuvabitch."

"It couldn't hurt," Saga said, eyes also locked on the cliff, though he also sounded somewhat reluctant.

"You don't think it's very convenient my bracelet suddenly takes us to *her* cave, rather than Asgard?" Magni asked, a frown marring his forehead. "You know how the fucking Norns love to meddle."

"What are you even talking about?" I asked,

squinting at the rock to try to work out what had the two of them so agitated. Apart from looking particularly grim in the already desolate landscape, I didn't see anything special about the cliff.

"That is where the Norn Verdandi brought both our fathers, once upon a time," Saga said, pointing up toward the top of the cliff.

"What's a Norn?" I asked.

"A weaver of fate," Magni said, mouth still pulled into a displeased line. "And notoriously incapable of butting out of other people's business."

"Be that as it may, if you were capable, you would have used your bracelet to try to get into Asgard again. Since you haven't, it's obvious you're as stuck here as I am," Saga said. "And since we can agree that Jotunheim isn't the *best* place for a mortal with a god's claim on her neck to hang around, maybe we should just walk up there and ask what she wants."

Magni heaved a deep sigh, his grip around my hips tightening. "Fine. But once she's confirmed that Annabel is mine, there's nothing you can do to stop me from taking her to Asgard."

"You can try," Saga said, his fierce smile terrifying rather than comforting. "And you will fail. I was not prepared before, but I am now. You will not get an advantage on me again. And when my brothers find us, you can forget all about taking my mate to Asgard. She belongs with us, and us alone."

"And what about what *I* want?" I growled, anger

finally cutting through despair like a hot knife. "You bicker like children over a toy. I am not a thing! I don't want to go with either of you. I want to go back to my own world."

"You'd die if we let you." Saga sighed, patient exasperation in his voice. "You don't want that."

"You don't know what I want!" I snapped.

"We do." Magni moved his hand over my back from my hips, brushing over his bite on my neck. "You're a part of me now, Annabel. I know your every desire, even if you still refuse to accept it. You're an omega, with an omega's yearnings. You will bear the offspring of true gods, and once we get to Asgard, you will come to see this as the gift it is."

I kneed him in the sternum. Hard.

The redhead grunted and doubled over, and I stumbled to the ground to the sound of Saga's peeling laughter. Immediately, the chill bit into the soles of my feet, but I was too angry to care.

"I will not! I swear it! I will *never* have your children. I may be an omega, but I was not raised as one and I refuse to accept your archaic views of what I'm *supposed* to want. You can force me to follow you, but you will never force me to become a glorified broodmare!"

Magni straightened from his keeled-over position, rising to his full height. Sparks flashed in his eyes, like fissures of lightning behind the green of his irises. It took everything I had not to shrink back from his intimidating figure, but when he spoke, his voice was quiet.

"I already mated you, omega. If you do not carry my child in your womb now, you will after your next heat. Or the one after that. You may spit and claw as much as you please, but the outcome will be the same: you will give me what I need. You will surrender. And in the end, you will obey."

10

GRIM

"When I get a hold of that low-class thundercunt, I'm breaking his neck," Bjarni growled as he plodded along next to Dragur.

Unlike our other brother, it was rare that Bjarni let his temper get a hold of him, but apparently our run-in with Magni's lightning powers had done the trick. Not that I blamed him—my teeth still smarted like I'd been chewing on tinfoil.

"We have to find them before you get the pleasure of murdering Thor's bastard, and if Saga's still alive he may already have beaten you to it." I stared into the falling snow. It was hard to make out anything but pure white, but when I squinted I could see the vaguely familiar outline of a rock formation up ahead. "It didn't look like that portal opened up into Asgard."

"It was Jotunheim," Bjarni said. "The twat went to *our* domain."

"How... curious." Why Magni hadn't taken the omega to the gods' realm I wasn't sure, but Jotunheim? He wasn't welcome in the land of the Jotunns, not after his betrayal.

Ahead, the rock formation grew the nearer we came, until I could finally make out our farm below. Every fence and building was covered in snow, but the hills shielded it somewhat from the worst of the blizzard.

Two dark birds sat on the roof of the main house, a stark contrast to the powdery landscape.

"Arni and Magga are here," I said jutting my chin at the ravens patiently waiting for our return. "Maybe they will have news of our brother."

Bjarni lit up—he was much fonder of the birds than I. "And Annabel. Poor thing must be scared out of her mind."

I remained silent, driving Draugr down the hill with my knees. I didn't care about the troublesome omega's state of mind. I didn't care much for her at all. But both my brothers did. They'd lost their damn minds the second the girl arrived, sniffing and pawing at her like adolescent alpha pups, and we didn't have time to argue about her. Again.

I took a moment to ensure Draugr was well cared for, before I followed Bjarni across the courtyard and in through the front door.

Our guests were already inside, each perching on one of Bjarni's sweater-clad shoulders. Magga was cooing excitedly, nuzzling against Bjarni's neck in a bid for affection. Bjarni, soft as ever, stroked the treacherous bird along the beak and chittered back, much to the raven's delight.

"We bring news from Valhalla and beyond," Arni said, his hoarse voice sounding much like the creaking of rusty hinges. "The omega is in danger—Thor's son has stolen her to Jotunheim."

"We know," I said, smothering an eye roll at how Bjarni cooed at the flying rat nibbling on his earlobe. They were supposedly messengers of the gods, not obnoxious pets, but you wouldn't know it from how he treated them.

They'd been Odin's, once. Before our father stole them from his rookery and gifted them to his sons. One each for Bjarni and Saga.

I came later, but there'd been no raven to mark my birth. I preferred horses anyway.

"What we don't know is why he didn't call on Bifrost and take her straight to Asgard." I crossed my arms over my chest, schooling my impatience into a hard stare.

"Or where exactly we can find them. Jotunheim is a big place," Bjarni rumbled, finally pulling his focus from the raven on his shoulder.

Magga squawked with dismay, pulled on a tuft of his beard as punishment and flapped her wings.

"The bastard son can't cross the rainbow bridge

without an escort," Magga crowed. "Daddy hasn't given him the keys to the kingdom."

"Magni's been with them for centuries. He betrayed his own mother to join Thor. Why would he not be able to access Bifrost?" Bjarni frowned. It didn't surprise me that my golden-haired brother wouldn't understand how even a son who'd shown his allegiance by betraying his own mother could be considered an outsider.

"Odin," Arni creaked. "The Allfather doesn't trust him. He crosses the worlds with a dwarf-made bracelet given to him by Thor himself."

"He thinks the omega will redeem him," Magga agreed. "Make Daddy proud."

"And where is he now? Where's Saga?" I asked.

"Both are with the girl," Arni crowed. "Headed for Verandi's peak, last we saw them."

"The Norns," Bjarni muttered. "Why would they...?"

"Because the omega, who's supposed to save our entire bloodline, is now mated to *both* Magni and Saga," I said, my jaw working despite my best effort to stay calm. "A detail *she* forgot to mention when the Norn spied our future and told us the only way we'd survive Ragnarök would be if all three of us mated that girl."

And if they were headed to Verdandi's mountain, it was because she wanted them there. Which meant the seer planned this. And why wouldn't she have? She was a fucking Norn—a weaver of Fate.

If anyone could have fooled Loki, it would be her.

"We need to get to them," Bjarni said. "Norn or no, Saga's gonna need our help to get rid of that ginger prick."

I sighed. Whatever game Verdandi was playing, I was sure she'd interjected Magni into our plans on purpose. She wouldn't make it easy to get rid of him. But Bjarni was right, our brother needed us.

"Ooh, time to play with the map?" Magga chirped, flapping her wings with excitement. "Do you even remember how, little godlings?"

I shot her a glare. "Never you mind, fiend. Go find our brother. We will meet you in Jotunheim."

The black bird cawed at me, eyes predatory sharp. "We do not fly on your command, misborn."

Hot anger flared in my chest at the hated nickname. It'd been a thousand years, and their shrill voices still felt like claws in fresh wounds.

Grim the Misborn, they'd called me as a boy. Picking at me, like a swaying carcass in the wind, reminding me every day how I was our father's biggest regret.

"You will fly, or you will regret the day you clawed your way out of your shell," I snarled, clenching my fists to suppress the dark energy within.

"Oh, not this again," Bjarni sighed, deftly stepping between me and Magga. He brought a hand up, bopping the female raven over the beak. "Find Saga. Once we are through, lead us to his side."

Arni squawked, flapping his wings.

"As you command, son of Loki," Magga said. I

sneered at her, and clenched my fists at the sound of their mocking laughter as they disappeared up the chimney.

"They only taunt you because you still give a shit," Bjarni said. "They'll keep pecking until you learn to ignore it."

I shot my golden-haired brother a glare. "I don't care about the opinion of flying rats. Now, can we find the damn map before Saga gets himself killed by lightning?"

Bjarni cocked an eyebrow at me, but thankfully dropped the subject. "Fine."

The map was another gift our father had given his sons, besides the stupid ravens. A map over the nine worlds, and the secret passages through them.

The gods had their rainbow bridge to Midgard, the realm of the humans, and clearly Magni had his magic bracelet, but there was no other official way to cross the fabric of reality. The other realms had different paths between them, but the trickster god had wanted a way to sneak in the backdoor without detection. Our father'd never told us how he'd had the map of the nine worlds crafted, but he'd given it to us when we left for Midgard.

It was our ticket back.

Not that I ever wanted to return to Niflheim.

The map lay hidden in the barn, where we kept the few items that betrayed our immortality. Of course, no human would understand what they saw if they came across this particular magic relic.

The effigy still burning low with Jotunn magic from our ritual last night was another matter. I sneered at the horn-crested figure as we entered the barn. Odin's beard, I hated that thing and everything it stood for.

I'd been content in Midgard, taking care of our farm and tending to the horses. It'd been the closest to happiness I'd ever known.

And then *she* came. And ripped it all away.

My eyes caught on a strand of dark hair snagged on one of the hay bales closer to the door. Frowning, I crouched down and touched a hand to the faint indents in the scattered straw covering the floor. When I inhaled deeply, I caught just the most delicate whiff of honey and thyme. And omega.

Annabel.

"What are you sniffing at?" Bjarni rumbled from behind me as he drew the door shut, shielding the barn from the icy winds.

"The girl saw us last night," I said, standing back up again. "She must have witnessed the ritual. I'm guessing that's why she ran."

Bjarni snorted, an amused sound. "Crafty little thing."

"I'm not sure why you find it so funny. Because of her, our brother's in danger, and so are we. You said there was no one else. If we don't mate her in time...."

"We die. I know." Bjarni clapped a massive hand to

my shoulder before he made his way further into the barn. "But it won't come to that. Once we've taken care of Magni, we bring her back, wait for her next heat, and then we claim what's ours. Simple."

Simple. Everything always was, for my golden-haired brothers. They thought nothing of taking a mate they hadn't chosen for themselves, hadn't even blinked at the prophecy that revealed we had to *share* an omega if we wished to survive. If we wanted our father to survive.

"Stop brooding and come help me look. You were always better at this damn thing," Bjarni called. He'd cracked open the chest hidden deepest in the barn and unfurled the large, yellowed map over a bale of hay.

I sighed and crossed the room. Whatever my reluctance to mate the girl, there was no other way. We had to find her, and Saga as well, if we wanted to survive. In the end, it *was* simple.

Death, or my immortal life.

At least by sharing her with Bjarni and Saga I would have no need to tend to her, after. They could coo and pet and dote on the omega if they wished—I had nothing to give her.

I flattened the map with a brush of my hands and looked at the flat representation of the Nine Realms for the first time in centuries.

None of which I'd ever wanted to see again, really. They held no promise of home for me. Midgard had its faults, certainly—namely, that the end was nigh—but at least here, the feud between the gods was far enough away that my brothers and I could live our lives without the specter of our father's misdeeds looming over us.

"There." I brushed my fingertip over the aged parchment, placing it on top of the rivulet of ink promising a thinning in the fabric of reality. "The gateway is there."

"Then let's go get our brother."

11

SAGA

Thor's son was an idiot. Hotheaded and lost on instincts, he'd told the little omega everything she didn't want to hear, and then proceeded to force her back in his arms and over his shoulder, where she now hung in his unyielding grip, misery and fury in her brown eyes. But he couldn't see that—he'd slung her over his shoulder as he pushed up the mountain with all the furious intent of an alpha determined to force his will through. And he didn't see the steely determination forming in my pretty mate's gaze.

Right then, she hated him, and I knew she'd do anything to get away from him and his demands of surrender. She may regret it later, when his blasted mark on her neck called out for him, but by then it'd be too late.

He'd only had a short time with Annabel—while she'd been in the throes of her heat and as submissive and eager for dick as any other omega. He didn't know what she was truly like—hadn't had the short introduction to her willful personality as I and my brothers had gotten. We'd come on strong as well, eager to claim our promised mate and high on her enticing scent. Even Grim, unhappy about the prospect of a mate as he'd been, had been aching to mount her. But now, after how thoroughly she'd drained my balls in that cave, it was easier to think clearly again.

She hated me for what I'd done. But she was lost in a foreign world, and if I played my cards right, she would soon come to see me as the lesser of two evils. As much as my own instincts roared to rip her from the other alpha and ensure she understood who was her true mate, I had to keep them contained.

In the end, Annabel would think she chose me of her own free will.

The air was cooler up on the cliffside, and I shot my mate a concerned look. She might've been wrapped in my clothes, but her bottom half was still bare, and even I felt the chill as we climbed. Humans were so damn frail, especially the females. But one glance at Annabel, and it was clear her seething anger was keeping her plenty warm.

I smothered a smirk at the fury in her chocolate eyes. That idiot Magni had no clue what he'd done.

His naked ass flexed below her scowling face, his own annoyance at the situation apparently keeping him warm, too. Not that he was in any danger of dying from hypothermia, what with his divine lineage. Didn't stop me from wishing he'd get a nasty case of frostbite on the dick, though.

He'd had the omega meant for my brothers and me before we did, tried to take her away from me and use her to salvage his own pathetic family while putting a serious kink in our carefully laid plans. And now he'd gotten me stuck in Jotunheim with an omega carrying a god's claim, risking her life as well as that of my brothers.

Yeah, he was going to regret what he'd done—but right now I needed him to help me protect our shared mate. It was plenty obvious from the fact that he hadn't tried to zap me with lightning again that he was tapped out, but having him by my side in case I needed to defend Annabel from Jotunheim's more savage inhabitants was vital. Until my brothers found us.

I didn't know how long it'd take until they came for us, but I knew that they would. And when that time came, I needed to have convinced Annabel that I was the better choice. If she came willingly, it'd be so much easier to settle her into her new role as omega and mother.

Hopefully Loki would be able to help us get rid of Magni's mark. Despite Annabel's current levels of anger, I still felt the redheaded buffoon in our bond, like a warm buzz cocooning the fresh connection between my mate and me. His anger, his frustration... his urge to protect the small woman currently wrapped over his shoulder. It was all there, etched into the sacred space that was supposed to be for just me and her. And, later, my brothers.

Mating the same omega had always been in the cards for Bjarni, Grim, and I, ever since our father tracked down that prophecy. And we didn't mind—well, Bjarni and I didn't mind. Grim was another story. But if I had to share this vulnerable elation with anyone, it would be my brothers. I'd die for them, after all.

Magni... Magni not so much. And yet there he was, an uninvited interloper, my enemy laid bare in ways I'd never wanted to see. I wasn't going to pretend not to know that, on his end, he saw me as I did him. Felt my heart stutter in my chest whenever I laid eyes on Annabel. The most private and personal of moments, shared with a man I hated just as much as he did me.

And I hated him all the more for having ruined my bonding with my omega.

"Not much further," Magni grunted from ahead of me, probably more for Annabel's benefit than mine. No matter how boneheaded he was, he had to be aware of the gnawing presence of her anger in our shared bond.

I held back a snicker. He might not want to admit it, but I knew he had to be squirming, instincts neither of us could control pushing him to please his omega despite his own annoyance. It was a bit of a shock, this insistent tugging from behind my ribs to pet and soothe my unhappy mate.

I'd fucked many a woman over the years, mortal

and otherwise, and never had my interest in their mood stretched beyond getting them willing to take my dick. When I first saw Annabel, my cock had ached for her so intensely I hadn't been able to think about much else. Until she was stuck on my knot, and all I wanted to do was purr for her and promise her that I would protect her and care for her until the end of time.

I'd never not loved being an alpha. The strength, power, and status it brought made life easy, betas and omegas alike bending readily to our natural superiority. Except I was starting to think that maybe I'd gravely miscalculated a mate's impact on instincts I had no control over.

At least there was some pleasure in watching Magni struggle with similar emotions. And so long as I could manipulate my mate into thinking she was choosing her place by my side, there would be no need to deal with the unsettling sensation of her unhappiness humming out of tune in my chest.

Annabel ignored the redhead, and he grumbled something under his breath I didn't quite catch but had her eyes narrowing even further. Odin's beard, he was a moron.

"Verdandi has a long history of meddling in the affairs of gods, but she's also been known to help show the path that must be taken. If she's in the mood," I said. It was becoming increasingly clear that Annabel's greatest desire right about now—maybe except for pants—was to feel like she had some say in what was going to happen to her. She didn't, of course. And she wouldn't, ever again. That was the lot of any mated omega, and most especially one whose fate had been interwoven with gods. But that didn't mean I couldn't share a few things with her along the way, to make her believe she did.

Annabel gave me a hesitantly interested look. "Is she a goddess?"

"Not really." I grimaced. "But don't tell her that. She's one of the three main Norns—she and her two sisters weave the fates of men and gods alone, and my father swears he's seen her snip a man's life-thread short because he didn't show her proper respect."

"And you think she'll be able to tell us where to go to get to safety?" Annabel asked, eyebrow raised.

"Well, that... and hopefully explain how exactly you can help us protect our families from Ragnarök."

Her eyes widened in outrage. "*How?* I thought you wanted to knock me up and that was magically gonna fix everything? Are you telling me you mated me and kidnapped me, and there might not have been any fucking reason?"

For an omega, she sure had a nasty temper.

"No, the prophecy was very clear on that part. The joining of our bloodline with yours is the answer. But prophecies tend to come with a certain lack of... shall we call them *general instructions,* and since Verdandi seems to want to speak with us anyway, we might as well ask her for a few pointers."

I reached out and stroked my hand over her chin, reveling in the electric buzz my digit had with the contact with her skin. "Maybe we can ask that she helps you understand, too."

"Fat chance of that," Magni muttered, taking a few steps forward at a quicker pace so my fingers touched nothing but air. Fucker.

"You don't know if you don't ask," I sing-sang, keeping my urge to growl at being separated with even a few feet from Annabel down.

"How long as it been since you spoke with a Norn?" Magni asked as he finally made it to even ground. "They come up with half of these stupid prophecies. Good luck getting a clear answer out of her."

"If you don't think she'll help, why did you drag me up here?" Annabel bit. I smirked at her irritation.

"Because I have to try," he growled. "I need to bring you to safety, and if my bracelet isn't working the only other way is to hike across enemy territory. Verdandi may be playing games, but she's a Norn. She can tell me how to protect you. I just need to ask the right way."

I rolled my eyes at his possessive alpha bullshit, but some of the anger in Annabel's eyes seemed to soften. *Shit.* Apparently the little hypocrite liked *some* aspects of having an alpha mate.

My cock gave a needy spasm at the memory of how she'd milked my knot despite her anger at being mounted against her spoken will. Yeah. She may not like getting bossed around, but she couldn't get around the fact that she loved alpha dick and alpha protection as much as any other omega. And I could use that to my advantage... so long as I didn't allow Magni to win her over using the same tactics.

Magni finally made it to the top of the cliff, and I climbed up after him just as Annabel let out a startled gasp.

The black rock had looked like any other form below, but from here it was carved into the very realistic portrayal of a black dragon. Its open maw was just over eight feet tall, and through it lay the cave we sought. I remembered my father taking me here when I was still green. The Norn hadn't been present that day, but the eerie quietude of the place had still chilled me to the bone. There was magic, and then there was *magic*. The kind these creatures of Fate wielded was most definitely in the latter category.

"Was that... Was that *alive*, once?" Annabel breathed as Magni slid her off his shoulder. She was staring wide-eyed at the stone dragon, carefully reaching out to trace the scales etched into the side of its face.

"No one knows for sure," I said, stepping forward so I could put myself between her and Magni. I placed my hand on her lower back, ignored the redhead's warning growl and guided her toward the entrance. "But it's been stone for eons. I wouldn't let you walk into danger, sweetling. It's quite safe."

Magni shot me a dirty look, but for once decided not to argue. Instead, he pushed in ahead of me, leading the way through the dragon's gaping maw. Undoubtedly an attempt at showing our mate he was the alphaest alpha of them all, taking the lead and having us follow, but it left Annabel in my care.

I wrapped my arm around her waist and pulled her close. For once, she didn't object, seeming almost grateful for my attention.

The throat of the stone beast was dark. The wind whipping through it birthed a hollow shriek, a blood-curdling wail far more terrifying than the low and grinding roar a real dragon could produce.

"It's so dark," Annabel whispered by my side. "Why is there no light?"

"Because some of us are trying to sleep," a hissing voice rasped too close for my comfort.

Lights flickered in the cave, like a bright candle in the wind, and suddenly the large room was illuminated by a myriad of golden orbs attached to the black stone walls.

Right on top of us a woman hung from the ceiling like a large bat, her blonde hair dripping from her skull in thick locks. Her black as midnight eyes were much too wide for her face, and her thin lips revealed sharp pointed teeth.

Annabel screamed and jumped back, jerking hard on my arm—and on Magni's. She'd clasped on to both of us, evidently trying to pull us away from the monstrosity but failed due to the difference in our body mass to hers.

A flicker of something warm and confusing bloomed in my chest.

"What the hell is that?" she shrieked, batting wildly at me as I tried to pull her back into my arms—and closer to the blonde woman.

"*That* is Verdandi," Magni said. He turned to the broadly smiling Norn. "We have come to seek your guidance, wise one."

Verdandi's smile widened further, revealing even more sharp teeth and then skittered across the ceiling and down the side like a spider, limbs inverting in wholly unnatural ways. Annabel shuddered in my grasp, halfway trying to burrow into my side and halfway attempting to disappear behind me. I'd never admit it out loud, but seeing the Norn up close like this didn't exactly do wonders for my gut, either.

Verdandi finally landed on the floor, looking somewhat less like an oversized spider when upright. She pulled a hand across her face, and her features melted underneath her fingers.

"Oh, God," Annabel croaked, horror plain in her shaky voice, but when the Norn removed her hand, her eyes were normal sized and a pale blue, and her teeth looked humanly blunt.

"Which one?" Verdandi asked, head crocked to one side as she stared unblinkingly at my mate.

"W-what?"

"Which god are you invoking?"

Annabel blinked, taken aback by the curiosity in the Norn's voice. "I... no one in particular."

"Huh. How odd." Verdandi broke out in a smile again. It was still somewhat too wide for a human face—it'd clearly been a while since she'd had to to conceal her true form. "It's been a while since we last met, little omega. How are you?"

"I'm very sure we've never met before. I would remember you," Annabel said as she stared at the Norn, and I quelled a grin. Even Magni's lips twitched.

"I was there when you were born," Verdandi said, unfazed by the Annabel's denial. "You found me frightening then, too." And then, as if it was the most natural thing in the world, she reached out and pressed a finger to my mate's nose.

"Boop."

"That's enough," Magni said, pulling Annabel from my grasp and tucking her against his own body. "She's mortal. She scares easy."

I snarled at having my mate taken from me, the sound rumbling through the cave before I could clamp my teeth shut around it.

Annabel shot me a glare. "Stop that," she hissed, before she pulled away from Magni enough so that her side wasn't smushed against his. "Both of you." Then she refocused on Verdandi. "You were at my birth? How? *Why?*"

"The prophecy, of course." The Norn blinked, a

puzzled expression on her face. "Someone had to shield you until you were ready."

"Shield me? How? From *what*?" Annabel's eyes were almost as wide as Verdandi's had been before she changed her form. "I don't understand what any of this has got to do with these idiots thinking I'm their broodmare."

The Norn turned to stare at Magni and me, the jerk of her neck too sharp. "Does she not know? Have you not told her?"

"Told me what?" Annabel insisted, the quiver in voice complete gone now, wiped away by thirst for knowledge.

Verdandi closed her eyes and hummed, before her face fell solemn.

> *"On the day the first snow falls,*
> *And Ragnarök looms dark,*
> *To save the kin of gods,*
> *Their sons must ride to find,*
> *The mortal omega with fate divine,*
> *And bind her to their side."*

She blinked her eyes open, smiled wide and booped Annabel on the nose again. "That's your prophecy, little omega. You are the one with fate divine."

"What?" Annabel said. "It doesn't say one word about it being me! It could be any omega."

Verdandi's brow creased in a frown. "No, no, no. Not any omega. You. I weaved your fate myself."

"That's some bullshit," Annabel growled. "What kind of a prophecy is this anyway? It doesn't explain anything. It doesn't even say anything about me having to pop out some demigod to save the world."

"That's seers for you," Magni said with a shrug. "And Mimir always gets kind of poetic about his prophecies. That's why Loki went to Verdandi—to get her help interpreting it."

"And how do *you* know what my father did?" I asked, eyes narrowed at the redhead. "He told no one but my brothers and I."

"Oh, that was me." Verdandi shot me a brilliant smile.

"What? *Why?*" I blinked at her in shock. "That twat kidnapped Annabel before Grim and Bjarni could mate her!"

The Norn looked from me to Magni, eyebrows raised in surprise, as if I was asking the most obvious of questions. "For the prophecy."

"It doesn't say a word about Thor's bastard needing in on this," I gritted out, only narrowly managing to keep my tone above insolence. "You told my father that Grim, Bjarni, and I needed to claim the omega as our mate."

"But of course." She blinked at me, twice, then shook her head, dismissing my protest to refocus on

Annabel. "Come, shiny. There is something you must see."

Annabel took a hesitant step forward, and Magni followed—but Verdandi stopped him with a hand on his shoulder. "Not you, godling. Neither of you. Just the omega."

"There is absolutely no way Annabel will be out of my sight," I said, stepping up to flank Annabel's other side.

Magni crossed his arms over his chest, lips pressed into flat agreement.

For the first time since our arrival, the Norn's face lost all traces of good humor, her expression darkening into something bordering on terrifying. "Did you not come here for my help?"

"Yes, wise one," Magni said, and the hoarse note to his voice let me know that his blood probably also suddenly ran a degree or two cooler. "But she is our mate—"

"And do you think, after how much time and effort I have spent shielding her from danger, how I ensured you both found her before Ragnarök is upon us... that I mean harm to befall her?" Her voice was quiet, but still rang with the strength of a hundred drums.

"No, wise one," I said, suppressing the urge to rip Annabel behind me to protect her from the powerful being in front of us. "We need your guidance to keep our mate safe. Please." I kept my tone demure, because I knew Thor's hotheaded son wouldn't be capable of such a feat. And this being in front of us might be all-seeing and eternal, but my father had also warned me that she was quite the diva.

"Good!" Verdandi lit up in another too-wide smile, the eerie darkness surrounding her thinning to wisps. She held her hand out to Annabel. "We won't be a minute. Come along, shiny. Let's go have a look at your fate."

Annabel hesitated for a long minute, before she drew in a deep breath and gingerly placed her palm against the Norn's.

It took everything I had not to follow, pulled along by the aching string stretching between my heart and hers, as she disappeared into the dragon cave's throat.

12

ANNABEL

As angry as I was with the two alphas who'd mated me against my will, a very large part of me wanted nothing more than to turn around and run back to their protection as Verdandi led me further down the stone dragon's throat, our only source of light a small flame hovering over her free palm. And it wasn't entirely because of the two new bonds in my chest humming irritably at being separated from my mates, either.

"You are so fearful," Verdandi said, her tone unconcerned. "You have no need to be. I've watched over you since you were a babe."

"Like my own personal fairy godmother," I muttered, suppressing a shudder at the thought of the Norn hanging upside down in her true form in my nursery.

"But your instincts to seek protection with the

godlings is good," she continued, as if she hadn't heard me. "I am glad. Your thread was... difficult to weave together with theirs. Such a willful soul."

"My thread?" I asked.

"You will see," she simply said. "Come."

Not that I had much of a choice whether or not I came along. She still had my hand in hers, her grip light but with a quiet strength that told me I wouldn't be able to break away if I tried. We walked for a long time, always down through an ever-spiraling corridor. The stone floor slapped against my bare feet, but it wasn't as cold or rough as the terrain outside the cave.

When I was certain we had to be deeper than the roots of the cliff we'd scaled, Verdandi finally stopped. A veil shimmered in front of us, gossamer thin and interwoven with delicate strands of light. The Norn finally released her grip on my hand and brought it forward, drawing a finger down the length of the veil.

It parted in two, opening a rift into the darkness beyond.

"Come, shiny," she said, before stepping through. The darkness on the other side seemed to swallow her hole.

"I'm... I'm not sure...." I hesitated on the edge of the flowing veil. Magic might be an everyday occurrence for this Norn and the two demigods above us, but I was still having a hard time wrapping my head around it all. I'd dedicated my life to finding facts, not diving head first through magical portals. And this was already the second of the day!

"Be brave, Annabel." Verdandi's voice gusted through the gap in the veil, like a cool breeze on a summer day. I stiffened as memories flickered for my mind's eyes. I'd heard those words before.

"Be brave, Annabel."

Every time I'd been scared, when I was a kid and feared monsters lay in wait for me under my bed, when I fell through the ice and thought I was going to die, when I'd had exam jitters. Those words had echoed through my mind. It was Verdandi's voice. She truly *had* watched over me.

I sucked in a deep breath and stepped through to the darkness beyond. The veil caressed my skin, setting every hair on my body on end as tingles of sensation ran across my skin.

Then I was through, the musty scent of earth and decomposing plants enveloping me, but before I could take in my new surroundings, an agonizing hollow spread behind my ribs.

"No!" I keeled over, pressing a hand to my chest, the very clear memory of the pain and loss I'd felt the first time I stepped through a portal sending panic through my brain. But as I gasped and wheezed, the rendering I'd felt that first time until Saga came through with me didn't set in. It never deepened to more than a numb, deep hollow that gnawed at my gut.

"Your mates can't follow us," Verdandi said. When I

looked up at her from my bent-over position, she gave me a sympathetic smile.

"Is that why I feel like this?" I asked, forcing myself back upright again. I pressed a hand to my chest, trying to soothe the emptiness there. "It was worse... when Magni took me from my world to here. Until Saga came."

"He took you from another plane. We are still in Jotunheim—there's just a barrier separating us from them now," the Norn explained. "The connection between you—it is your greatest weakness."

"I don't know why they had to mate me at all. That so-called prophecy didn't mention mate claims or some twisted, polyamorous relationship! And also," I pointed a finger at the Norn, my ire with the whole situation mounting exponentially, "I'd really like an explanation for why you all think *I'm* the omega you're looking for. A logical, based-in-facts explanation, please."

"As you wish." Verdandi turned her back on me. "Come, and you shall find the answer you seek."

I finally looked up then, for the first time focusing on the room beyond. It was a great grotto, the space so vast I could only make out the nearest wall made from soil and held together by a net of tree roots. The majority of the room was filled out by a myriad of strings dangling from the ceiling high above, all glowing with the faintest of lights. There were thousands upon thousands of them, in all lengths, some as thick as a finger, others fine as spider silk, weaved together in places and drooping singularly in others. Most were in mossy, earthy tones, but a few here and there shone in silvery and golden hues.

"What is this place?" I breathed, stunned awe at the display making me whisper, as to not disturb the sanctity I felt hum through the grotto.

"This is where my sisters and I weave the fate of man and god alike. Every strand is someone's lifespan," Verdandi said as she led me through, nimbly moving between the long strands in pathways I'd never been able to find on my own. "And every dwarf, elf, Jotunn and what else have you, of course." She paused, letting her finger run up along a sienna-toned string that reached just around my sightline, tutting as she caught it between index finger and thumb. "Well, now look at this." Without pausing, she reached into a fold of her clothes and drew out a gilded pair of small scissors, snipping the thread. Its faint glow dimmed instantly, the thread shriveling into a dried husk. When Verdandi brushed past it, it crumbled to the floor in a small pile of ash.

"Was that... did you just *kill* someone?" I stared at the ash—then noticed multiple other mounds scattered around the ground nearby.

"He made a terrible choice. Went against his destiny. It was his time. Every string here will end up nourishing the ground one day, bringing life to the mighty world tree. Well... almost every string." She wrapped a finger around a golden one, tugging demonstratively. "Some are fated for eternity."

"The gods," I murmured, looking at the golden string that seemed to shine brighter than many of its neighbors.

"Well, gods... and a few others here and there." She glanced at me again. "Of course, Ragnarök may still change all of that."

"Will everyone really die?" I asked, following her when she began walking again. "Is there no way to stop it?"

"Of course there's a way to stop it," she said, as if that was the dumbest question to ask. She finally paused and stepped aside, pointing at a fine cluster of strings tangled in an intricate pattern. "That's why you're here, shiny."

I frowned at the strings she'd indicated. One of them lit up with a bright, rosy glow. Surrounding it was a number of silvery and golden strings. "Who's that?"

"You, silly," Verdandi said, giving the rosy string a poke. My spine tensed in response, an echo of sensation running up along it. "Why do you think I had those young godlings bring you here? You are the shiny one. You can stop Ragnarök—if you choose to."

"W-what?" My heart thudded unevenly, a sucking sensation setting in in my chest, as if a black hole had suddenly opened up in my sternum. "But they said— I'm just here to—"

"To save *their* bloodlines by popping out a kid or

two? Yes, I told them that." Verdandi let her finger slide down to one of the golden strings wrapped around mine. "They needed to tie your souls together, and for an alpha, that means mating. Much easier to get them to accept a shared mate claim if they think they're helping their own lineage. Which, they would be. Just not quite how they anticipated."

"I don't understand." I croaked. "Why me? What am *I* supposed to do to stop the literal end of the world? Isn't there... someone better qualified? Like literally *any* god?"

The Norn sighed impatiently, poking my thread again. Another ghostly chill ran up my spine. "I told you. You are the shiny one. There *is* no one else. Look here—" She trailed her fingertips down the rosy thread to where two golden strings, one slightly more of a champagne than the other, wrapped around it. Further down another two glowing threads of gold coiled, and below that again, one of pure silver. They all entangled with each other in a mesmerizing pattern, but all along the rose-colored one ran as the center core, tying them all together.

"The five godlings will support you, and you them. Only together can you defeat the darkness. There is so much treachery in Asgard. I have shielded you from those who sought to destroy you before you could grow into your power, but the time has come to fulfill your destiny."

I stared at the coiling threads, my heart hammering

so hard in my chest I could feel my pulse in my ears and taste iron on my tongue. "I don't have any power. I'm just a human. Just an *omega*. Also... *five?* I'll have *five* mates?"

"You have more power than you think, Annabel," Verdandi said, voice solemn. "But you need their help to unlock it. All five of them."

I shook my head, fighting back tears that welled without warning. "You're wrong. All they've done is hurt me. I don't even have power over myself now, let alone enough to save the whole fucking world! You said I can choose to follow my supposed fate—and I'm telling you I can't. Someone else, someone with actual power, will have to step up."

Verdandi looked at me for a long moment, her face betraying nothing. Then, she reached out and laid a careful finger between my eyes. The grotto flickered, and my vision darkened.

"I want you to see what your choice means, Annabel," she said softly as the world faded from my vision.

Then everything turned black.

I BLINKED MY EYES OPEN, and was hit in the face with a howling wind that sent a chill deep into my bones. All around me was a wasteland of snow, engulfing me up to my waist, and more came tumbling from the gray skies.

"We have to keep going, Anna!"

I turned in the direction of the male voice shouting to be heard over the wind. Magni was there, snow and ice crusting in his red beard now much longer than the scruff he'd had the last time I saw him.

"W-where are we?" I asked. He didn't answer, only wrapped his arm around my shoulders and hunkered down over me, protecting me from the icy winds as best he could. I looked down and realized I was no longer wearing Saga's donated clothes, but a complete set of winter gear. It did little to protect me from the plummeting temperatures.

A shadow appeared ahead, almost completely wiped out from the falling snow.

"Thank Odin," Magni gritted as he pushed us forward, using his strength and size to plow the dunes of snow aside for me. It took so long to make it a dozen or so steps, but finally the shadow turned into a person. Despite the thick coat and drawn hood, I recognized Saga's features and a measure of anxiety eased at the sight of him.

"Is help coming?" Magni asked.

Saga shook his head, his mouth tight and eyes drawn with... with grief, I realized. My heart thudded unevenly, and I reached for him without thought.

He wrapped me in his arms and buried his head against my hood, breathing deeply. "There is no one. They're all gone. We are the last."

"No," Magni whispered. "No, we can't be."

"I saw them die," Saga said, not lifting his head from

me. It was hard to breathe in the tightness of his embrace, but I clung to him nonetheless, too scared and confused to battle against the instincts who told me my mate needed me. "It's over."

There was nothing but the howling of the blizzard for a long while, until Magni finally said, "We have to keep going."

"There's nothing to keep going for," Saga said.

"There is our *mate*," Magni hissed. "We promised to bring her to her parents. Don't you dare go back on your word, Lokisson!"

Saga finally lifted his head then, and there was despair and fury in his eyes. "Didn't you hear me? Everyone's dead! *Her* family, *our* families—*everyone!* This is the end, and there's nothing more we can do!"

"What? No!" Grief threatened to suffocate me, the shock of his words squeezing my sternum flat against my breastbone. "They've got nothing to do with this!"

"My mate," Saga whispered, touching a cold glove to my cheek. "I'm sorry. I'm so sorry we couldn't protect you. He won."

I stared up at him, and in his eyes I saw the truth. This *was* the end. Of everything.

Ragnarök had come.

A deep rumble shook the earth underneath us, making me stumble and fall away from Saga just as the soil and snow burst apart mere inches from where we stood.

I shrieked in horror as a gigantic larva-looking

monster rose from the ground in a cascade of dirty ice, rising above us so high I had to crane my neck to see it in all its terrible magnitude. Its gaping maw had gleaming teeth the size and shape of daggers.

"Anna, run!" Magni roared. He leapt in front of me, drawing a sword from his belt as he took stance next to Saga, who also pulled his weapon. The air crackled with electricity.

But I couldn't move. My feet were leaden, nailed to the ground as the two men who'd each claimed a part of my soul attacked.

The monster shrieked, a piercing sound that made my ears ring, and dove for them. Magic seared the air, thunder deafening the shrieks of the beast, but even their divine power wasn't enough.

Blood splattered the ground as the larva bit savagely into Magni, rendering him in two. My heart gave a spasm and then a searing pain I'd never known existed tore through my chest.

I fell to my knees, screaming in agony and denial as the light snuffed out of Magni's green eyes.

Saga roared his fury out and leapt at the beast, burying his sword in its side. It shook him off, the blade still buried in his flesh, and turned on him as he fell to the ground.

Dark magic rose around his fallen figure, but it wasn't enough to ward off the next attack.

"Saga! No!" I cried his name into the storm as the

last shred of my soul was torn from me, and nothing was left but agony and despair.

"Annabel."

The sound of my name made me blink and open my eyes.

I was in the cave once more, the earthy scent of decaying plants filling my nostrils as the icy grip of the blizzard released my body.

I stared up at Verdandi from where I'd crumbled on the floor of the grotto, my body trembling as if fighting off seizures.

"Every being has a choice if they wish to follow their fate or not," the Norn said softly. "For some, it means an unfulfilling life of regret. For others, an early death. For you, Annabel... it means the end of everything there ever was and everything that would have been. There is no one else. It has to be you. You will find your power with the men destined to be yours. Only then, only if you surrender your fears and claim your birthright will the events of your vision not come to pass."

"My vision?" I whispered. "You mean... you didn't... make that up?"

"Of course not," Verdandi said, head cocked. "I only helped you see. Your power of sight unlocked earlier than it should when you fell through the ice as a child. You will need to find a way to control it."

"How?" I asked. "I don't...." The image of Grim's

mismatched gaze glowing with fury as he stood over me flashed for my mind's eye. Not a "daymare."

A vision.

She closed her eyes for a moment, then opened them again. "If you choose to accept your fate, you must find Mimir. He will guide you on your path. And you must allow the three remaining godlings to mate you. Only united will you stand a chance."

"It has to be five?" I asked, choosing to grasp on to the random number rather than the implications of what else she'd said.

"Five mates for the shiny omega," she said with a nod, pointing at my thread entangled with five others. "Any less and—"

"And the world gets covered in icy doom," I interrupted, rubbing my hands across my face. "It's not much of a choice."

"But it is yours," the Norn said.

13

ANNABEL

The sky was dark when we left the stone dragon's maw.

I got to walk down the mountain myself, thanks to Verdandi. After she brought me back upstairs to the two waiting—and pretty peeved—gods, she handed all of us clothes. Even Saga, who was the only one who'd managed the trip through time and space somewhat dressed to begin with, pulled on the thick leather gear she provided. Apparently the denizens of this land weren't familiar with Earth's high-tech fabric and fashion.

I, however, would have given a lot for a parka and jeans. The outfit Verdandi presented me with was made from soft black leather decorated with feathers cascading down over the shoulders. It clung to my body like a second skin, and made me look like some avian version of Cat Woman.

Crow Woman. Not particularly dangerous but very feathery. And apparently with the ability to see the future.

Christ.

I scrubbed my hands over my face, promptly tripping over a rock on the narrow path and nearly hurtling face-first over the jagged cliff edge. Saga's hand on my shoulder stopped my fall before I'd even managed more than a startled gasp.

"Do you need me to carry you?" he asked, and I felt his other hand brush down to my hip, undoubtedly to lift me up like I was some unstable toddler in danger of stumbling out into a busy road.

"No. Thanks. I think I can manage," I gritted, pulling my shoulder out of his grasp so I could continue down the path. I was still pissed with both of them for kidnapping and mating me against my will, but my experience in the grotto had altered the emotions churning in my gut since we passed through the portal to Jotunheim.

I'd been filled to the brim with misery and despair on the way up this mountain, along with hatred of the men who'd brought me here. I still was, to some extent, but... not quite like before.

The echo of the pain I'd endured as I saw the worm-like monster murder both my mates panged in my chest, and I rubbed at the feather-covered leather. They might have forced their marks on me in a mistaken attempt to save their respective families, but I knew the truth now. They'd give their lives for me.

The connection that tugged and pulled at me where two bonds were anchored deep in my heart was as strong on their ends. They'd tied themselves as much as they had me—had altered their own lives almost like they had mine, even if they didn't seem to realize it yet. How cruel of the Norn to play into their alpha instincts to claim and possess, when in the end, they were equally as enslaved to Fate as I.

Perhaps at least the idea of Fate and magic was easier to swallow for them than the human who'd just gotten sucked through a portal and told she had to save the world.

I wanted to cling to denial something fierce, grab hold with firm disbelief of anything as nonfactual as visions and magic and *gods* coming to life—but after what I'd seen in Verdandi's cave, I no longer had that luxury. She'd called it a vision of the future—if I remained adamant in denying the fate she'd weaved for me—and I knew she was right. Something in the very fabric of my being had known the truth as I lay gasping on the grotto floor below the shining threads representing the souls of myself and the alphas vying for the right to claim me. It wasn't a trick. It was real.

And I was the only one who could change it.

Despite everything, despite how absurd that a human—and an omega no less—could be the difference between the end of the world and its survival, the knowledge of it filled me with a quiet strength.

Yes, I'd been ripped away from my life and forced to mate with two strangers, but I wasn't here to be a mindless breeding slave. I had power. And purpose.

I just had to figure out how to unlock it.

"How much further until we get to Mimir?" I asked Magni, who was leading the way down the mountain. As opposed to me, he seemed to have no trouble with the treacherous path—but then, I supposed he was a god. Or maybe part god, part mountain goat.

"Mimir's Well isn't far," Magni said as he cast a look at the giant tree trunk rising up high above the clouds. "It sits in a glade by the roots of Yggdrasil. A day's travel, at most."

I eyeballed the World Tree. "His... Well? Do you mean his house?"

"He wouldn't have much use for a house," Saga said, an amused note to his voice. "Any who wishes to seek the knowledge of the Well will make an offering there, and if Mimir's so inclined, he will accept. Hopefully he's not in the mood for an eyeball this time around."

"An eyeball? He might want an *eyeball*?" Just what kind of fresh hell was this? I'd gotten the impression this guy was going to help us save the damn world, but there was a chance he'd start demanding body parts in return?

"He did once," Magni said. "Of the Allfather."

"The who now?"

"Odin, most supreme of the gods, the one-eyed ruler of Asgard, god of wisdom and magic and war, to name but a few. And, of course, your esteemed grandfather-in-law," Saga said, the complete lack of respect in his voice in sharp contrast the accolades of the god he was talking about. "Surely you've heard of him, little historian?"

"Of course I have," I snapped. "I just...." *Never thought of him as real.* Then something he said struck me like a bolt of lightning. "Wait—what do you mean he's my grandfather-in-law?"

"He's Thor's father," Magni said. "My dad."

"And technically the father of all the gods, hence the whole Allfather title," Saga interjected.

I don't know why it'd taken me this long to process —but it had. Thor was my *freaking father-in-law. Thor.* Images of Chris Hemsworth in a red cape flickered uninvited for my mind's eye.

"Odin wanted all the wisdom Mimir possessed. In return, Mimir asked for an eye," Magni said, as if it were no big deal to ask people for such an offering. "We're asking for far less, so we should be fine."

"Oh yes, we're just asking how to save the world," I muttered.

"We're asking how to safely return to Asgard," Magni corrected, and I rolled my eyes behind his back. He still thought he was going to put a magic baby in me that would sort Ragnarök right out.

"You mean, we're asking how we can keep Annabel

safe while you and I sort out your illegitimate claim," Saga snarled behind me, the sudden change to his demeanor startling.

Magni whipped around so fast I didn't manage to stop in time and smacked right into his chest, but he didn't focus on me—his green eyes were locked on Saga, fury sparking within. "Threaten me one more time with how you're going to separate me from my fucking mate, and your head's ending up in that well alongside Mimir's!"

I didn't hear Saga's reply. Blackness swarmed my vision, ripping my consciousness away.

THICK FOG COVERED THE GROUND, making it near impossible to see more than five feet ahead, though the sky no longer seemed darker than a stormy gray. What looked like gnarly, oversized roots rose out of the fog to the left. Yggdrasil's roots.

"It's here," Magni said from beside me. I jolted as his large figure emerged from the fog. He placed a hand on my lower back, and despite myself I found comfort in his touch. The eerie quietude of the mist-blanketed glade made my nerves stand on end.

"This is not like I remember," Saga murmured from my other side.

"*Annabel!*" The sound of my name boomed through the air, coming from all around us. I spun around, trying to locate the source, my heart thudding into overdrive.

"Annabel!" It was a roar, so loud the ground shook and dark dots danced for my eyes.

"Annabel!"

I blinked, the sound of my name now coming from much closer. When I opened my eyes, I stared right up into Saga's worried, gray gaze. Above him the sky was dark, a single star twinkling through the cloud cover. That is, until Magni's face appeared, blocking out the sky. His red eyebrows were pulled down as he scanned my face.

"W-what happened?" I croaked, fighting to sit up. Saga didn't let go of my shoulders, but instead of pressing me back down, he supported my weight so I could get up.

I could make out Verdandi's cave as a black void against the dark sky high above us, and when I looked to my right the vastness of the world tree's trunk was also visible. The fog-covered glade was nowhere to be found.

"You passed out," Magni said, voice gruff. "Probably from lack of food."

"Did you even eat before you snuck out this morning?" Saga asked, tilting my face up to with a finger underneath my chin.

This morning. Somehow the creepy ritual at the

Lokissons' farm and my ordeal in the cave back in Iceland seemed like eons ago. In some ways, I guess it was a lifetime ago—because the girl who'd run out into the snowstorm this morning didn't exist anymore. That girl hadn't known about Ragnarök or Norns or visions.

"No, I didn't eat," I murmured, frowning as I tried to remember the details from the glade. I was pretty sure that'd been a vision, but... nothing had *happened*. I'd just had this unshakable sense of foreboding. A sensation that still lingered. I rubbed my arms, trying to ease the goosebumps covering them. "How long was I out?"

"Ten minutes, maybe." Magni straightened up and cast a look over the landscape. "We need to get you fed."

"I'm not leaving her alone with you, so don't even ask," Saga warned, not taking his eyes off me.

"As if I would let you hunt for *my* mate," Magni huffed. He turned back, giving us both a lingering look. It seemed like he was trying to weigh his options and coming up short. "But she needs food. Humans are...."

"Fragile," Saga sighed. "Hunt for her, I'll stay and protect her."

"If you try to take off with her—" Magni growled, eyes narrowed.

Saga rolled his eyes. "She *just* face-planted from lack of food. I'm not about to take her anywhere before she's been fed. Besides, the Norn made it quite clear we need to find Mimir. It's not like you don't know where we'd go."

Magni didn't answer the blond alpha. He just stared

hard at him for another moment, then returned his focus to me. "I won't be gone long. If you need me, scream. I'll come."

"Sure thing," I muttered, trying not to hold it against him that he was incapable of seeing me as anything more than a swooning damsel in distress. If some form of monster *did* happen to swing by, I'd be happy to swallow my pride and scream for both him and Saga, but it was still infuriating to be treated like....

Well, like an omega.

When Magni left, Saga helped me to my feet and led me to a trickling spring of water. I drank greedily from it, and briefly considered washing up as well. I was still caked in semen and dried sweat underneath my new outfit, but the temperature wasn't exactly great for bathing. In the end I decided against it, vowing to get clean when I could do so without losing a nipple to frost bite.

"Fucking Magni, coulda' at least started a fire," Saga muttered by my side as he stacked tinder and branches into a small circle by the side of the spring. "Use those damn lightning fingers for something good, for once."

I remembered the fight in the cave and how Magni had zapped Saga while he was still coming inside of me, and cracked a half-smile. "They seem to be pretty useful for deflating knots, too."

Saga shot me a dirty look, and I snickered. "Sorry. It's just... You kind of had it coming."

"I know you're upset about how everything went

down," he said, sighing softly as he stared at the pile of branches on the ground. "And that you don't trust me all that much right now. But I promise you, it was never mine or my brothers' intent for your claiming to be this traumatic."

"You just wanted to gangbang me against my will and force me into a three-way marriage I didn't want," I said pointedly. "Nothing too unpleasant."

He looked at me over his shoulder again, but there wasn't anger in his gaze this time. Only gentle regret. "I know you didn't want this, Annabel. But I felt the change in you when you came back with Verdandi. Whatever she showed you, you now understand why we had to do what we did. Don't you?"

The infuriating thing was that I did. "It doesn't absolve you for being such an asshole," I said. "And for thinking that the only way I could possibly be helpful was to spread my legs and give you an heir. She tricked you, you know? The Norn. She has this great big plan that involves you, me, your brothers, and Magni and some other dude, and she figured the best way to get you to accept sharing a mate was to make you believe you all needed to impregnate me."

He stilled, his eyes widening slightly as he stared at me. "What?"

"Yeah. She played you. All of you." I rubbed a hand over the back of my neck, wincing as both the marks there stung slightly at the too-harsh touch. "She believes we can stop Ragnarök. But only together."

He regarded me quietly for a long while. "And you believe her," he finally said.

"I do. She showed me... the alternative." I shuddered at the memory of the monster in the snow.

"And what makes you think she isn't tricking you?" he asked. "That she isn't telling *you* what you want to hear to get you to accept her plans for you? Norns are tricky creatures... And it is unlikely she could have fooled Loki when she first interpreted that prophecy for him and pointed out which family this omega would spring from so he could make his deal with your ancestors. My father is the god of mischief and deceit, after all."

I frowned. "That's not... possible." Everything she'd said—the vision—it'd felt so very real. But he had a point. If Verdandi had tricked them, what was to say she couldn't have tricked me, too? But to what purpose?

Saga sighed and got up from the unlit fire. He crouched back down by my side, wrapping an oversized hand around my arm. "Annabel, I'm not saying that whatever she told you was a lie. Most likely, it was a half-truth. And I promise you that if there is a way for us to stop Ragnarök, then I will walk that path with you. Even if it involves not murdering Magni and his asshole brother for trying to steal you away from me."

"But?" I asked, because the tension in his tone told me he wasn't done.

"But Magni isn't going to see it that way. He's dead set on bringing you to Asgard to take your role as his mate. Nothing either of us say is going to sway his mind."

I arched an eyebrow at him. "I mean, it wasn't like you seemed all that keen on changing your mind. Maybe he'll surprise you. If he knows there's a way to stop the end of the world, surely he'll go for it. He might be a dick, but he's a god, after all."

Saga released my arm and trailed a finger up along it, caressing the nape of my neck where his bite still lingered. His touch warmed my skin. "The problem is he won't believe you. He won't entertain the possibility that Verdandi might have told you the truth while she manipulated him."

"But you want me to believe you will?" The humming in my chest at his nearness was distracting. I tried to keep in mind that this was the guy who'd lured me across the ocean to force me to accept his claim, but the damn bond was murmuring about how he only wanted to keep me safe. Hadn't he proved that by refusing to let go when Magni tried to separate us and pulled me through the portal?

"I do. Because I will, Annabel." His voice was quiet and intimate, a hypnotic murmur that contradicted the swaggering alpha I'd met in Reykjavik's airport so sharply he may as well have been a different person. Gently, he pulled me into his arms and nudged my head up with a finger, locking my gaze in his. Perhaps it was the lack of food, but I felt woozy all of a sudden. But also... warm. Safe. I stared at him, my mouth half agape, trying to collect my thoughts and finding it impossible to with the blond alpha so close. *My mate.*

"All I want is for you to learn to love me," he whispered, letting his finger slide up to caress my cheek. "I know it will take time for you to trust me after all that's happened, but I promise you I will never lie to you. Ask him—ask Magni if he will abandon his quest to bring you to Asgard even if Mimir confirms Verdandi's claims. He may be the son of Thor—but he is no hero. He will let your parents and every single other human die, if it means he gets to protect his own family."

14

SAGA

The one good thing about the bond thrumming in my chest night and day, forcing me to open my soul to the stubborn human I'd claimed, was that it made it so much easier to manipulate her.

I didn't shoot lightning from my fingers like Thor's redheaded bastard—my magic was subtler.

Loki had many children, many I'd never even met and all of whom had inherited something from the god of trickery that sired us. For Grim, it was his guile and lethal darkness. For Bjarni, his ability to make a friend out of any enemy. And I... I'd received the gift of deceit.

I hadn't thought of using it on Annabel, not at first. She was just a human after all, and there'd been no need.

But that was before fucking Magni had ruined everything, and now—now our plan's survival relied on my ability to convince my omega that her other mate would never allow her the freedom she'd grown so used to while she was raised as a beta.

To my delight I'd found the bond that tied us together left her more vulnerable to my influence than any other I'd ever used it on. I'd told her half-truths while I petted and comforted her, and she'd not so much as registered my magic wrapping around her will and easing her defenses.

All I needed now was for Magni to bluster about how she would learn to obey him a few more times, and the girl would choose me without a second thought when the time came.

"The well isn't far," Magni said from up ahead. He was once again leading us, allowing me to bring up the rear. I normally wouldn't have allowed a hostile alpha to take the lead, but the more she experienced the controlling asshole he truly was, the better.

Besides, I had a fabulous view of Annabel's leather-clad backside from here. Magni was only cheating himself.

"This doesn't seem familiar," my mate mumbled, taking in the dense forest lining the western path around the outskirts of Yggdrasil's roots.

"I would be surprised if it did," I said, amused that she thought it would. "Guessing you haven't swung by Mimir's Well before, hmm?"

"No," she said, but the hesitance in her voice suggested she was confused nonetheless.

Poor girl hadn't had an easy twenty-four hours.

We walked for maybe half a mile more before the path twisted sharply to the right, through a thorny thicket. The glade beyond wasn't more than maybe thirty feet across, covered in blackened, dead vegetation, and in the center stood the familiar stone well, pointing toward the gray skies above.

"It's here," Magni said, coming up beside Annabel to place a hand on the small of her back.

I moved in on her other side, instincts to protect swelling for some unknown reason. Probably because I hadn't fucked her since her heat. Fucking alpha hormones. If Magni hadn't been around I'd have flipped her over and taken her until she liked it before we got going for the day—but I wasn't about to give him any advantages in her eyes.

"This is not like I remember," I said, frowning at the clearing. When my father'd taken me here decades ago, the grass surrounding the well had been lush and emerald green. Of course, that was long before the Fimbulwinter set in. Jotunheim might not be hit like the human world was, but it was foolish to believe any of the nine realms would be untouched by Ragnarök's arrival.

Annabel jolted between us, her gaze flickering up to mine and then back to the well. "I... I don't think we should go any further," she said. "I've got... a bad feeling about this."

"The Norn told us to find Mimir," Magni said,

letting his hand stroke up her back in a soothing motion that should have pissed me off but somehow didn't. "You've just been through a lot, pet. Your nerves are overworked."

She shot him a glare he didn't notice as he stepped forward, making his way to the well.

I put a hand on her shoulder and gave her an encouraging smile. "This is what you wanted, right? A chance to prove your role in this."

She frowned up at me, uncertainty flickering in her chocolate eyes. "I guess. It's just... Something's *off*. I had this... well, I thought it was a vision, but...." She looked around the clearing, shoulders slumping in defeat. "But it didn't look like this."

Vision? Had Verdandi told her she could see the future? Something stirred at the back of my skull—the first sliver of doubt that just maybe the Norn hadn't lied to the willful omega to get her to accept her fate. If she had magic... it would make sense that *she* was the human fated to save Loki's lineage.

"What do you mean it didn't look like this?" I asked.

"There was a thick fog everywhere... but you and Magni... you were the same."

I sighed, oddly disappointed as I grabbed her hand. It was better this way—a mate with magic was more trouble than a weak human. "Visions are very clear— they don't deviate from the details. Come, sweetling. There is nothing to be afraid of—at most, Mimir might tell us a long and boring story before he gets to the point. He doesn't get out much—but he isn't dangerous."

She didn't respond, but she let me drag her toward the well where Magni was already waiting, bent over the side of it. His long, red hair danced in the wind as he stared into the depths below.

"He home?" I joked as I stepped up on the bottom rim of the stone construction and peered down.

Fog swirled below, thick and languid, its tendrils slowly creeping up the inner sides of the well. Instantly, my breathing slowed down as my brain hazed over.

Fight it.

The thought came from faraway, as if moving through molten molasses, and I blinked stupidly at the swirling mist below.

Fight... what?

An urgency that didn't belong to me shot through my nervous system, and in a daze I realized I felt *him*. Magni. The bond that connected me with Annabel tugged urgently on me from within, but the desperation was muted and didn't come from her. It was him.

That's when I saw it. The creature hiding behind the fog, its features hidden by the swirling mist. It wasn't Mimir. It was something else... Lurking. Waiting.

I tried to jerk back, but my body didn't react. I stayed locked in place, unable to move. Unable to shout a warning when Annabel came up between us and leaned over the side of the well, peering down.

"Hello. Mr. Mimir?" she said, squinting into the

well. "I'm Annabel Turner. We've come to seek your advice."

"I've been waiting for you," a voice that definitely didn't belong to Mimir said.

Down in the yawning void, something dazzled with a strange sort of half-light, once more hiding the creature from view.

"Guys?" Annabel whispered between us, looking to first me and then Magni. "I kind of don't think I should be leading the conversation here."

The blackness congealed around that single point of brilliance. *"They are frozen, shiny one. You cannot rouse them."*

"What?" Annabel jerked back, her hands reaching for each of us. When shaking us did nothing, she stared back into the well. I felt the swell of her fear in my chest.

Run, Annabel, run, I prayed silently. Whatever was hiding below the fog, it was powerful enough to have blocked not only my access to my physical body, but my magic too. And Magni's along with it.

But she didn't run. My stupid, brave little omega clenched her hands around the edge of the well, staring into the mist. "Why? What do you want from me?"

"Your coming was foretold. I want to help you, and they would never let me," the voice said.

Annabel arched an eyebrow. "Well, yeah. *You* foretold it, as far as I understand. That doesn't explain why you've frozen Saga and Magni."

The voice grew nearer, as did the solidifying void. *"They seek to shackle you, shiny one. They will use your magic for their own needs. But what about your plans? What about everything you desire? Let me help you, and you will be a slave no longer."*

My heart thudded unevenly in my chest. Whatever this thing was, it knew her deepest wish.

I wanted to scream when I saw Annabel lean further over the edge, parting her lips in an expression of desperation. "You can do that? You can... remove the marks? But what about Ragnarök? Verdandi showed my... our fates. They're intertwined. And your prophecy—"

"They brought you here. That was their only job. They're selfish creatures, unconcerned with your wants. They took what they needed from you, and if you let them, they will keep taking until there's nothing left. Nothing but an empty shell. You don't need them, shiny one. Let me help you break free from your chains."

"I...." She hesitated, one delicate hand reaching for the marks emblazoned on the back of her neck. My heart shuddered when she brushed her fingers over mine, the sensation sending a vibration through our bond. Then, her face hardened and she gripped the edge of the well again. "What do you want in return?"

No. No, no, no!

The fog swirled, tendrils shooting higher up the side of the well. *"Just a sip of your essence. It has been so long... since I tasted magic."*

Annabel bit her lip. "Will... will it hurt?"

"*Yes.*" It was a breathless whisper, and it chilled me to the bone.

The dark-haired omega swallowed noticeably, but seemed to steel herself. "And if I do this, you promise you will break my mate bonds and help me stop Ragnarök?"

"*Yes.*"

"Okay, then. How...?"

"*Lean closer,*" the creature pressed. "*Let me reach you.*"

I strained with everything I was, fighting against the invisible bonds. By my side and through the bond I shared with Annabel, I felt Magni's desperation flare as urgently and knew he was clawing at his own restraints in our shared need to get to our mate before whatever was in that cursed well either kept its word and broke out connection—or worse.

Oblivious to our desperate fight, Annabel leaned further over the edge, trying to look through the fog. "I can't see anything."

"*I see you,*" the voice said. "*Just a little closer.*"

Light reflected off the white blanket, sparking in multi-hued splendor. It reminded me of an aurora draping the stars in radium ribbons. Annabel reached out, stretching a hand toward it, mesmerized by the deceitful beauty.

And that's when I finally saw what was lurking underneath.

It rose through the fog, dark tendrils snaking up

with a speed too fast to counter. It wrapped around Annabel's wrist, pulling taut as the mist finally dispersed.

Teeth. So many teeth flashed, too many eyes focusing on the woman in its grip.

"*Shit!*" she screamed, pulling hard on the tendril around her wrist. "Let go of me!"

The creature yanked harder on her, nearly pulling her shoulder from its socket as it breached the edge of the well. Another tendril snaked up, wrapping around her throat and yanking her head up and back.

"*You agreed. A deal is a deal,*" it hissed. "*Give me your essence.*"

The fear and pain shooting through my mate bond was blinding, and in my head I screamed her name as the creature's black mouth covered hers.

Annabel jolted hard, and with her free hand punched the inky monster square in about five of the eyes covering its head.

It pulled back with a hiss, quickly grabbing the offending limb to restrain her fully.

"No! Help! Saga—Magni! Help me!" It was a desperate shriek and died on a groan when the creature attached itself to her face once more.

The world around us convulsed hard, and I felt all my divine power swell up without my conscious thought, hammering at the invisible bindings keeping me locked in place. By my side, I felt Magni's essence tearing at his own, saw the air quake as we both fought with everything we were—but it wasn't enough.

Panic clenched my chest as *something* drained from the other end of my bond. Something that sapped the light out of the world and opened a chasm where my heart should have been.

Her life essence.

My mate was going to die.

And I didn't have the strength to save her in time.

Magni's pain echoed through the bond, mirroring my own as he came to the same conclusion.

In the end, neither of us were strong enough to protect the mate we'd claimed. Neither of us were worthy—

The realization struck like lightning from a clear sky.

Neither of us were enough to save her—alone.

Without waiting to think it through, I drew my power to me—and then forced it at the bonds keeping Magni frozen.

A crack like a falling tree snapped through the glade, followed by the familiar stench of ozone.

Magni roared his fury out, his battle cry echoing like waves of thunder. His hands lit up like a pair of Roman candles, and then he lunged at the creature and grabbed onto its face.

The air ignited in static arcs around the redheaded alpha, followed by another blast of thunder as lightning shot through the slimy flesh.

The creature brayed, its howl splitting into a chorus of discordant tones. Annabel dropped to the floor as the monster thrashed, releasing her to fight off the furious god.

But it was too late—Magni wasn't letting go. He funneled his power through it, lighting it up from the inside. But in its fury it snaked its tendrils around his torso and tore its teeth into his arm.

"Magni!" Annabel stumbled to her feet and threw herself at the beast, fists aiming for its many eyes. She was a small whirlwind of fury, kicking and punching at the terrifyingly powerful creature as if her puny human strength could do any damage to a being such as this.

But somewhere along the way she must have gotten enough of a lucky shot in to startle it, because it drew back from Magni with a howl.

The other alpha snarled, blood dripping from his arm as he lit into the creature with another crack of thunder.

Bright light flashed, blinding me with its sharpness and making Annabel stumble back, one arm raised to shield her eyes from the light.

When it dimmed, there was nothing but a pile of ash where the monster had been.

The bindings that had kept me in place snapped just as Magni sank to his knees with a groan.

I pushed off the well and spun around to Annabel.

"Are you all right? Did it hurt you?" I grabbed her

face between both hands, turned it to both sides and peered into her eyes to ensure the spark was still there.

"I'm... I think I'm okay," she whispered. "It didn't take much. That wasn't Mimir, was it?"

I laughed, mostly because the relief of her survival had my head spinning, and crushed her to my chest to soothe our still-quivering bond. "No, it wasn't. I don't know what that thing was, but it's gone now." She smelled like ozone too, like *Magni*. But as I buried my nose in her hair and breathed in deeply, I found that I didn't mind, because she was safe and that was all that mattered. "Don't ever do something that dumb again."

"*Dumb?*" She protested, pushing against my chest. I held on. "*You* brought me here! *You* told me it was fine, after *I* said I had a bad feeling about this!"

She had a point. "That fucking Norn. We should get going. We don't know if there are any more of its kind around."

"Where do we go?" Magni said, his voice strained. "Mimir's gone. How the fuck do we find him now?"

I turned around to where he was sat slumped against the well, and the shock of it made me finally loosen my grip on Annabel.

His face was ashen, trickles of blood still leaking from where the monster had bitten him. He looked... weak. Sick.

"Magni," Annabel whispered. She pushed out of my grip and knelt by his side. Hesitantly, she brought her hand to his cheek, careful not to touch his arm. "Are you... okay?"

He grimaced, mouth pulled into a grim line. "I'll be fine."

But he wasn't fine. He looked halfway to the grave, and with a wave of gratitude I realized what he'd given to save Annabel.

That creature had wanted her essence—her life force. Evidently, it'd taken Magni's instead.

"Saga's right," he said, each word pronounced carefully, as if it caused him great difficulty. "We need to get out of here."

Annabel reached for his hand to try and pull him up, but she was no match for his weight.

I pushed her aside before she could hurt herself and clasped my hand in Magni's. His fingers were cold against mine, but he managed to get to his feet. He didn't protest when I took the lead.

Nor did he seem to notice the ravens circling up above us.

15

MAGNI

I made it maybe two miles from Mimir's well before my body's scream for reprieve became too much to bear. Judging from the low set of the sun, it'd taken more than five hours to cover the short distance.

"We need to rest," Annabel said. She'd been walking behind me for the past mile or so, taking up a position of protection I should have offered her. Not the other way around.

Saga looked over his shoulder at me, and I gritted my teeth in expectation of his challenge.

"I'm fine," I sneered. "We push on." I'd rather die than he know how weak I was right then. If he did, there'd be nothing stopping him from taking Annabel.

My lungs constricted at the thought, and I pushed down a wave of nausea.

If he took her from me, the gods would perish.

"No," Saga said, surprising me. "It's late. We need to make camp." He motioned toward a clearing half-covered in sprawling brambles.

I stared at him for a moment longer, trying to figure out what his game was. If I were him, if he'd been the one so weakened, I'd have pushed my advantage. If he wasn't, he was up to something—he was Loki's son after all.

The muscles in my arm spasmed, and I nearly faltered. With a grunt, I nodded. "Fine. We rest."

Annabel put her arm on my back to support me, as if her small body could do anything to keep me up. But her touch through the nubile leather of my clothes felt good, and somehow I found the strength to walk the few steps. I sank down against a tree, eyes fluttering closed before I could stop them.

This was better. Not good. But better.

"I'm going to hunt," Saga said.

I cracked my eyelids open to look up at him. He stared down at me, an expression across his face I couldn't quite decipher. It looked almost like... pity. But no. I was the son of Thor—no one *pitied* me. And *he* was the son of Loki—he was incapable of such emotion.

"With what?" I asked. "Your magic isn't offensive and it's not like we have weapons handy."

Saga's lips hiked up at the corner, a haughty smirk playing across his face. "Well, at least the meat won't be singed this time, eh?"

I didn't have the energy to argue—and Annabel

needed to eat. As much as it killed me not being able to provide for her myself, a small part of me was grateful her other alpha would.

I should have been infuriated at the thought, humiliated I needed another man to care for my omega—but I didn't have the strength. Instead of answering him, I leaned my head back against the trunk and closed my eyes.

"Stay hidden," Saga murmured, the softness in his voice indicating the command was directed at Annabel. "I'll be back soon."

His footfall retreated out of the glade. Annabel shuffled around for a little while, and I wished I could have lit a fire for her. But my magic was gone. Pulled out of me like marrow sucked from a snapped bone.

"Why?" she asked.

I forced my eyelids open again to look at her—the sound of her voice pulling on me like a siren's call.

"Why did you get in between me and that... that thing?" she insisted when I didn't answer.

Pain pulsed from my arm where the well creature had sunk its teeth into me.

I'd asked myself why since we left Mimir's well. As the blight crept up my arm, tainting it cell by cell and twisting the divine helix of my DNA, I thought long and hard about what had possessed me to put myself in harm's way for Annabel. I'd had other options at my disposal—gods usually did—and if I'd stopped to think about what I was doing, I would have likely chosen a fate that didn't involve this slow, agonizing torment.

But that was just it... I hadn't stopped to think. Seeing her so close to danger, perhaps near death, had filled me with an urgent and insurmountable need to protect her. I'd reacted on some stupid, involuntary instinct, one which left no room for hesitation, and now here I was, weakening with each passing second.

"Magni?" Annabel said. She was staring at me and had been for some time, her dark hair loosed from its braid and tumbling wild over her shoulders. It had been a tough day and a half since I took her through the portal, filled with arduous treks and near-death experiences, and every bit of that was reflected in the pinched corners of her eyes and the grim set of her lips.

And still, she was beautiful. Despite the way the wind had beat against her, or how tired she was, Annabel was as radiant as ever.

It worried me, how difficult it was to dim her shine. I'd been banking on a female more easily broken, one who would accept her fate. I realized now that she was not that girl, but it was too late. She was already mine. We were stuck with each other.

Which would have been fine—she may be spirited, but I was a god. At my full strength I could break her in fully until the fire in her simmered down to a comfortable warmth. But right now, with my arm throbbing dully and my magic dried in my veins, there was no way I was going to let on how bad it really was.

She would rebel if she knew—and Saga would take her from me in a heartbeat.

Still, she was staring at me. Waiting for an answer.

"You were about to die—or worse," I reminded her, grimacing as another fissure of pain bloomed beneath my skin. "There is too much at stake to let that happen."

"You could have used your magic," she pointed out, gaze dropping to my arm where I cradled it against my chest. "But you didn't."

I shrugged, turning away. "I might have hit you."

"You had no problem shocking me before."

"Do you never just accept an answer?" I hissed. "Must everything be a battle?"

Annabel shrugged. "I spent years in college learning to ask questions and hoping they'd be the right ones— the ones that would get me answers to the things nobody else knew. It is... it *was* a huge part of my profession."

I snorted. "A skald."

"A *historian*."

This crawling sickness had infiltrated my bones now, setting fire to my marrow. Sweat clung to my temples as I curled in on myself. "I fail to see the difference."

"Skalds were storytellers and poets," she said, inching closer to me and trying to pull my arm into her grasp to inspect it. "They made up stories just as often as they told the truth."

"Don't," I growled, shifting out of her reach again. "It could be catching."

Annabel narrowed her eyes. "It could be *killing* you."

"You think I'm weak?" I asked.

"I think you're sick," she said, withdrawing from me. I grabbed her wrist, my hand encompassing her bones easily.

"I am not *sick*," I growled, ensuring she remained on her knees. "I am as strong as I have ever been. I am still a god, an alpha, and your mate. You will treat me like all of the above."

Annabel tried to wrench away, and I thanked the stars I hadn't been bluffing as much as I'd felt I was. She remained in my grip, twisting futilely. "You're hurt. You're clearly in pain—"

Now I did let her go. She fell back onto her hands, staring up at me with wide eyes. "Must you argue? I saved your life. You admit as much. I know these realms better than you do. I know what fiends lurk in every corner of them. Has it not occurred to you I might be right?"

But I'd not doused the fire in her yet. Setting her jaw, Annabel sat back up.

"Except you don't know what *this* is," she reminded me, tugging my arm. It was a dirty move. I was momentarily gobsmacked by the pain, allowing for Annabel to push up my sleeve and survey the damage. Her face paled. "Jesus Christ...."

Coils black as a cuttlefish's ink squirmed under my flesh like a feast of worms. Some of them had fattened on what they'd devoured from me and were now swollen to the size of leeches, their undulations so pronounced I was mildly concerned they might break the barrier of my skin. If I tensed my muscles hard enough, I could beat them back, force them to retreat closer to my bones, but when I did, they burrowed into my elbow, misery lancing up into my shoulder and spine.

All the fight fled from Annabel's body then, and when she met my gaze, hers was so stricken as to rob me of my own fury. She may as well have kicked me straight in the heart, eyes rounded with fear and what looked to me like actual, genuine concern.

"I'm...." Her words caught, and she had to clear her throat to free them. "I'm sorry."

Tempered now, I muttered, "It's not your fault." Snatching my arm back, I hid it from her view. "You couldn't have known."

She nodded, but nothing in her expression made me believe she was convinced. After a glance in the direction Saga had stalked off in, she asked, "What was that thing? What did it want from me? And what did it take from you?"

I snorted. "Well, it certainly wasn't Mimir."

"I know that," she sighed with an earnest, exasperated look. "I don't know what it was. I've never encountered anything like it, or heard tales of it. It was... pure darkness. And it wanted your essence. It took... some of mine instead."

Annabel stared at my arm for a long moment. Finally, and in a soft voice, she asked, "Will you die, Magni?"

I eyed her from the corner of my vision. "Do you *really* think it's that easy to kill a god?" It shouldn't have been. We were supposedly immortal, or as good as. Yet I wasn't healing. The well within where my life force sprung wasn't refilling, like it always had when I'd been injured in battle before.

Silence yawned between us once more, opening a gulf neither of us wanted to cross. And why would she? She was tired and far from home. I'd dragged her out here into hostile territory, brought us to the wrong *fucking* place to begin with, and now I wasn't sure I could get us to where we were going.

"You should rest," I finally said. "Saga will return soon, and once we've eaten we press on."

"Magni," she said, exasperation in her voice. "You can barely stand. You might be healing—but it looks like it'll take a while. And I'm... I'm *really* tired. We've been walking, climbing, and running for *hours*. Maybe you've forgotten, but I'm not a god."

I liked the little crinkle she got above her nose when she was irritated with me. I hadn't noticed it before. There were other parts of her I'd taken stock of—the heavy swells of her breasts; the perfect slope of her waist; the way her hips fit easily in my hands—but that detail had escaped my attention. Now it was all I could look at.

"I'll carry you," I said, but Annabel only rolled her eyes.

"Not with that arm, you won't."

I reached out, ensnaring her ankle this time. She yelped as I yanked her toward me, turning onto her back and sitting up so close our noses touched.

"Do not tell me what I can and cannot do," I murmured, sliding my hand toward her knee. "Whatever you come up with, you will be wrong."

She flinched from me, face flushed. "I... I'm just worried about you."

"That's the second time you've called me weak," I said, grasping her opposite knee with my free hand and parting her legs. "You should be concerned about what might happen to you if you say it a third time."

She was so warm between her thighs. It penetrated her breeches, hotter and more inviting than the sun. And her scent—it was thicker than smoke, yet rising just as steadily. Sweet and heady, it curled in my nostrils and bid my cock to attention.

Annabel gasped as I pressed my thumb to where her clit lay beneath all those clothes. "How is your heat?"

"It's... it's passed," she stammered, trying to close her legs around me. I tore them open again, increasing the pressure of my thumb until she bit her lip.

"Really?" I asked her. "No more urges?"

"No," she lied through her teeth. When I began to stroke her, she grabbed my hand. "Magni... wait. You don't have to do this."

I paused, lifting my brows at her. "I am doing exactly as I please."

But Annabel shook her head. "That's not what I mean."

I searched her face. Something in her tone was... different, enough that it made me hesitate. Slowly, I moved my hands to her hips instead. "Go on."

She pushed herself into a more upright position, and though I would not let her go, I allowed her to curl her legs beneath her. "You don't have to fuck me just to prove you're not weak. Not to me, and least of all to Saga."

"Gods, pet," I laughed, trying not to show my alarm when it thinned into a wheeze. "You really do think too much."

Annabel cupped my cheek. Her palm was... soft. And just as warm as her pussy. She glided her thumb across my skin, tentative but tender, and I found myself rooted to the spot. She'd never touched me like his before—not that I'd given her much of a chance to. It was... disturbing.

I leaned forward, intent on putting her on her back, but she took my face in both her hands and stopped me again. "Magni... at the well... you saved me."

I regarded her again. She was serious. Whatever this

was, it wasn't a mere ploy to stall me. "And that means something to you, does it?"

"It does." Slowly, she threaded her fingers into my mane. "You didn't have to do what you did. You didn't have to let it hurt you instead." Swallowing, she added, "You could have let it hurt me."

"No," I told her, and meant it. "I couldn't."

She breathed in deeply and looked up at me, brown gaze searching for something in mine. "Magni... I want to tell you what the Norn showed me. When she separated us."

"She showed you your fate," I said, because it was what made sense. Verdandi was a Norn, after all, and Annabel had seemed less combative about her situation since. "Why your sacrifice is needed."

"Yes," she said. "But not how you think. She said... she tricked you, Magni. You and the Lokisson brothers. She used your instincts against you to make you share a claim with them. She said we cannot fight Ragnarök if we're not united. And *that's* our fate. To stop it. To save everyone—not just your bloodline. *Everyone.*"

There was so much passion in her eyes, so much desperation. Her cheeks were still flushed from my manipulation of her clit, and long wisps of brown hair framed her face. And for a moment, I wanted to believe her, just so I could bathe in her shine for a little while longer.

But I knew the trickery of Norns. What Verdandi had claimed was a rouse for me, was clearly a snare for the annoying little omega in my arms. Her desperation to have agency over her fate was her greatest weakness —and the easiest thing to manipulate. What better way to get Annabel to comply than to tell her her fate was to save the humans she so loved?

I'd been called many things over the centuries, many of them less than kind, but I wasn't heartless. And letting Annabel believe that there was any hope for her world, or any need for her besides what lay between her legs would be too cruel. The sooner she accepted her fate, the sooner she would settle into her new life and, eventually, find some measure of contentment.

I bit down on the pain throbbing through my arm and up my shoulder, and forced her onto her back.

She squeaked from surprise at the unexpected movement, arms flying up to grab my shoulders as I hovered over her, trapping her beneath me.

"I am your mate, Annabel. I may not be what you wanted, but I am still that. No wishful thinking, no deceitful promises from the Weavers of Fate, and no son of Loki will ever change this. You are my omega, you will sit by my side in Asgard, and you will fulfill your destiny when you birth me a son. *That* is your fate." I brought my injured hand to the side of her neck, brushing over my mark. The agony lancing through the injured limb made me hiss, but the throb of desire in my blood at the touch of her skin against mine was unhindered by the pain.

"Why are you so goddamn *stubborn?*" she growled,

eyes flashing with anger at being put into such a submissive position. "Are you really trying to rape me while your arm is withering away, just to prove how alpha you are?"

"No, pet," I growled, showing her my teeth when she dug her fingers into my injured arm but holding fast. "I'm proving to you exactly where your place is, and reminding you how much you like it. I may be injured but I'm not *weak*. I'm your alpha, and I'll never stop reminding you. You will come to accept your fate for what it is, Annabel. And I will help you."

"Stop it, Magni! I'm not in heat anymore!" she hissed when I snaked a hand between her legs, coming to rest on an elbow to push her resistance down. She was scalding hot, and when I shoved down the front of her pants slickness met my fingers. She might not be in heat, but her body was still responding to my closeness and dominance. I slipped my fingers between her folds to find her clit, biting back on a pained moan when the dark fissures in my arm dug deeper at the flexing of muscles.

"Magni!" Annabel whined, a breathless sound halfway between protest and pleasure. "Stop! I don't want this!"

"You may not want it," I growled, rubbing the little pearl in firm circles. "But you need it."

"Stop being such an idiotic alpha stereotype!" she hissed, swallowing a whimper when I pinched her clit. Her legs kicked in a futile attempt at pushing out from underneath me, but her pelvis canted up for more. "You're sick! Goddammit, Magni, stop!"

"*I'm. Not. Weak,*" I snarled. Without waiting for permission I shoved two fingers into her sheath, stretching her heat. She was damp enough to take it, but not nearly as wet as she'd been the day before—and she responded with a wail.

When I looked into her beautiful brown gaze again she was no longer glowering at me. Her eyes were wide with shock, understanding finally sparking in their near-golden depths. She got it, now. What she was. An omega—born to serve her alpha. Nothing she could say and nothing she could do would change that.

"You're *mine,*" I growled, desire at seeing her on her back for me and the slick noises I forced from her pussy as I slowly pumped her making my own desire take over. It hazed out even the intense agony, soothing it to a dull throb.

Odin's beard, she was beautiful. Small and delicate, plump lips parted for every gasp, and so incredibly soft against my fingers. The perfect omega.

My perfect omega.

"I said *stop!*" The punch came like lightning from a clear sky, smacking against my nose so hard bright lights burst behind my eyes. If I'd been at my full capacity her puny human strength wouldn't have made me blink, but I wasn't.

"Shit!" I groaned, pulling my hand from between her legs to my face. The ripe scent of her body's desire mixed with the pain from her aggression, fueling instincts as ancient as my blood. I snarled, deep and rich, a threat and a promise to the feisty little omega who thought to *challenge* me, and lowered my hand to see her quiver when she realized her mistake.

But we weren't alone in the glade.

"Well, well, well," Saga drawled as he watched us on the ground, head cocked. On each side of him stood his brothers, one light, one dark. Weapons were in their hands.

"I leave you alone with *my* mate for but a moment and you think you can maul her like a lusty bear? You're going to regret this, Thor's son."

They are going to take her from me.

It was the only thought that thundered through my head as I hunched over Annabel's prone body. The next second, they attacked.

16

ANNABEL

It was like mountains colliding on top of me.

The three Lokisson brothers charged at Magni, slamming into him full-force. Above his shoulder a sword gleamed, and I screamed.

"Stop! You might hurt her!" Saga snarled from somewhere above me. He gripped the sword-slinger by the wrist, staying his hand.

Someone else kicked Magni square in the side, finally getting him off me. The injured god rolled, groaned on impact, and fought to get back up, but Bjarni planted a heavy boot on his back and shoved him back down on his stomach, raising his axe above his head with a snarl.

"No! Don't!" The words were out of my throat before I could even think them, my heart slamming into over-drive. Everything had happened so suddenly, my emotions were still in a tailspin from the softness I'd felt only moments before when I realized just how much Magni had sacrificed to save me, mixed with the fury and disbelief that he'd still rather fuck me into submission than entertain the thought that I was more than a broodmare. But the sharp edge of Bjarni's axe dulled both my anger and gratitude into nothing as sheer panic burst through my frantic heart.

"Don't kill him!" I pleaded, throwing myself on top of the redheaded alpha to shield his body with mine. It wasn't a conscious choice—it was pure animalistic instinct, a desperation for survival—because every cell in my body understood that if my mate died, I would cease to exist.

"Don't kill him? He was trying to *rape* you!" Bjarni snarled, his normally so kind face twisted into battle rage. At that moment he was every inch the ruthless alpha—and nothing at all like the gentle giant who'd given me hot chocolate with marshmallows what felt like an eternity ago.

"It's not like you weren't going to do the same!" I reminded him. "Every fucking one of you, if you remember."

The complete confusion on the blond alpha's face would have been amusing under different circumstances. "What?"

"Don't give me that look—I know everything now. You lured me to Iceland so you could all mate me against my will." I pointed a finger at him. "And your brother went through with it."

"That's enough," Saga said. He sounded irritated as he stared down at me laying prone across Magni's crumbled body. "We can't kill him. Not as long as his claim is still on her. It will break her."

A strange trickle of relief traveled through my veins. Saga understood. He might still hate Magni—but he understood.

"She'd get over it," Grim murmured. He drew a nail along the blade of his sword when I twisted to glare at him. "We've wasted enough time thanks to Thor's bastard, and it's not like we can bring him."

"We leave him," Saga said. "He's too weak to follow us. If he wants to survive, he'll crawl back to Asgard and stay there." His gray gaze flicked over me, a silent offering in it.

I sat up on my heels, the need to protect Magni easing now that his death wasn't imminent. Carefully I looked over the three brothers, from their sharp weapons to their grim determination, and I knew what I said next would determine the rest of my life.

If I went willingly, they would likely let Magni live. And as long as he lived, I wouldn't be broken into a thousand pieces. The echo of the vision in Verdandi's cave shuddered up my spine. As angry as I was with the redheaded alpha for his attempts at forcing me into submission, I wasn't going to survive his death.

And if what the Norn had shown me was true... neither would my world. Or any of them.

My heart ached and spasmed at the thought of leaving him behind in his weakened state, but that was nothing but the bond he'd forced on me. He was a god. He would heal.

"Let him live and I'll come with you willingly," I said softly.

"Annabel, no!" Magni hissed. He forced his way onto his back and gripped my arm with his healthy hand. The other he clutched against his chest. "Your place is by *my* side!"

I jerked back from him and got to my feet. "Even now, you can't see it! I am not a *thing,* Magni! I am not a toy for you to bicker over. This is my decision."

Magni's verdant eyes flashed with anger, but instead of shouting at me he turned to Saga. "So you're not just a coward," he said coolly, a sharp contrast to the anger I felt snapping through our bond, "you're a scavenger too."

Saga cocked his head as if he hadn't heard him, but I knew he had—the vein in his temple was throbbing. "Come again?"

"It was true in the cave and it's true now," Magni continued, staring him down. "You couldn't mate Annabel on your own merits; you had to wait for me to turn my back first. And now... to take a female you've claimed from me, you have to have the help of your brothers *and* I have to be incapacitated. Do you hear how pathetic you are? Do you truly think you can be a satisfying mate for her?"

"Can we not?" I said, trying to avoid bloodshed, because Saga's face was turning red with rage.

They both ignored me.

"Your sole advantage," Saga hissed as he glared down at Magni said, "is that you got to her first. That's the only reason you're still alive!"

Magni smiled thinly. "But that's not true, is it? I didn't get to her first—*you* did. But she didn't want you. She rejected you. She was in heat and she *fled* from you. She doesn't *want* you, Saga. No one does."

Saga opened his mouth to lay into his enemy, then stopped as his words sank in.

"You're outclassed," Magni told him, "and you know it. All you can do is sit around waiting for table scraps."

I'd thought Saga would fly into a rage then, but instead he looked Magni over from head to toe wearing an infuriatingly inscrutable expression.

At length, he said, "You'd know all about that, wouldn't you? Waiting for scraps, I mean. Even if that *was* my fate, at least I wouldn't be begging off my own family. How many times have you had to beg and plead to not be kicked out on your ass?"

A white-hot flash of anger seared through the bond I shared with Magni. Whatever Saga was referring to, it'd clearly struck a nerve. He struggled to get up, undoubtedly to do something monumentally stupid, but Bjarni stepped in. He put a large hand on Magni's shoulder and pushed him back down again, raising his axe in silent warning.

"We don't have time for this bickering," Grim said. "We got what we came for. Either kill the bastard or don't, but we need to leave."

Saga breathed in deeply, then turned his focus on me. "Are you ready, Annabel?"

I tried to ignore the clenching in my gut as I glanced back at the wounded god on the ground. There was nothing more I could do for him, other than lead the alphas itching for his death away.

Silently I nodded and stepped away.

"Annabel—I'll find you again. I promise!" Magni's desperate call followed me as I walked out of the clearing, haunting me for every beat of my aching heart.

I SHOULD HAVE BEEN happy that every step led me farther and farther from the alpha who'd refused to consider me as anything but a walking womb, a means to an end—but I wasn't.

Our bond stretched thin in my chest for every mile, writhing like a worm, reminding me of how he'd sacrificed himself to save me. How good it'd felt when he helped me through my heat. How, even when I'd told him to stop, I wasn't in heat, some part of me had wanted him again when he tried to show me he wasn't weak. I knew it was just biology—my unwanted mate-bond clamoring to be reunited with the alpha who'd claimed me. But it still hurt like a bitch.

"It should be here," Bjarni growled, pulling me from my miserable thoughts. "Why the fuck isn't it here?"

They'd stopped in a small indent among the looming cliffs. We were a few hours out from where we'd left Magni behind, and the guys had left me alone to brood in quietude while they talked magic portals and gods and our encounter with the Norn.

"The portals move sometimes," Grim said. He swung a leather sack off his shoulder and reached in. When he pulled his hand back out again, he brought what looked like an ancient, folded map back out. "We should be able to locate it again."

"What's this?" I asked as the dark-haired alpha spread the map across a large rock.

"A map of the nine worlds," Saga said. He let a hand brush up my back, coming to rest on my shoulder. "Our father stole it from the dwarves a long time ago, and gifted it to us when he sent us to the human world to wait out the coming of Ragnarök. It shows all the secret passages between the worlds. It'll show us the way home."

"*Home?*" I jerked back from his touch. "You're taking me back to Iceland? What about the prophecy and everything Verdandi told me? How are we going to stop Ragnarök from the human world?"

Grim and Bjarni exchanged a look, both of them arching an eyebrow at Saga.

My mate grimaced. "Look, we can't stay here. Not with you—if anyone sees Magni's mark on you, they're likely to kill you."

"You promised!" I said. "You said—"

"I said I would help you stop Ragnarök if there was a way. And I will. But until Fate deigns to reveal how we can do that, my *only* priority is to get you to safety, Annabel." He wrapped me in his arms, the warmth of his body soaking through my clothes and into my flesh in a soothing wave before I could resist.

"Nothing's more important than stopping the end of the world," I said, doing my best not to swoon like a ridiculous virgin at her alpha posturing. But it felt good—his closeness, his promises of protection. Even the hollow in my chest where my bond with Magni was tethered didn't hurt so bad so long as my other mate held me like this. "Do you think Fate's just gonna hand us an easy way of saving the world if we go hide in a corner? That's not how it works."

"And you're an expert on how Fate works now, are you?" Saga asked, his tone sardonic even as he dragged his nose up along my neck.

"Perhaps not, but I do know that if you want anything in this world—human or not—you have to fight for it." That was how I'd gotten my education—I'd worked my ass off. It was how I'd achieved everything in my life. "Have you—any of you—ever gotten anything by just leaning back and waiting for the world to hand you what you want on a silver platter?"

"We're not leaning back," Saga said, and as he spoke *something* pulled on my mind. Something that felt like warm fleece wrapping around the urgency churning in my gut to do something to prevent the death of everything and everyone I knew. I blinked, and suddenly it didn't seem so... important.

I swayed, and he tightened his arms to pull me in closer.

"It's best if we travel home to Iceland for now, Annabel," Saga murmured, his voice soothing and deep resonating in my chest, making my ribs hum. "Everything will be okay. Just give in."

"Yes," I mumbled, resting my head against his chest because it was suddenly too heavy to hold up on my own. "You're right."

When I forced my eyes open, I saw Grim and Bjarni stare at me, Bjarni with a small smirk curving his lips, Grim with a look of disgust.

The dark-haired alpha chuffed through his nose and returned his focus to the weathered map. "Regardless, we'll have a long travel. The portal to Midgard is nowhere near Yggdrasil."

"What? Where is it, then?" Saga snapped, some of his irritation piercing my cocoon of dazed contentedness.

Grim brushed his palm over the middle right section of the map. "I'm not sure... but it looks like it's well past the Spine."

"Fucking Hel," Saga growled. "You want me to climb

a fucking mountain range with my human mate?"

"She's *our* human mate, if you remember," Bjarni said, eyebrow raised at his brother's temper.

"I don't control the portals between worlds," Grim growled. "And you should be careful—your control's slipping."

Saga muttered a curse but drew in a deep breath and returned his focus to me. "It's all right, Annabel. You'll be safe. I promise."

The swathe of fuzzy calm that'd started to lift snapped back in place around my mind like a rubber band.

But this time, I saw it.

Dark energy wrapped gently around my body, leaving hazy comfort wherever it touched, creeping along my skin and sinking into my bones.

Magic.

Saga's magic!

I pushed away from him with a gasp, ice-cold realization pushing the contented daze from my brain as effectively as a bucket of water.

"*You!* You've—" I grasped for the right words. What exactly had he done? Used his power to calm me? But no, it wasn't just that. That sense of woolly compliance... it'd been there before, as well. Subtly, worming its way into my brain, aided by the bond in my chest tying me to him.

"You manipulated me!" I hissed, the sense of betrayal closing around my lungs like a curtain of lead.

He'd made me think he believed me—that he might be able to see me like something more than a broodmare. But he'd just told me what I wanted to hear, so I'd be easier to take from Magni. "You're even worse than *he* is! At least Magni had the decency to be honest with what he wanted from me! But you—you think you can trick me to be your obedient little omega? I will never trust you again, and I will *never* submit to you, Saga Lokisson!"

Saga's face grew dark, the shadows playing across it reminding me all too much of his brother Grim as he stared me down. It took everything I had not to shrink back from him, the bond between us vibrating out of frequency, setting every hair on my body on end.

"I tried to placate you, Omega," my blond mate growled. "I tried to help you understand your place the easy way. But you don't want that? Fine. You'll get to be a victim, since you love the role so much. *I* claimed you. *I* fucked your little cunt and let you ride out your heat on my knot, and you belong to *me*. Your place is on your knees for me, and I swear by every *fucking* branch on Yggdrasil, you're gonna learn to obey!"

I stared open-mouthed at him, my heart hammering in my chest. Anger welled from a fountain deep within, but as I stared at the furious god fear kept me from taking a swing at him, however much my knuckles itches to connect with his stupid face.

"If the world ends and we could have stopped it—I will *never* forgive you," I hissed.

He didn't respond, just gave me a hard stare before he turned to Bjarni. "Call on Magga and Arni. Have them scout for the portal. The sooner we're home, the sooner you and Grim can mate the omega. It's time she learns her only purpose is to serve."

17

BJARNI

"He's gonna come around, sweetie." I offered the sulking omega a smile and patted her on the shoulder. Saga had stomped up ahead, taking up the lead, leaving it to me and Grim to ensure Annabel followed along. And since Grim was a grumpy git, it was up to me to smooth things over. As always. "And even if he doesn't, I ain't about to let him treat you bad."

She shot me a withering glare. "Oh? So you're gonna knock his head into a rock until he realizes we can't hide away like freaking cowards while the world *ends?*"

"Might do," I hummed, amused at the little thing's fire. She definitely was an omega, but she sure didn't have the temperament of one. "He's not wrong, though. There isn't much we can do about Ragnarök right now, except ensure you don't get eaten by Jotunns before we can get you out of here. Doesn't mean we aren't going to help fulfill this prophecy of yours, if we get the chance."

"You're just like him, aren't you? Like Magni. All you really think of me is that I'm some whore for you to fuck. That I live to *serve*. At least he was honest about it—and, excuse me, but it seems like going to Asgard like he wanted, versus hiding out in a remote farm in Iceland might bring about *slightly* better chances for saving the damn world," she said.

I shrugged. "Perhaps. Perhaps not. Ragnarök has been predicted since the dawn of time, yet the gods sit in their walled-off little kingdom. They've done exactly nothing to prevent it."

Annabel frowned and looked down, and I reached out to poke one of the inflamed marks on her neck. She flinched away, hand quickly coming up to cover the sensitive skin. "Don't do that!"

"You left one of your mates behind, sweetie. Right now, his mark is fucking with your brain something fierce, trying to convince you to return to him. Saga's an idiot sometimes, I'll give you that, but you're fooling yourself if you think Thor's bastard would treat you any better." I cracked a smile. "And I'll be here to keep my brothers in check. Pinky swear."

"I just...." She rubbed her mark and shuddered, blunt teeth making indents in her plump lower lip. "I feel like every step is breaking me in half. It *hurts*. And I... why am I here? Why am I doing this, leaving him, when this is no better? I came with you because

Saga promised he'd help me end Ragnarök. But if there is no difference, then—" She stopped abruptly. "This was a mistake. I'm going back for him. He needs me."

I was honestly surprised she'd made it this far. No mated omega liked to be away from her alpha, least of all when he was ill like Magni'd been. I assumed the dual-bond eased some of the discomfort, but mostly it seemed her dedication to stop the inevitable end of the world was what'd allowed her to push through the instincts that had to be tearing at her to get her to turn around. It was admirable, really. She was stronger than most, even if she was just a tiny human.

Carefully, I wrapped a hand around her chin, keeping hold of her even when she tried to jerk away. "Annabel, you can't do that."

"The fuck I can't!" she hissed.

"If you do, we'll kill him," I said, because there was no point in sugarcoating it. "You don't understand the hatred between our families. The only reason he lives is that you swore to come with us willingly. And—as much as I would love to lob off that fucker's head—I'd hate to see you hurt like that. So no, you can't go back."

She stared up at me, hurt and desperation dancing in those chocolate pools. "Why? Why do you hate him that much?"

I sighed. "It's two-fold. His father accused ours of trying to sneak the Jotunns into Asgard to overthrow the gods and prematurely start Ragnarök some centuries ago. It was disproven, but the mistrust among the gods toward our father and us remains.

"And Magni... Magni was born of a Jotunn mother, just like us, but Jotunheim wasn't good enough for him. He wanted to sit among the gods in Asgard. But because of his lineage, they didn't trust him. So, he decided to prove himself. His uncle was a chieftain, and he raised Magni in his halls despite how hated Thor is among Jotunns. Magni repaid him by burning down his house, slaughtering his sons, and putting their heads on pikes. Only then did the gods deign him worthy. But we... we won't forget what he did. We had friends among that chieftain's sons."

Annabel frowned. "But... but the Jotunns are evil... right?"

I snorted. "Are humans evil?"

"Well, sure, not all, but... I thought Jotunns were the opposite of everything that's divine and good? Like... really vicious giants ruled by chaos."

"Ha! Firstly, we are not giants. We come in all sizes. And sure, some are not the nicest, but I can guarantee you, the same hold true for the mighty gods and goddesses of Asgard. Jotunheim is the land of the wild. There are few rules and much freedom. But it's a harsh world with many dangers too." I released her chin and touched my fingertips to her cheek. "I might be a half-god, but I'm also a Jotunn. And so is Magni, yet he turned his back on his people. There is no honor in what he did, and there is no honor in how he tried to steal you from us."

She shook her head, stubbornly jutting out her chin, and I fought back urge to bite it—and then tumble her to the ground and give her something else to think about. That she'd mated my brother—and my enemy—did little to quell the need to bed the willful omega. She smelled like stale sex, sweat, and semen, and all it did was remind me how I'd been cheated out of partaking in her heat.

"Come up here! Arni and Magga are near," Grim shouted from up ahead, distracting my focus from Annabel. I jerked my head in the direction of my brothers. Two ravens were circling up ahead.

"Come, sweetie," I said, offering her my hand. "Don't let your bond fool you into going back on your word. You swore you would follow us willingly if we let Magni live. Prove to me you honor your word, and I will in return swear to you that I will do whatever you ask to stop Ragnarök. Deal?"

She hesitated for a moment, searching my eyes for something. Then, swallowing, she nodded hesitantly and put her hand in mine. It was so small, it practically disappeared in my palm. "If you swear it. And no more tricks."

"No more tricks," I agreed, turning to catch up with Grim and Saga. "Though that's more Saga's thing, anyway."

"Bjarni?" she asked.

"Hmm?"

"Who *are* Arni and Magga? If not your parents, then—?"

"This is Arni and Magga." I pointed up at the circling ravens.

"The birds?" she asked, confusion plain in her voice. "You had *birds* play your parents for the past decades? I don't understand."

I laughed and stopped as we reached my brothers, offering an arm to our winged messengers. Arni dove down to perch on the offered limb, but Magga chose Saga's shoulder instead. She nuzzled up against his cheek, cooing sweetly.

"Only in name. They are our eyes and ears. Our messengers. They cross the veil of the realms and bring us news from near and far. This is Arni. Arni— Annabel." I lowered my arm so the raven was about eye height with the small woman by my side.

"You named a raven *Eagle?*" she chuffed, reaching out to stroke Arni's gleaming feathers. He immediately bit at her fingers, only narrowly missing the tips of them when I yanked my arm back.

"Behave!" I scolded. "She's Saga's mate and she'll soon be mine. *Let* her."

Arni shot me a withering stare. "Do you want our scouting report, or do you want me to play petting zoo with your mortal?"

"Oh my God, he *talks!*" Annabel's eyes widened

comically as she stared at the raven. "Is he... what *is* he?"

"Just a raven with a voice," Grim said, voice dry as tinder. His dislike of our birds wasn't a secret. "And an annoying one, at that."

"Don't be rude!" Annabel chided. Judging from the awestruck expression on her cute little face, she was as excited about our talking birds as she had been the horses on our farm. "Does that... does that mean Draugr can speak too?" she asked, confirming her thoughts had been on Grim's black stallion.

"Draugr is a dumb animal. We're messengers of the gods," Magga cawed haughtily. Grim shot her a glare. He'd always been absurdly obsessed with his horses, especially that one-eyed stallion of his.

"Draugr isn't dumb," Annabel muttered, lips drawn down in disapproval of the raven's comment. I stole a glance at Grim to see if her defense of his beloved horse might soften him a smidge, but no. There was nothing but dark displeasure in my youngest brother's mismatched eyes.

"Enough," Saga broke in. "Have you seen anything useful? Is the Spine passable?"

"There are passages," Arni said.

"But the spires are whitening more and more each day. Soon, they will close and not open again until Ragnarök has eaten the world," Magga finished.

"And the portal to Midgard? Did you see that?" I asked.

Magga ruffled her feathers. "We saw a portal."

"But not to Midgard," Arni supplied. "To Asgard."

"Then we need you to scour the lands until you find the one for Midgard," Saga said.

They both flapped their wings, ready to take off, but I lowered my arm to get Arni's attention. "Not you. You need to find Loki and tell him we have the omega, but Thor's bastard got in the way. Tell him we need his advice on how to rid her of the illegitimate claim."

"He's going to lay an egg," Magga cackled. She set off Saga's shoulder and flew a loop around our heads before she swung high into the sky. "Good luck with that message, brother."

"Wouldn't be the worst thing he's birthed," Saga muttered.

I smothered a chuckle and jutted my chin at the bird still perched on my arm. "Off with you now. The sooner he knows, the sooner we'll have a fix."

Arni sighed deeply, a very human sound, and set off without another word.

"They're not very polite, are they?" Annabel asked.

I chuckled. "No. It's not in their nature. But in Arni's defense, the last time he had to deliver bad news to Loki, it took him a month to regrow his tail feathers."

Saga looked up at me from his broody stare into the

still-crackling fire. It was long after sunset, and he was supposed to be asleep like Annabel and Grim while I took first watch. But he wasn't.

"I'll sulk for exactly as long as I please," he said pointedly.

I chuckled low, conscious of the curled-up woman resting on the other side of the fire. Grim slept like the dead, but Annabel'd had a long day, and she was mortal. She needed her sleep. "It's not winning you any favors with our mate."

"So far she's *my* mate," he said, pressing a fist against his chest. "Don't preach to me about my omega. I know her far better than you."

I rolled my eyes, not taking the bait. Saga was usually very easy-going, but occasionally he would get in a *mood*. The last time was when he'd failed to convince Annabel to come to us when she reached her eighteenth birthday. Loki had been less than pleased with the son he put in charge of securing the bloodline.

Saga'd spent a month wrestling mountain trolls in the Spine after that one.

"You sure about that? Because all you've managed so far is to alienate and antagonize her."

Saga shot me a glare. "Don't start with me."

I sighed, glancing at the sleeping girl. She looked... troubled, as if she were plagued with bad dreams. "Look, all I know is, if it'd been my mark on her neck, I'd have spent the night under her blanket, keeping her warm and making sure she doesn't miss that prick Magni too bad."

"You think I don't want that?" he snapped. "It's not that easy. She isn't one of your doe-eyed farm girls. I try to give her the comfort of an alpha, and she hates me for manipulating her. I save her from that asshole, and she says I'm *worse* than he is! She's... *difficult*."

I cracked a grin. "Not really, brother. She's just a scared little girl with a nasty temper and nowhere to turn. I don't care what nonsense you've heard about omegas needing a firm hand. She's a spitfire, and if you don't start appreciating that, you're going to ruin it for yourself. And for Grim. That sorry fuck's going to need both of us to not absolutely screw up his bond with her. And you can't do that if you're at odds with her too."

Saga sighed, flicking his gaze to our sleeping brother. He lay several yards from the fire, with his back turned and his black hair spilling over the hard ground. "I don't know how."

"For starters, don't be a prick," I suggested with a small smile that earned me a scowl in return. "She's female—she's going to act out. Let it roll off your back. And then... I think we need to do some damage control. She's been through the wringer, and honestly, it's not so weird she doesn't really trust us."

"And how do you suggest we do that?" Saga asked, eyebrow raised.

I shrugged and leaned forward to poke the fire with a stick, ensuring the logs would stay at a comfortable smolder so the omega didn't freeze. "We take her to Mom's place. If we're crossing the Spine, it's on the way, and I think it'd be good if she sees us as something other than her kidnappers. Don't you?"

~

"No."

I rolled my eyes at Grim's firmly pressed lips, as Saga heaved a sigh.

"She's not going to beat you with a spoon, Grim, you're old enough to know not to get in the way of her livestock this time."

"Who's not going to what now?" Annabel came through the bushes from where she'd spent some time cleaning up in the spring that trickled by our makeshift camp. I caught myself inhaling to test her scent, and found the traces of sex replaced by her natural scent of honey, thyme, and woman. It did little to still my desire for her. She may not be in heat anymore, but I'd never been around an omega without fucking her this long before. And Annabel... she was more than just an omega. She was mine. Or, she was supposed to be.

"We're stopping by our mother on the way to the mountains," Saga said, and I didn't miss how much gentler his tone was today. "Grim's scared of her."

"Why?" she asked, blinking at Grim in clear surprise. I imagined she found it hard to think of Grim as scared of anything. Or having any emotions other than hatred. Most people did.

"I am not scared of that woman," Grim said, a suppressed snarl in his voice. "She is nothing to me."

"Great! No reason to avoid her house, then," Saga said with a cheerful smile. "Let's pack up and get going."

I smothered a smirk at the dirty look Grim shot in Saga's direction and grabbed my backpack. The thing about being an emotionally constipated ball of barely contained rage was that it made you awfully easy to manipulate.

~

"WHY DOESN'T GRIM WANT to see your mom?" Annabel asked me, voice politely lowered.

I glanced up ahead at my black-haired brother who'd taken the lead, and sighed. "It's not his mom—it's Saga's and mine. But he grew up there for some of his younger years. Was a moody little bastard even back then, and got into a heap of trouble every other day. And Mom's quick with the wooden spoon. We all got a good few whacks over the years, but Grim especially. And he's not the type to let go of a grudge."

"Oh." She frowned as she followed my line of sight. "Poor guy. If she beat him, I can't say I blame him for not jumping for joy at the prospect of seeing her again."

I shrugged and lopped an arm around her shoulders, ignoring the small stiffening in her posture at the uninvited contact. "Perhaps not. I just never saw the point in holding on to old pain. Makes it hard to enjoy life if you drag around every slight."

"Says the man who's willing to murder another god over old hatred," she said, arching an eyebrow in my direction.

I laughed and gave her a squeeze that nearly knocked her off course. "Fair point. And had it been anyone but Mom who took a spoon to him, I'd have killed them for putting a finger on either of my brothers. But that's just how child rearing goes here. A firm hand is the only thing that'll keep young Jotunns in check."

"I'd never hurt my child—nor one that was placed in my care," she said, giving me a hard look. "Not even a Jotunn."

My gaze flickered to her stomach of its own accord. Yeah, she was fierce. And protective, even over hypothetical kids that she'd gone to great lengths to declare she didn't want.

Since before I came of age, I'd known my mate would be whoever this prophecy deemed the right one. For centuries I'd known I'd share her with my brothers, and that who she was as a person didn't matter in the slightest. I'd accepted it without complaint, because I'd do anything for my family, and keeping them alive through Ragnarök was the most important thing I'd ever do.

And here she finally was, all fire and claws, telling me she'd never hurt a child. *My* child. Or my brothers'—it was the same to me.

Warmth I hadn't anticipated bloomed in my chest as I stared at the little mortal that I'd never before worried about if I'd like or not.

And I knew I would love her.

"Don't even think—*Oh!*" Annabel's combative voice died on a groan.

"Annabel? What's the mat—?" My own question faded into nothing when her eyes turned upward, showing only the whites, and she omitted a sickly keening noise before she collapsed in my arms. Lifeless.

18

ANNABEL

Dark clouds whirled above me, barely visible as a swathe of charcoal gray through the blanket of heavy rain pelting down on me.

"Annabel!"

I jerked at the frantic sound of my name and saw Saga come running toward me from several hundred yards away. As far as I could tell, we were in a flat and wide valley, hills rising to our left and—in the far distance—white-tipped mountains rising to the right. A far cry from the rocky woodland we'd made camp in.

"What's the hell?" I muttered, squinting against the rain to try to make sense of my surroundings.

"The dam is breaking! Get her out of here!" Saga roared, and despite the distance, the sheer panic in his voice carried loud and clear.

Large hands clasped my shoulders, pulling on me.

"Let's go," Bjarni growled.

"What's happening?" I asked, a tightness in my chest making it hard to breathe. The bond between Saga and me was tight as a bow string and vibrating with frantic intensity.

"There's no time for your harebrained questions!" Grim barked from my other side and another hand carved from granite closed around my bicep. "Run!"

But my question didn't go unanswered.

Behind Saga a gray wall of churning water burst forward out of nowhere, sweeping toward him with roaring speed.

No matter how fast he ran, he would never outpace it. And neither would we. I stood frozen as the flood swept Saga away on its path to swallow me, too.

Annabel!

I GASPED FOR AIR, my eyelids fluttering open as someone shook me hard.

I was staring up into a gray sky several shades lighter than it'd been just a second ago. Saga was bent over me, worry painted in every angle of his face.

"Sweetling, are you okay?"

I wasn't sure what was more astonishing—opening my eyes and realizing I wasn't dead, or the gentle tone of the alpha who'd only yesterday growled at me that I'd learn to kneel.

"I think... I had a vision," I said, pushing him away so I could sit up.

"Again?" he asked, but despite the exasperated tone, he continued, "What was it this time?"

"There was a storm... And a flood. A dam broke. We... I think we died." It was so surreal, talking about my own future death after having already experienced it. And his. My heart clenched hard, and I rubbed at my ribs at the same time as Saga brought his hand to his own chest, pressing his knuckles in where it attached on his end.

He frowned at me. "Where were we? Can you describe the area?"

"You're actually taking a mortal's claims of having visions seriously?" Grim asked, and even though I couldn't see him, his tone made it more than clear what he thought of my claims.

"You weren't at Mimir's Well," Saga growled with a scowl over his shoulder. "She saw it, even though that *thing* tried to shield itself. If she's had a vision of dying, I'm going to listen. And so are you."

It was an odd sensation, hearing him defend my supposed powers not twenty-four hours after he'd made it clear he wasn't interested in them. Odd, but... nice.

"We were out in the open. A large valley, I think, hills on the left, mountains on the right. I couldn't see much for the rain," I said, frowning as I tried to recall the details.

"The White River dam," Bjarni mumbled. "We'll be there in about five hours at this pace. If the lady can stop fainting, of course."

I shot him a glare that only earned me a grin in return.

Saga lifted his head and looked up. The clouds were ever-looming, but seemed thicker toward the east. "There's definitely a storm coming. *Fuck!* If we take the other path it'll be three weeks before we even get to the foothills."

"Really? We're doing this?" Grim heaved an impatient sigh. "We're going on a three-week detour because your omega fainted and had a nightmare?"

"It wasn't a nightmare," I snapped. He only offered me a cocked eyebrow in response.

"You should be pleased," Saga said as he got up from his crouch, grabbing my hand to pull me up along with him. "It means we won't be stopping by Mom's house."

"No, but we will need to find shelter before the weather gets bad," Bjarni said as he cast a long look at the gathering darkness on the horizon. "If it's enough to make the White River dam burst, it's gonna be a bad one."

"The only place not through the valley within a twenty-mile radius is Udgard," Grim said, lips pulling into a firm line. "Bad enough to bring an omega there—if anyone spots Magni's mark, we're all done for."

"What's wrong with being an omega in Udgard?" I asked.

Saga grimaced. "The human world isn't the only place with a shortage of omegas. And Udgard has a lot of warriors hanging around. Alpha warriors. And few rules, except the strong take what they want."

"*Oh.*" I was partly surprised that he was trying to be delicate about it, but mostly I was fighting back horror.

"They usually leave a mated woman alone, but even if we could show off my mark without revealing Magni's, they'd know who you were," my mate continued. "Fuck! If it's gonna get that bad, we can't stay outside. Jotunheim is not a safe place for a mortal in the best of circumstances. During a storm...."

He didn't finish his thought, but he didn't need to. I'd already seen what happened during a storm.

"But why does it matter who I am?" I asked, having about zero desire to try and huddle up underneath a tree during the torrential downpour my vision had shown me. "I'm just a human—remember?"

"You're also the omega fated to protect her mates through Ragnarök," Grim said. "If Saga suddenly shows up with a claimed omega in tow, some will realize why. And they'll see it as us trying to stop Ragnarök."

"And that's... a bad thing?" I asked.

"The Jotunns want Ragnarök to come," Saga said. "It marks the time where they will finally overthrow the gods."

"And screw the rest of us?" I shot Bjarni a pointed look. He'd been so busy telling me Jotunns weren't evil, he'd apparently forgotten to mention how they were jockeying for the end of the world to roll around.

He ignored me, giving me a thoughtful once-over. "What if she wasn't an omega, though?"

I crossed my arms over my chest when his gaze lingered for a bit too long. "Why, do you have a cure that'll turn me beta again? Because then I'm all for it."

~

"I'M GONNA MISS YOUR TITS," Bjarni sighed. He handed over the piece of ripped cloth he and Saga were busy wrapping tightly around my chest, skimming my exposed skin in the process. His hands were so warm compared to the chill of the air, it sent a shock all the way into my blood. They were both so close to me, I was practically swarmed in their heady alpha scent, and despite the awkwardness of being half-naked in front of all three brothers, I had to fight not to let their nearness distract me.

Not that I wanted anything they had to offer.

"I'm not gonna miss you ogling them," I replied tartly. "But breathing was nice."

Saga chuckled, his warm breath ghosting over my nape and setting the small hairs there on end. "We'll free them as soon as the storm's passed and we're on our way to the Spine again."

"I'm sure you will," I muttered.

Another chuckle rumbled from Bjarni this time, as Saga secured the cloth and pulled one of the extra tunics his brothers had brought in their packs over my head. It was so long, it hit my knees. I cast a sad look at Verdandi's black leather top stuffed into the bag—it might have been overly feathery, but right now I felt like a little kid playing dress-up in her dad's clothes.

"Let's cover that pretty face, hmm?" Bjarni said, offering me a cheeky wink. And then he bent to scoop up a handful of mud, and proceeded to smear it across my cheeks and forehead.

"Ugh, is that really necessary?" I complained. "Does being dirty *really* make me look less like an omega? Or are you just being a massive sexist right now?"

"It'll help with the disguise," Saga said, spinning me around to face him. "Grim, give me a hand."

The dark-haired alpha, who'd been waiting on the outskirts while Bjarni and Saga tied my breasts flat, sauntered over. "Can't do a little illusion work on your own, brother?"

"Shut up and get to it," Saga said as he grabbed my face lightly between both hands and studied it much like an artist would a lump of clay. "I'll do her face— you do her hips and ass."

Cool, strong hands landed on my hips from behind, and every hair on the back of my body stood on end when Grim stepped in close. I could feel the odd chill from him, as if his strong body was Neptune, gravitational pull tugging on me. But in front of me Saga radiated with alpha heat, like the sun warming my front and stabilizing the uneasy drag from Grim's frigid presence.

I was so preoccupied with the warring sensations of heat and cold I didn't notice the magic before darkness interwoven with sparks of light swept around my body.

Saga touched his fingers to my cheek bones, directing the dark energy in a smooth flow along my features. He caressed my jaw and brushed against my lips, smoothing his hand down the column of my neck in a light but firm grip that—completely uninvited— made me remember his dominance when he'd claimed me.

Behind me, Grim dragged his knuckles up from the swell of my hips, working his fingers over my waist and up to my bottom rib in slow, gliding movements. I breathed in deeply and tried to ignore tingling sensations of awareness spreading from the chilled bite of his fingertips sinking through my clothes. An exercise that wholly died when he smoothed one hand down the front of my stomach to rest over my sex.

I jolted hard, the sheer shock of the intimate touch making me gasp out loud, but Grim's touch was clinical —detached. He pressed against my mons, then slid his hand back around to my hip and over my backside to join with the other.

Heat radiated from my cheeks as he rubbed over my ass and down my thighs with the same precision of a doctor assessing a patient. Maybe if it'd just been him, I would have been fine—but his cold yet intimate touches were underlined by Saga's warm, gentle caresses to my face, and my body lit up from the inside like a Christmas tree.

Heat rushed from Saga's fingertips through my skin and down my body to warm every place Grim touched, sending my blood through my veins in heavy pulses until I was acutely aware of every single inch of my skin —and the way my nipples strained against their confines.

Holy damn, how long can a bit of magic take to finish?

Just as I was certain I wasn't going to be able to keep it together any longer, they both stepped back from me, the darkness fading from my body as swiftly as it'd come.

"Well, that's certainly something," Bjarni rumbled, a lopsided grin lighting up his scruffy face as he took me in. "But I'm still aching to bury my head between your legs until you gush." He adjusted his cock through his pants with a large hand, but not before I saw the beginning of a swell at the front of them.

My blush heated up about a million degrees as uninvited flashes of what he'd suggested tore through my mind, spurred on by the lingering sensation of his brothers' touches. Without looking in his direction I turned and walked to the slow-moving creek we'd been following since morning and bent over it to catch a look at myself.

The transformation was startling. I still looked like me, but... also not. More accurately, I looked like I would have, if I'd been a twelve-year old boy. My lips were slightly narrower, the Cupid's bow less pronounced, my cheekbones softer and my jawline sharper. From what I could see of my waist and down, Grim had evened out the curve of my waist and hips. And—I blinked twice and leaned closer to double-check. Yup. I had a hint of a male form at the apex of my thighs.

"It's her scent," Grim said, pulling my attention back from the jaw-dropping image in the water. "No illusion's gonna cover that."

"I can wash," I suggested. But when I turned around to look at them, the dark-haired alpha just gave me a dark look.

"It won't help," Saga rumbled, and I didn't miss the hoarse note to his voice. I wish it didn't affect me—but it did. It pulled on something deep inside, laid bare by the heightened sense of awareness his and his brother's touches had left me in. As a—most unwelcome—result, the rasp of Saga's voice sent shockwaves through my body and into my clit.

"Not when you smell like *that,*" he continued, advancing on me with a single step that spoke of agility to rival a large cat's.

My heart slammed into overdrive, mixed instincts vying for dominance as I found myself caught between an urge to run and a need to surrender.

"Stop that," Grim hissed. "You're making it worse. It's not going to be long before the storm's on us, and we still have a couple of hours to Udgard."

I blinked, heat of an entirely different kind reaching my cheeks when I realized what, exactly, it was they could smell: my arousal.

"Goddamn alphas," I muttered, hiding my face in my hands to regain my sanity.

"We need to find something to mask her smell," Bjarni rumbled. His voice had also taken on a distinctly raw note, but the devilish grin on his face was more mischievous than anything else. "And I think I have an idea."

19

SAGA

I had to give Annabel credit—for a woman her size, she put up a Hel of a fight when it dawned on her what Bjarni's plan was.

In the end, though, it didn't matter. My blond brother was much faster and much stronger than her, and he simply pinned her down on the forest floor as he rubbed deer droppings in her armpits, hair, backs of knees, and inner thighs while she kicked and cussed and promised him a lifetime of misery.

She spent the rest of the walk quietly seething, only offering Bjarni the filthiest of glares whenever he tried to charm his way back into her good graces.

I didn't mind, though. His plan actually worked; she no longer smelled tantalizingly like omega and *Annabel*. And—instead of walking by his side as she had since I lost my temper with her—she stayed near me as we made our way to Udgard. Not quite by my side, but hovering around my vicinity, drifting nearer when she was too preoccupied snarling at Bjarni to realize.

I'd regretted my earlier harsh words the instant they were out of my mouth, and I felt the painful yank from my bond as her trust in me shattered into a thousand pieces. But it had to be done. I had to use any means necessary—including my magic—to get her to follow me. Anything to make her pick me over him.

As if summoned by my thoughts, the *other* end of the connection shuddered, and I gritted my teeth to refrain from rubbing at my chest. A few feet away Annabel gasped and pressed her hand to her chest.

Magni.

He was only an echo for me, and that was closer than I'd ever wanted to be to that prick. The sooner Loki found a way to rid Annabel of his claim, the better. Perhaps then she'd finally see that I only wanted what was best for her.

That I wasn't her second choice.

I clenched my fists when Magni's words echoed through my head. *Waiting for table scraps.*

All my life I'd had to fight to prove that I was good enough, worthy enough, and even now, after I'd claimed the omega who would save my bloodline... even she hadn't picked me first.

He was right—she'd been on the cusp of her heat, and she'd still fled into the wilderness to escape me. Into *his* arms.

And now, the only way she'd truly be mine was if Magni's claim was annulled.

"Saga?" Annabel's quiet voice sounded from my side. From almost as close as she'd been while I'd disguised her, and the beautiful scent of her need rose heady in my nostrils. Even her desire I wasn't able to quell, because if I gave her what she truly needed, she'd only hate me more.

"*What?*" It came out angrier than I'd intended, and I felt her recoil a step. I kept my gaze on the path ahead.

"I... Never mind."

Regret flared hot in my chest, but she was already dropping further behind, putting physical distance between us mirroring the strained bond pulled tight in my chest.

"We're here!"

I snapped my attention up at the sound of Grim's call, every muscle in my body tensing as I spied Udgard's walls in the distance. Now was not the time to worry about my frayed bond.

The first drops of rain began to fall as I stared at the stronghold, praying that I'd be able to keep Annabel safe.

We weren't the only ones seeking refuge from the storm in Udgard. Jotunns poured through the tall gates of the fortress to the mead hall within, while others rushed around outside to finish up their chores before the weather got too bad.

Annabel stared wide-eyed at everything from the many gruff-looking Jotunns to the impressive stone and timber structure rising up above us. The door was maybe thirty feet tall, and the sprawling building itself representing an oversized version of some unholy marriage between a large farm and a fortress. The function was something similar.

"Keep quiet and close," I muttered to my brothers as we entered the hall. "The less attention we draw, the better. And you—" I looked at Annabel. "—do not move from my side under any circumstance. Got it?"

She nodded instantly, pushing up close against me when an eight-feet-tall Jotunn shoved his way past us. He looked like there was more than a few drops of troll somewhere in his ancestry.

When I offered her my hand, she clung onto it with no hesitation and my bond hummed in my chest, because despite everything, she still sought my protection in times of danger. Magni might have frayed our connection, but it wasn't damaged beyond repair.

The mead hall sprawled out wide and huge. It was the center of activity in Udgard, workers, warriors, and travelers from near and far finding their way here every day of the year. Udgarsloke, the chieftain, opened his halls for everyone who passed through his desolate land—though not everyone made it out again. Those too weak to protect themselves often found a slave collar around their necks as payment for their host's hospitality.

"Over there," Bjarni said, nodding to a quiet corner far from the roaring hearths. It was past several rows of long tables already more than half full of laughing, shouting men. Warriors mostly, it looked like from their armor and weapons.

My brothers closed in around Annabel, Grim to her other side, Bjarni in front, shielding her from view as we crossed the mead hall. We might have disguised her, but the less anyone got a chance to look at her the better. It was the first time my mate had been this cooperative since I picked her up at the airport what felt like eons ago, and I felt her anxiety flutter in our bond. But also something else—curiosity.

I glanced down at her, and saw her peeking out between the bulk of Grim's arms and his body, taking in everything with her mouth half-open in wonder.

"Are you *enjoying* this?" I asked, frowning at the great hall to try and guess what'd piqued her interest enough to challenge her natural sense of danger at being surrounded by so many violent brutes.

"No. Well... it's just... everything looks like it's from the Viking era. It's like seeing living, breathing history," she said, then grimaced when the troll-blooded shoved past us to sit down on a half-empty bench. "Or at least living, breathing legends...."

I eyed her quietly as she took in Udgard's mead hall with an unmistakable curiosity, despite the looming danger of the aggressive Jotunns around us. She might have been disguised as a boy, but the flush in her cheeks and gleam in her eyes still brought my cock to attention. Not many humans ever crossed the fabric between Midgard and Jotunheim, but of those who did, none had held their head high in the center of Udgard, surrounded by Jotunns. Yet Annabel did. She wasn't cowering, and despite her strong grip on my hand, the looming danger didn't quell her curiosity.

I'd never considered I'd be interested in the Turner girl promised to my lineage for anything more than the sweet pull any omega offered. But Annabel was something more. Something *different*.

Underneath the steady urge I had to bend her over and shove my dick up her cunt I'd battled since the first time I saw her, intrigue slowly grew. Bjarni was right—she was fierce. Like a warrior. Even if she was just a human blessed by the Norns with clear sight.

"I'll grab us something to eat," Bjarni said as Grim and I sat down, keeping Annabel between us. "And if you give me a smile, I'll find you a honey cake too, sweetie." The last bit he said while looking at Annabel, a hopeful smile on his bearded face. She completely ignored him.

Bjarni's smile faltered at her silent rejection and he turned to fetch the food. Poor sod wasn't used to having to work for forgiveness. He'd usually flash a smile and have whatever womenfolk he'd upset forgive any and all transgressions. A not small part of me was decidedly gleeful that Annabel wasn't that easy. At least I wasn't the only Lokisson she was mad at.

"Who's that?" Annabel asked, bringing my attention to the front of the hall with a nod.

I followed her gaze to the dais, where a large Jotunn sat leisurely sprawled on a low throne made of wood and animal hides.

"That's Udgardsloke. The chieftain of Udgard. And it's best if he doesn't notice us."

"Why?" she asked, frowning as a young woman wearing nothing but a slave collar and a skirt made from sewn hides kneeled by his side and offered him a large horn full of mead. "Because you're the sons of a god?"

"Not exactly," I said, smirking as the slave girl reached between Udgardsloke's legs and freed his cock, causing Annabel's cheeks to flame red before she quickly averted her gaze. "We're on good terms. And he's been known to even host Thor on occasion—he's a lot less prejudiced than the mighty gods of Asgard. But he's also one of the most conniving men in all the worlds. He's outsmarted even Loki on more than one occasion—and I don't want to take my chances that he won't be able to see through your disguise."

"Oh. Right." She pointedly kept her eyes away from the dais as the slave girl bobbed her head up and down between the chieftain's thighs. "Looks like he's too busy to worry about us anyway."

I chuckled at her obvious discomfort. She may be a

warrior at heart, but she was also still just a human girl —and I found her embarrassment at basic needs adorable. "Not everyone would rather run through a blizzard than have their needs tended to, sweetling."

She shot me a glare. "I thought you were going to murder me in a heathen ritual."

"I'd never hurt you," I murmured, stroking a finger along her cheek. "None of us would."

"No, just rape me," she said, but despite the anger in her voice she didn't move away from my touch.

"This song and dance again? We both know you wanted it. Do you not remember how your body begged for my cock? How hard you came on my knot? Why do you insist on playing the victim, Annabel, when we both know you're anything but?" I slid my thumb down to her lower lip, smirking when her breathing turned just a bit uneven.

"You need to stop playing with the girl," Grim growled quietly from Annabel's other side, his voice terse. "Her scent is seeping through."

I inhaled deeply and caught the first delicate whiff of female arousal and shot my mate a knowing grin. Yeah, she liked playing the unwilling party, but she couldn't hide her body's instinctive response.

Annabel, apparently realizing what Grim had referred to, turned beet red and pulled away from me with a jerk, hissing some insult I didn't care enough about to listen to.

"I'm starting to think you like to play pretend, sweetling," I murmured, not allowing her to squirm away from my gaze.

"Saga, stop!" The growled command didn't come from Annabel—but from Grim. He'd twisted around in his seat to stare me down, fury simmering just behind his blown pupils. "If one of these pricks catch her scent—"

Either Magni's mark would be discovered, or she would be fucked to death. I'd seen it happen before—some hapless omega dragged to the dais and forced to service every single man present until her body gave out. It wasn't Grim's words but the dark heat in his eyes that made me pull away from Annabel, sick dread churning in my gut. My youngest brother tried to deny his physical yearning for our omega, but judging from his blown pupils, her scent was getting to him already.

"No need to look so dour." Large plates of food were plonked on the table in front of us, followed by mugs and horns filled with foaming mead. Bjarni sat down directly in front of Annabel and flicked a copper coin at the serving wench who'd helped him carry the food. "We've got food, we've got mead, we've got a roof over our heads... dig in!"

Bjarni'd always been fond of the simple pleasures in life. It spoke volumes of his attempt to woo Annabel that he hadn't added the serving girl to the list. I arced an eyebrow at him, but he only shot me a grin and grabbed the thigh-sized hunk of meat on his plate with a pleased hum.

By my side, Annabel seemed to be taking in the serving size with a bit more hesitation. Bjarni'd gotten her a full leg of lamb, with a few measly root vegetables pushed off to the side of the plate. She'd eaten fresh kills roasted over the fire with no protest since we arrived in Jotunheim, but in all fairness, this particular hunk of meat was about half the size of her.

"I can't eat all this," she said. "It's way too much."

"I got you the most tender leg," Bjarni protested, the look of genuine hurt making me bite back a snort of laughter. My blond brother was very particular about his food—a leg of perfectly roasted lamb from the hearth of Udgard was definitely a courting gift from him.

Annabel opened and closed her mouth several times, undoubtedly wanting to bring up food shortage and wasteful spending, or whatever human argument she was used to considering. Finally, after a long look at Bjarni's disappointed face, she sighed and grabbed the leg with both hands. "Thank you. It looks delicious."

Bjarni brightened and bit into his own sizable portion with a pleased hum. I envied his carefree attitude to life. In his mind, the woman he was planning to mate had accepted his courting gift, and that was the end of that problem. Whereas I... I had the blasted mating-bond shuddering in my chest, one moment humming with contentedness at being near the woman I'd claimed as mine... and the next tightening with suffocating agony when Annabel made her lack of trust in me clear.

"Well, I'll be damned! If it isn't the Lokissons feasting on Udgardsloke's meat and drink!" a booming voice echoes overhead.

My heart stilled in my chest as a Jotunn sat down on the bench next to Bjarni, slamming his oversized mug of mead on the wooden long table. His beard was long and braided in two, but the dark brown hair tumbling over his shoulders was wild and unkempt. Over his back hung a long bastard sword, gleaming from within.

"Surtr," Bjarni said, offering the Jotunn a hearty slap on the back. "What're you doing in Udgard?"

"Gathering the troops. I'm traveling all across Jotunheim looking for volunteers for the army." He nodded at my blond brother. "You three finally going to take on the Asir?"

"We will. But we'll have to catch up with you when you're closer to the border—we've got an errand to run first," Bjarni lied smoothly, taking a casual swig of his own mead.

"And what errand would keep the Lokissons from joining forces with the mightiest Jotunn army to ever see the light of day?" Surtr asked, narrowing his eyes in suspicion. "I know quite a few of us would be mightily unimpressed if you tried to pull a stunt like that godlover Magni Thorsson."

"I suggest you don't go making accusations that we'd have anything to do with Thor's bastard," I said, arching an eyebrow at the Jotunn. "We have little love for the gods, or the half-bloods who betray their Jotunn brethren."

"We're taken the little one to our mom's place," Bjarni said, nodding his head at Annabel.

For the first time, Surtr let his gaze slide over my mate. He arched both eyebrows in surprise. "Is that a human boy?"

"Half-human," I said, patting Annabel on the shoulder. "Grim got a bit too acclimated during our stay in Midgard. Sired a son. With Ragnarök coming, we need to get the little guy out of the way."

"Ha!" Surtr shoved an elbow into Bjarni's ribs and leveled an amused look at Grim—who was busy shooting silent daggers at me over Annabel's head. "Grim's fathered a half-human bastard? Now I've seen it all! I thought his kind were too frigid to get it up, let alone produce an heir. Even if it's a scrawny one."

"We were also surprised," I said, offering Grim a smirk. "But lo and behold."

"And here I thought the ice-kindred procreated asexually," Surtr guffawed. "Grim Lokisson a father, huh? And giving enough of a shit to pull the half-blood out of Midgard. Come here, boy. Let me have a look at ya!"

Annabel shot me a wide-eyed stare, but there was no way around it that wouldn't raise the Jotunn's suspicion.

"Do as you're told," Grim growled, not even bothering to look at Annabel. Father of the year, right there.

Slowly, she got up from the bench and walked around the end of the table to stand by Bjarni's side. She was so small next to him and Surtr, standing barely level with their eye-height while they sat, and the pang to protect her was nearly insurmountable as I felt her uncertainty in our bond.

"Does Daddy teach you how to fight like a Jotunn?" Surtr asked, prodding at Annabel's spindly arms with a finger nearly as thick as her wrist. "Or did you inherit his nefarious magic? You don't look like much, but if those three've dragged you all the way from Midg—" His amused voice died mid-sentence, and every muscle in my body tensed when his pupils suddenly dilated, nostrils flaring wide.

"You sneaky bastards!" Surtr said. The amusement was gone in his voice, washed away by a rich growl. "Trying to save such a ripe little omega pussy all to yourselves."

20

ANNABEL

Ice-cold panic seized my spine when the giant of a man grabbed me by the upper arm. Rage flared from Saga's end of our bond and he shot up out of his seat, already halfway across the table before Grim caught him by the shoulder and yanked him back.

"Will you keep your voice down? We're not looking to share with all of Udgard," Bjarni said, casually resting a hand on my hip. His warmth made my nerves simmer down just a smidge—even if the blatant intentions written all over the Jotunn's face made my hackles rise.

"Udgardsloke isn't going to be pleased if he hears you've kept an omega from him. You know he claims a stake in any omega snatch that crosses his halls," Surtr said, not taking his eyes off me. It was like being watched by a predator—and yet it gave me none of the pleasurable goosebumps I'd come to associate with an alpha's attentions since arriving in Iceland. Only sick, cold dread.

"He wants a piece at any pussy, regardless if it's omega or not," Bjarni said, still keeping his tone light, as if the subject bored him. "So let's just cut to the chase—what do you want, Surtr?"

The Jotunn smiled a slow, wide smile. "What do you think I want? It's no fair you three get an omega all to yourselves—the least you can do is share her for a night. The way I see it, I get her for a full night instead of a quick romp while fighting off every other fucking alpha in here—and you get to keep your little knot warmer for all the cold days ahead."

Bjarni narrowed his eyes in thought, rubbing his beard with the hand not still resting on my waist. "It would seem this requires further discussion. Perhaps somewhere more private?"

I gasped in outraged. "Excuse me? You think you can just rent me out?"

Surtr shot me a heated look. "I see you've yet to show her her place. I suppose I'll help you out with that little problem, too. Teach her to hold her lip."

"Yeah, she's a feisty little thing." Bjarni smirked, slapping my ass with a large hand. "Saga, bring her in, will you? Grim, get us some mead. Surtr and I have business to discuss." He got to his feet, casually silencing my protests with a warning finger on my lips as he held out his other arm toward the back of the room, eyes locked on the Jotunn. "Shall we?"

Surtr glanced from me to Saga. "There better be no tricks, Lokissons."

Bjarni roared a booming laugh and slapped him on the shoulder. "And leave me to face the wrath of Surtr the Swarthy? Nah, man. She's a good piece of pussy, but she's not worth my life. C'mon. Unless you want to share her with the entire hall, we need to get moving."

I stared after the two as they disappeared behind a leather sheet suspended between two arched pieces of timber. Then I turned to Saga—and found him alone. Grim'd silently disappeared, undoubtedly to get the mead needed for the *negotiations*. "If you think I'm going to let that creep touch me—" I began through clenched teeth.

"If you think I'd let another alpha have you, you still don't understand what it means to be my mate," he said gruffly as he walked around the table.

"You seem plenty keen to have me fuck your brothers," I hissed. "And right now, Bjarni's apparently negotiating the *price* you'll charge for me!"

Saga sighed impatiently. "Fuck's sake, it's a ploy, Annabel. Grim's poisoning the mead as we speak. We just need to play along until he passes out."

"And then what?" I asked, crossing my arms over my chest. "There's a storm out there."

"If Grim does his job, Surtr will be out for at least a day. He's too busy gathering his army to hunt after a bit of pussy, so as long as we're a few hours away once he wakes up, we'll be fine. We can weather the storm overnight and set off in the morning." Saga brushed his fingers along my cheek, then lowered his hand, casting a glance around us to make sure no one saw him fondle what was *supposed* to be his nephew. "I won't let any harm come to you, sweetling. I swear it."

There was a lot I could say about Saga Lokisson, most of it less than flattering. But one thing I couldn't deny, not with the quiet throbbing of the bond in my chest, he would never let me get hurt. "And what about Bjarni? If Grim's poisoning the mead...?"

Saga snorted and grabbed me lightly by the arm, leading me toward the leather curtain the others had disappeared through. "Don't worry about him. Grim poisoned him so often while growing up, he's mostly immune these days."

I blinked, mouth already halfway open to ask why on earth Grim had been *poisoning* his own brother, but Saga put his finger to his lips and pulled me through to a hallway, nodding toward another leather curtain. From behind it, Surtr's booming laugh could be heard.

Right. Time to play pretend.

Saga pulled back the other curtain, revealing a small room with nothing but a wide, fur-covered platform. Bjarni and Surtr sat cross-legged on each side, shaking what looked like pieces of carved bone in a horn before spreading them on the furs.

"Dice?" Saga asked, arching an eyebrow at his brother.

"We decided to up the stakes a bit," Bjarni said, a

broad smile on his lips as if he didn't have a care in the world. "I win, we get gold. He wins, we join his army and go smack some gods over the head."

"Ha! Not a bad bet," Saga said, smacking me on the ass to shoo me toward the side opposite Surtr.

"Not so fast," Surtr said, pausing briefly to let loose a burp strong enough to make the leather curtain stir. He snatched out an arm and grabbed me by the wrist, yanking hard enough to make me stumble a few steps. "I need me a lucky charm. C'mere, omega, and warm my lap!"

I shot a panicked look at Saga, my instinctive response to search out my alpha for help, and the look on his handsome face spelled absolute murder.

"*Release* her," he snarled, closing his hand around my shoulder as if to tug me back from the Jotunn.

"Don't be silly, brother," Bjarni said, a quiet note of warning in his otherwise carefree voice. "Let the man get a feel of the goods. Far be it from us to complain if he wants to sniff at her while we roll the dice. Just means we'll get more gold lining our pockets."

"So possessive over a piece of human-grade omega cunt," Surtr rumbled, an unspoken challenge in his tone. "Now why is that?"

Saga stood frozen for a long second, and I felt his warring emotions roiling in our bond. Everything in him ached to attack the male who'd put his hands on me—and oddly enough, that calmed my own anxiety right down.

Yeah, he wouldn't let anyone hurt me, least of all this big goon. But we also needed their ploy to play out, which meant playing along.

I placed my free hand on Saga's chest, willing the fire in his blood to cool enough so he remembered what he'd told me only moments before. "It's okay," I murmured.

"Ha! Look at that—even the girl knows she needs a good knotting by a real alpha," Surtr, guffawed. "Don't you worry, sweetheart, I'll teach ya to take it."

Saga's eyes narrowed to slits, but I saw reason slowly return to his gaze, overruling the instincts undoubtedly roaring to fight the alpha trying to lay claim to what was his. Without a word he released his grip on me and sat down next to Bjarni.

Surtr gave another yank on me, and I fell into his lap with a startled squeak.

"There ya go, princess," the Jotunn laughed, letting his hand roam down my front. "Get nice and comfortable now."

It was impossible to ignore the hardness pressing up against me, and his oversized hands on my body made my skin crawl, but I gritted my teeth and dealt with it. Once he was knocked out, he was so getting more than one kick right in the balls.

Grim appeared within minutes with two giant mugs of mead. He offered one first to Bjarni and then the remaining to Surtr.

"Not so fast," the Jotunn said, the hand on me finally

leaving to snatch the mead Bjarni was already drinking from from his hand. "I know you Lokissons and your tricks. You've inherited far too many traits from that god of mischief who spawned you."

"Suit yourself," Bjarni said with a shrug, grabbing the mug first meant for the Jotunn. "Now, are we going to roll some dice, or are you going to squabble over free mead?"

They rolled dice and drank mead and laughed as if nothing was amiss for a good hour or so. I didn't understand the marking on the pieces of bone, but from Surtr's growing irritation, it seemed they kept coming up stalemate.

One look at Saga's face, tense with concentration, and it dawned on me that the outcome wasn't by happenstance. Thankfully, Surtr was deep enough in his mead—and hormones from repeatedly sniffing at me, judging by the lewd comments he growled in my ear—that he didn't notice.

However, the third time in a row he rolled what looked like a bird to Bjarni's four jagged lines and then two circles, he'd clearly had enough. Roaring with frustration he tossed the dice to the ground and put a hand on my back, shoving me forward and onto all four on the bed.

"Enough!" he snarled, the richness of his growl drawing nothing but panic up my spine. "We can gamble in the morning—I've waited long enough for a piece of this cunt."

Thick fingers brushed up against the juncture of my thighs, rubbing suggestively, and I kicked blindly. But before he could grab my legs and keep me still, a loud *crack* rang through the room.

Surtr swore, and I turned around just in time to see Saga swing at him again, this time impacting with his nose. Blood spurted from the Jotunn's face, and he retaliated with a mighty blow right to Saga's gut.

"Get off him!" I howled, rage reddening my vision as my mate smacked up against the nearest wall from the force of the impact and pain ricocheted through our bond. *Something* vibrated through my body, like an electric current, numbing my fingertips, but before the mounting tension could come to a head, Surtr snatched me by the back of my shirt.

"Such fierce loyalty you two have," he snarled, blood still flowing freely from his broken nose. "I wonder...."

Strong fingers pushed my hair away and pulled down on my collar.

I growl filled the small room as he bared my marks. "That... that's Magni Thorsson's mark! *Next* to yours?! You filthy traitors! I'm going to snap—"

Before he could finish his threat, another *crack* sounded from high above me. Surtr's grip on me slackened, and Grim yanked me away just in time to avoid getting squashed underneath the Jotunn's giant body as hit the ground. He fell over like a giant oak, revealing Bjarni standing behind him with the leftovers of the mug he'd used to bash Surtr over the head.

"Well, fuck," Bjarni muttered as I stared down at the fallen Jotunn. "Guess it's time to flee through a fucking storm then."

"Is he dead?" I asked.

"Unfortunately not. He's got a thick skull," Grim said, disgust pulling on his upper lip as he stared down. "Without the poison, he'd still be on his feet."

"We need to get out of here," Saga said, voice still strained from Surtr's blow. "He's seen the marks—he's not going to stop before she's dead."

"And us along with her," Bjarni muttered. "Fuck."

"And where do you suggest we go?" Grim asked, irritation clear in his voice. "He'll be on us before we ever reach Midgard."

Silence spread between the three brothers for a beat, before Saga clenched his hands, drawing in a deep breath. "Magni. We find Magni. He'll bring her to Asgard, and the gods will protect her. And we're going with them."

21

MAGNI

I hadn't thought it was possible to feel any shittier than I had when the Lokissons had bested me back in the glade—and yet there I was, sprawled alongside the road without even a view of the night sky. Not that I could have seen it anyway with the rain coming down in sheets that had soaked me through long before I'd toppled over like an old log. My face was in the mud, some of which had made it into my nose and mouth, and I was too weak to do anything about it besides wheeze.

I should have gotten my ass back to Asgard. I should have at least tried. With my arm the way it was and the rest of my body slowly deteriorating in kind, the last thing I needed was to pursue my wayward mate across what amounted to the Asgardian backwoods.

I needed healing. I needed rest. I needed to regroup.

But I hadn't done any of that. Instead, I'd set off in

pursuit of Annabel, and in doing so, had turned against my own best interests.

The worst part was that I didn't know why. Or rather, I didn't have a logical explanation for it. All I knew was that the farther she got from me, the worse my pain became. And not just the pain in my arm—this torment was far greater. It was the agony of distance, the excruciating experience of being separated from my mate.

Every inch that stretched between us was a knife in my gut. Had I gone to Asgard, it would have been unbearable.

And yet there was no physical reason for it, no tangible cause I could point to and rip out like a faulty organ. When it came to Annabel, the organ was my very soul.

"Gods damn it," I hissed, huffing as another spray of mud spattered my face. I closed my eyes, trying to at least will myself onto my back. It somehow seemed more dignified, even if it meant showing my belly to a passersby. What kind of man was I, traipsing about after a woman I'd already lost to three other men? What kind of god was I, lying here helpless?

Clearly a lovesick one. Shame it was a disease with no cure.

Except her.

She was all I wanted, all I craved. She was as potent a need in me as hunger or thirst, all at once the respite of sleep and the excitement of falling too far too fast.

Being with her brought me peace just as much as it brought me electric joy. Fucking Annabel was like riding the lightning.

Being without her was like drowning, but being unable to die—like bleeding out with no end. It was torture beyond imagining, a constant, crushing weight on my chest.

And all the while I scolded myself for having taken her as my mate in the first place. I longed for the sight of her, the scent of her—even just the lilt of her voice....

"Is that...?" someone said in the wake of a thunderclap, and my whole body jolted at the sound.

Her. It was her.

"Annabel...."

The earth trembled with her footfalls as she raced to my side, kicking up puddles in fierce sprays. Every step brought her closer, made my blood pump harder and hotter, until she put her hands on my body and turned me over, kneeling at my side.

"Jesus," she whispered, her braided hair framed by storm clouds and purple lightning.

"No," I said, trying not to wince. "But close enough."

She didn't laugh. Instead a strange parade of expressions flitted across her face—a caravan led by relief with anger and grief bringing up the rear.

"Idiot," she hissed, tumbling forward against my chest.

I sank back into the mud with a grunt. Given my

condition, I was worried the impact might break me, but instead of shattering, I felt suddenly... whole.

It was like the soft press of Annabel against me was welding me together, stitching up all the disparate parts that had been torn asunder. With great effort, I managed to lift my good hand to the back of her head, clutching it as I breathed her in. Despite the dampness clinging to her and the time she'd spent with the Lokissons, she still smelled like mine.

"You know," Bjarni said, his shadow falling across me as he caught up with the wayward omega, "I have a sheep who's a lot like you."

"I have a horse like him," Grim chimed in, his stark features coming into view. "Or at least, one end of the horse is like him."

Over top of Annabel's head, I leveled them both with my best glare. It must not have been very intimidating; they only smirked.

But the look on Saga's face was different. As he approached, there was a somberness to him, a sort of grim understanding. His cold eyes slipped away from me and to Annabel where she'd burrowed herself in my chest. Though I anticipated some raised hackles, all I got was a little nod of what looked like recognition.

My thumb passed over the twin sets of indentations on Annabel's nape. He knew. Better than anyone else, Saga knew what I'd gone through. After all, I'd spirited her away from him not so long ago. Was this how he felt?

An unexpected stab of guilt panged in my stomach and rattled my bones. I shifted uncomfortably beneath Annabel's slight form, but it wasn't the weight of her body that was pressing in on me—it was the weight of what I'd done.

I... actually felt bad for a Lokisson. And not just bad, but... there seemed to be a sort of kinship between us now.

Well, shit.

"I would have thought you'd have had enough smarts to get your ass back to Asgard," Grim said lips still tilted smugly, "but it seems I overestimated you."

Bjarni chuckled. "Alone and wounded in enemy territory... I'm afraid it's not a good look on you."

"It's not as stupid as you think," Saga snapped, stepping past them and to my side. "He didn't need Asgard. He needed his mate."

He reached down, but instead of plucking Annabel from my embrace, he merely offered his hand to me.

I blinked up at him, but took it. Annabel rocked back onto her heels, and together they helped me to my feet, though I hated that they had to do so.

"Thanks," I muttered, trying to lean more on Annabel than Saga, despite his obvious strength. "And... thank you for bringing my pet back to me."

Scowling, Annabel opened her mouth to speak, but Saga beat her to it. "We only came back for you because we need your help."

I snorted. "That must have hurt to admit."

He gave me a sidelong glance. "You have no idea."

"We need to get to Asgard," Annabel said, still pressed to my side. The longer she was near me, the stronger I felt. I looked down at her in quiet wonder as stability returned to my legs. "Circumstances have... changed."

I cocked a brow. "You mean everyone and their brother knows what you are, and they're after you now." I shot a look at Bjarni and Grim. "In some cases, literally."

Bjarni crossed his arms. "Maybe he's not so stupid." Then he grinned. "But he still missed the good stuff."

"The good stuff?" Annabel shrieked, whirling on him fast enough to test my balance. "What happened back there—at the mead hall—that was fun for you?"

"It's quite likely," Grim said with a shrug. "He's a simple man, and he wasn't the one getting auctioned off."

Now it was my turn to raise my voice. "Auctioned off?" Blood surged into my neck, hot and prickling. "You were going to auction off my mate?"

"You're all dense," Saga barked, throwing his hands up. "I've explained it time and time again. It was a ploy!"

Annabel narrowed her pretty eyes. "That doesn't mean I had any fun."

"Oh?" Bjarni's grin widened. "Are you sure?"

With a huff, she quieted, and the brothers shared a knowing smile. I didn't like it. The fact that they knew things about her I didn't, that they had inside jokes and stories... it rankled.

Fortunately, Bjarni put me out of my misery. "She kicked Surtr in the balls."

"You..." I stared at her again in shock. "You did?"

"I did," she confirmed, lifting her chin defiantly. "And he deserved it."

I looked her over, appreciating how much she'd changed in so little time. She looked good in her leathers bordered by raven plumage, a stark contrast to her fair skin. Though she'd seemed out of place in them before, now she looked comfortable in them, like they'd been made with her in mind.

And I supposed they had, but it wasn't only her body filling them out anymore—it was her attitude as well, her confidence. That challenging spark in her eyes set off another flood of heat in my veins, only this time, it all hammered south.

"Asgard," I murmured, finishing my assessment of my mate. "Yes. That would be nice... if it were possible."

All four of them turned to me with Saga the first to ask, "What the Hel does that mean?"

"My bracelet," I said, rattling it so he could see. "It's stopped working. And before you ask, no, I don't know why."

"Let me take a look at it," Grim offered, approaching with a frown. "I'm good with magic."

Warily, I offered my arm for his inspection. He ran his nimble fingers across the metal and runes, cocking his head this way and that as he examined them. His lips moved in nearly silent recitation of the spellwork meant to transport us to my home, but even though a few of the sigils flickered obediently, they did not hum with power as they should.

"Much as I hate to admit it," he said, stepping back, "Magni's not lying. Worse, I'm just as stumped as he is as to why the magic's failed."

"Which means we're talking about a month-long journey," I said, nodding to Grim. "All of it on foot or horseback, and all of it through Jotunn territory."

Bjarni rubbed the back of his neck. "Yeah, and a lot of them aren't happy with us right now."

Annabel's face fell in total devastation. I couldn't blame her. No doubt she'd sought me out as the solution to her problems. I hated to let her down, but it made me wonder if that was all she'd come after me for, and whether she'd have bothered if things were different.

As if she'd sensed the thought, she looked up at me, meeting my gaze. "It's probably because of what you did for me at the well... which makes this all my fault."

Carefully, I pulled away from Saga, laying both my hands on her shoulders. I practically engulfed her with just that tiny gesture, but it warmed my heart to see she no longer flinched at my touch.

"Whether it is or it isn't, I would do it again," I told her, lightly squeezing her through her armor.

She almost smiled. I pulled in a breath, touching my

mark just behind her ear... and rolled my eyes at the retching sounds Bjarni made.

"There's another option," Grim said, pushing at Bjarni to make him stop. He glanced at Saga, perhaps seeking permission, before training his eyes back on me. "We have a map left to us by our father. There's a closer entry point... though it's an unofficial one."

Given their father was Loki, I could only imagine what that might mean. Still, it was intriguing—and likely our best chance at getting the Hel out of here both quickly and in one piece. "How close, and how 'unofficial,' are we talking?"

"It's practically right under your nose," Bjarni said through an infuriatingly smug smile. "As to the rest, it shouldn't matter... as long as you're on board."

Now that was interesting—much as I needed them, it seemed the Lokissons needed me, which evened the playing field between us. Hel, depending on where in Asgard we ended up, it might even stack the deck in my favor. After all, once we were there, I didn't have to offer up any guarantees as to their safety. The moment we were all safe and sound, I could have them banished right back here.

But then I remembered how it felt to be parted from Annabel and guilt gnawed at me again. I wasn't thinking so much about Saga's feelings this time—now I was thinking of Annabel and what it would do to her to be parted from him, even for the time it would take to have his mark removed. And that made me think of what it must have been doing to her all along, how I'd already caused her so much pain, and....

"Whatever you need," I said, basking in the radiant glow of the hope on my mate's face, "I will provide. But you must agree that my brother mates Annabel as I'd planned. I won't give that up."

Saga chuffed, both his brows lifting. "You seem to think you're in a position to bargain here. I wonder where you got that idea."

"You do need my protection," I reminded him. "You've already admitted as much."

He pursed his lips. "Need is a strong word. I mean, it would be nice. But we could always just hang around until you die."

"Please. The moment I die is the moment you and your brothers suffer the same fate. The moment you so much think of setting foot in Asgard without me—"

Annabel pushed away from me despite my growl of protest. A cold flash of anger burned in her eyes—the prelude to the detonation of a nuclear bomb. "Am I cheese?" she said.

I blinked at her. "Are you what?"

"Cheese," she repeated. Okay, so I hadn't misheard. "In your godly opinion, am I cheese?"

I began several sentences, but in the end, abandoned each one. "I have no idea how to answer that." When she only continued to glare at me, I went with my gut. "No?"

"Am I flour?" she continued through her teeth. "Or fish? Or jewelry? Or a used car?"

"Oh," Bjarni said, nodding sagely. "I get it. What she wants to know is—"

"What I want to know is," Annabel snapped, cutting him off, "if I'm not just some market good to you, why the fuck do you insist on haggling over me like I am one?"

I gaped at her. The three other alphas present didn't seem willing to interject her glorious tirade, either. In the ensuing silence, Annabel continued. "I'm not going anywhere with any of you until you agree to save my family. Once and for all. No more tricks. If you want me to go along with this, you will give me what I ask."

I glanced at the three Lokissons, expecting them to protest, but no one spoke a word. Great. Seemed it fell to me to speak reason.

"Annabel... they're humans. If they're fated to survive this, they will, but—"

"You're not listening," she hissed, eyes flashing like lightning in a summer storm. "You can try to force me with you again. But I'm telling you right now—all of you—you won't succeed. Not unless you treat me like an equal. Not unless you help you save my family and stop Ragnarök."

I wanted to argue, only because I knew that agreeing would mean a deviation from my own plans. A wrinkle in my attempts to save my own family. But... I stared down at Annabel and felt the throb of her fury in our bond.

She was my family now, too, even if that'd never been a part of my plan when I set out to conquer her.

I felt a softening in my chest, where our bond was hooked, and it scared me. Here I was cooperating with the enemy, even going so far as to share a woman with one of them, and I knew I'd bend to her will on this matter too, even if it was at the cost of my own desires. This wouldn't sit well with my family. Hel, it still didn't sit right with me.

But she'd come back for me. Even if the Lokissons had only allowed it to gain access to Asgard. I'd felt her relief shuddering in sync with my own when she pressed into my chest.

Breathing deeply, I turned to the other alphas and said, "It's settled then. Together, we go to Asgard."

22

SAGA

Knowing where we were headed didn't make the prospect of arriving there any less daunting. First and foremost, there was the fact that we were using one of our father's "back doors" to enter into Asgard, an act I was fairly sure would be frowned upon, to say the least. Despite having Magni in tow—and therefore, an excuse—there would be no small amount of fury awaiting us, a pack of Jotunn interlopers, on the other side.

And then there was the undercurrent of dread to consider—the one that had been nipping at our heels since this ill-begotten journey began. Something wasn't right here, and we all knew it. All of us save for perhaps Annabel.

How could she know? She'd been dropped into the middle of this mess completely unaware of the ins and outs of godly affairs. Hel, even my brothers and I could barely keep up with it all, and we were descended from them. Magni, for all the eons he'd spent living in Asgard, didn't seem to be any wiser than we were. We'd known Ragnarök was coming—we'd prepared for that much—but now that it was here....

It was the end of the world as mortals knew it, sure. But something seemed... off.

I glanced over at Annabel as she walked alongside me, leading my brothers to the portal with Magni supported between them. She looked good in her leathers—damn good—but more than that, she looked *strong*.

What I'd heard about her from her parents paled in comparison to the reality. They'd said she was studious, dedicated to her work, and self-sacrificing, and so I'd prepared for a submissive mate to continue our lineage. The truth was that Annabel was all of those things, but she was also so much more.

I'd seen it at the mead hall and again when we found Magni lying in the mud alongside the road. She was confident and unwavering, brutal even, while at the same time capable of such compassion and tenderness it stole my breath. I'd already known she would be a good mother—that the instinct was there, as well as the disposition—but what I hadn't realized was that she'd be a good *woman*. She wasn't just some pretty plaything.

That thought frightened me. It was something else I hadn't prepared for, another complication that had cropped up where I least expected it. That seemed to be the running theme of our little adventure. It made me wonder if Fate weren't playing some kind of game with us.

Whether it was or not, we were about to cross yet another threshold. Before us lay the portal our father's map had illustrated for us. There was magic in the air, a low vibration that flowed soundlessly, yet tangibly through the spaces between our atoms and bones.

Annabel fidgeted by my side, clearly feeling it too. I placed my palm on the small of her back. It was a light touch, a small gesture, but the way her spine straightened meant so much more.

It meant she was mine—something we both already knew, but it never hurt to be reminded of.

In front of us, the world rippled and shimmered, a gelatinous membrane shuddering into being. Annabel inhaled sharply through her nose. She'd only been through a portal once before, and that had been something of a harrowing experience.

I cast a glare at Magni. He still needed to pay his dues for that.

But then again, maybe he already had. He was doing better now that he was closer to Annabel, but he was still pale, his lips still bloodless. Hopefully he'd survive, but not before having to withstand the knowledge that right now, he was pretty much useless.

"Is that it?" Annabel asked, drawing my attention back to where it belonged. "Is that Asgard?"

I peered past the thin tissue between realities to

bask in the glow of a golden city. I hadn't seen it in centuries—perhaps longer than that—but the sheer majesty of Asgard couldn't be mistaken for anything else. Gilt spires jutted past iridescent clouds beyond a sea of rolling fields. There was no grass so green in any of the other realms, each blade like a shard of emerald purloined from a dwarven mine.

And all around the image blazed a honeyed, runic script. It didn't say "TO ASGARD," exactly, but I knew enough to know that's what it meant.

Or I thought I did, because the moment I began to step through, Grim stopped me.

"Wait."

I turned to him, brows raised. "What for?"

"There's something... off about this," he said, squinting at the runes. Abandoning Magni to Bjarni's grasp, he cocked his head, coming to my side.

Great—something else that was just *wrong enough* to be unsettling. "Off *how*?"

Grim's lips moved, but no sound emerged from them for quite some time. Annabel looked up at me, searching my face for an answer, but I was unfortunately just as bewildered as she was.

Finally, he shook his head. "Entry isn't free."

Bjarni snorted. "Hel is *that* supposed to mean?"

Grim glared over his shoulder at him. "It means there's a cost. If either of you bothered to give magic the respect it deserves, you'd know there often is. Crossing borders like this, especially into a place as well-warded as Asgard, will require a phenomenal amount of magical intervention. We'll have to give up something of ourselves in exchange. We'll have to pay a sort of... toll."

"And the price?" I said, instinctively blocking Annabel from view. Grim was right—I didn't know a whole lot about the finer points of magic, but I did know that when it came to a cost, it was usually steep.

Grim's mouth formed into a slash. "I don't know. It doesn't say. The most I can tell you is that it will be exacted three times. Three trials, so to speak." He looked back up at the sigils. "But I'm not sure what they entail."

"Perfect," Bjarni muttered. "We'll just step through the magical doorway with no idea what's on the other side, then? Is that it?"

"I'm afraid that's it," Grim answered, turning to me once again. "I'm the scholar. I'll go."

Bjarni bellowed a laugh. "And if the trials don't involve brooding with your nose in a book? Then what will you do?"

Grim quirked a brow. "Are you volunteering?"

Bjarni shrugged, hefting Magni up off his feet without even the slightest hint of an effort. "I'm pretty useful in a fight."

"Put me down," Magni hissed.

"And if it isn't a fight?" Grim countered, gesturing to the portal. "Everything that's here leads me to believe it's something more esoteric than that. Something metaphysical."

They would bicker like this for hours if I let them, and that was time none of us had. I was the eldest. I was the most experienced. And that made me responsible.

"I'll go," I said, already stepping forward. "I'll let you know when it's over with."

"Saga!" Annabel said, grabbing at my arm. "Wait. You have no idea what's on the other side!"

"No," I told her, "I don't. But neither does anyone else, and that's not the point. The point is that we have to get you to safety, and we have to get him—" I nodded at Magni. "—to a healer. Because if you lose him, sweetling...." I trailed off, knowing exactly what words I wanted to say, which ones were true—and yet when it came down to it, I was utterly unable to say them.

If you lose him, then I lose you too.

"I'll be back," I said instead, gruffly shaking her off to deter her from pursuit.

But in true Annabel fashion, as soon as I was on the other side, she cried out after me, "I'm coming with you!"

And so the darkness swallowed us both.

I cursed, pulling in a lungful of mist. It was the only thing I could sense in this void besides Annabel herself, shimmering like a beacon behind me. Every echo of her footsteps incensed me. Gods damn her, I told her I would do this myself!

"Go back," I snapped once she was near enough,

whirling on her and taking her by the shoulders. "This is no place for you."

She shook her head. "You need me. You can't do this alone."

I stared at her in utter disbelief. Was she implying I was weak? That I needed the company of some *omega* to get through this?

Wasn't that what she was always implying, though? Every time I gave an order, she rebelled. Every time I made a suggestion, she had one of her own. Every time I wanted to take action, she just had to argue. And now here she was, following me into dangers untold because she thought she knew better than an alpha—than the son of a god.

The darkness yawned around us, fog thickening in my chest as I tightened my grip on her, walking her backward whence we came.

"I didn't ask your opinion on what I can and cannot do, Annabel," I growled, a palpable heat prickling my throat. "Just as I did not ask you to accompany me here. Go back with the others. *Now.*"

But she dug in her heels, reaching up to take my wrists in her delicate hands. "No. Saga, just listen to me. Please. I have this feeling...."

"I am not interested in your feelings!" I snapped, tightening my grasp until she winced. "You cannot listen, can you? What the Hel kind of omega doesn't know how to follow an order from her mate?"

Annabel's eyes darkened, growing nearly as pitch as

the rest of the room. "What the hell kind of alpha is challenged by his omega trying to support him?" She made a valiant attempt to brush my hands off her. "You know I can do this. You know I have some kind of ability, something that could help. Why won't you just let me?"

What was happening to me? The anger was rising so hard and so fast. The muscle in my cheek was twitching, my nostrils flared wide to billow as much mist as I took in. Another flash of heat, this one white-hot, seared behind my eyeballs until all I could see was red. I knew I was bruising Annabel now, but I couldn't stop. I didn't want to stop. Not until she obeyed me.

"Because I don't need your help," I told her through my teeth as she struggled to free herself. "What I *need* is for you to *obey me*. I need you to *submit*. I am not interested in any magic you might have, Annabel, nor am I interested in how you seem to want to play the warrior all of a sudden. You *aren't* one. *I* am. I've tolerated you playing dress-up because it means you keep your mouth shut, but even my patience for that is waning."

With surprising strength, she shoved away from me at last, stumbling a few feet toward where the threshold to the portal must have been. But instead of crossing it, she stopped short, staring at me with wide eyes and an unsettlingly blank expression.

"Is that what you think of me?" she asked, voice low and trembling, not just with hurt, but with cold, seething rage. "You think I'm just your... your weak little omega? Your subordinate? Your slave?"

The words tumbled from my mouth faster than I could stop them. "That is all I want you to be."

Annabel blinked in reply, just once. It was the kind of look I would have expected from someone who'd been slapped in the face. And the worst part was that I liked it. It felt good to see her put in her place.

"This is why," she whispered after a long moment. "This, right here—the way you see me, how you treat me, what I am to you at heart...." Tears were shrouding her gaze, but they did nothing to obscure the anguish in her eyes. "This is why I can't ever love you, Saga."

But she didn't have to love me—as far as our arrangement went, love was not required. I meant to tell her that too, to sneer it at her cruelly, but faster than I could stop her she stepped around me, heading into the black.

"Annabel!" I called after her, and as I did, the mist fled my lungs in a smoky plume, leaving me empty and cold. I put a hand to my chest, trying to recall where that anger had come from—all that hate and fear. It had bubbled up so rapidly, so readily, and....

What had I done? *Why?* What was this... this *rage,* clawing at my brain stem?

"Shit," I breathed, turning to follow her scent. "Annabel, I...."

But I couldn't say it. Once again, the words wouldn't come. They were so simple—*I'm sorry*—but no matter what I did, I couldn't say it. The words formed on my tongue and died on my lips.

Desperation mounting, I roared into the shadows. "Come back here!"

Annabel's only reply was a scream.

It wasn't fear. I'd heard terror before. I'd even heard it come from her own mouth. And this... this wasn't that.

This was pain. This was sheer, brilliant agony. The kind that stabs into you just as surely as any knife.

All too soon, it lapsed into wet, sticky gurgle.

"No," I whispered, every molecule in my body screaming at me to run. To save her. "No! Annabel!"

And yet all the while, I knew it was too late.

I was the son of a god. And not just any son—the eldest of them all. I was blessed long before the others with the powers of my father. I was the fastest. The strongest. If anyone could save her, it would have been me.

But no matter what I did—no matter how far or fast I ran into that darkness, following the waning echoes of a body choking on its own blood—I never seemed to get any closer. I was always just far enough away for it not to matter.

Until she was already gone.

I stared up at the spindle that had grown out of the rocks beneath my feet. It stretched three, maybe four times as high as I was tall, towering over me, so high up that Annabel's blood hadn't even dripped to my eye-level yet. Her body cast an eerie shadow; speared on the stalagmite, she rattled and spasmed. Her eyes rolled.

Then they set upon me. Confused. Accusing. Glazing over to cold, dead gray.

"S-Saga…"

My stomach lurched up toward my throat, then plummeted at the same moment gravity began to tug her down, down, down….

"*No!*"

I surged forward, grabbing the stalagmite with every intention of snapping it in two—but the damage was already done. As Annabel slid down the tapered end, the spire widened, ripping an even greater hole in her until….

Her legs fell one way. Her torso fell another. Ruined flesh scattered at my feet like confetti.

My *mate's* flesh.

With it, I was rent apart too, and not just my body—but my soul.

23

ANNABEL

"Please... gods, no. Please...!"

"Saga?" I said, blinking against the shadows draped from every corner of this dark, dank place. There was a smell to it, not blood or urine, but just as acrid.

Fear. It was the smell of fear.

The hairs on my nape came to attention. My chest clenched as a moment later, a scream, raw and jagged, shattered the cadence of heavy sobs I'd been following for what felt like an eternity.

It was that pain that had led me here—Saga's pain. I didn't understand it. I hadn't the first clue what had happened. All I knew in the very mantel of my bones was that one of my mates was is agony, and it was the kind that would have killed a lesser man by now.

That was what he was begging for, in fact—death.

An end to his suffering. To a torment neither of us had the words to name.

"I can't," he wheezed, making the air around me tremble. "I can't...!"

"Saga!" I called again, louder this time, but it came out more like a rasp. Our bond had wrapped around my throat like a noose, tethering me to him, tugging me along. "Where are you?"

Another scream served as my answer. It was too much to bear.

Knowing damn well I could end up face-first in a wall at any minute, I quickened my pace, first to a brisk walk and then a jog. Finally, I found the courage to sprint, spurred on by Saga's keening cries and the excruciating *twang* it inspired in our bond every time.

I called his name again and again, but there was no soothing him. Could he not hear me? Why didn't he answer?

At last, and so abruptly I nearly went tumbling over him, I found my mate on his knees hunched over a figure sprawled across the ground. Well, half a figure. The legs were gone, the pelvis in tatters.

He was holding it like it was the most precious thing in all the worlds to him, cradling it to his chest as he peppered desperate kisses along its face. "Please come back to me," he was saying, shaking like a leaf. "Please, you can't... you can't go...."

Slowly, giving him as wide a berth as I was able, I

approached. My fingers landed soft upon his shoulder. "Saga...?"

He spun, dropping the bundle in his arms. Porcelain shattered on the rocks, a doll cast aside and still spewing red threads into the dark.

The way he looked at me then... the shock, the horror, the relief... it stole any other words I might have said, and all I could do was change trajectory, cupping his damp cheek.

He leaned into my touch so hard it nearly brought me to the ground beside him.

"I don't understand," I blurted, coughing as he threw his arms around my waist. Pressing his face into my clothes, my mate—a god, an *alpha*—sobbed so hard his whole body shook with his grief. "I... I'm here. What happened?"

"Don't go," he answered, digging his fingers into my shoulder blades hard enough to leave bruises. "Please. I'm sorry. I'll give you the world. I'll give you anything. *Everything.*" Nuzzling in hard, he breathed me in, holding me so tight I was practically doubled over him. "Forgive me. Forgive me."

"I don't..." Bracing myself on Saga's huge shoulders, I pushed away just enough to look down at him, jaw slack in disbelief at his red-rimmed eyes and the brokenness in them. "I don't need to forgive you."

It was the first time I'd admitted so out loud. It might have even been the first time I'd admitted it to myself. But seeing him, with what he'd thought was my broken body in his arms, I knew then everything I ever needed to know about this man.

Saga just looked at me, brow furrowed, searching my face for the lie, but there was none. Closing my eyes, I continued, "I know I should. After everything you've done to me... taken from me... I should hate you, just like I should hate my parents. But I don't. All I know is...."

Slowly, I opened my eyes again. Once more, I moved my hands from his shoulders to his face, brushing his tears with my fingertips.

"All I know is that you're my mate. And that... that everything you've done, you've done to protect the ones you love. Your brothers. I... would have done the same."

Saga lowered his head again, something dark and terrible flickering across his face. A moment later, however, it was replaced by a warm glow.

We both shifted our gazes. Just beyond where we embraced, a woodland had come into view. Vast and lush, it surrounded an idyllic little cottage. Firelight spilled from its windows.

"What the hell is this place?" I murmured. With a deep breath, Saga stood, taking my hand.

"I think... it's the second trial," he answered, threading our fingers together.

He started toward the cottage with me in tow, kicking the life-sized doll out of the way and squeezing my hand as he did so.

"Do you know this place?" I asked as he led me up

the well-trod path toward the cottage's front door. The scent of vital foliage was thicker here, yet somehow too sweet, as though it were only the facsimile of a memory rather than the actual thing. I hated that dissonance immediately—how it was like we were walking through a scene someone had been told about, but never actually borne witness to. It made this place seem all the more foreboding and disturbingly alien.

"I know it," Saga confirmed, pausing only briefly upon the stoop. With a sigh, he wiped his eyes with his free hand and looked down at me with a mirthless smile. "This is home."

I began to say, "I don't understand," but perhaps he knew I wouldn't, because without giving me any further time to process he pulled open the door, leading me over the threshold and into a thick mist smelling of fresh-baked bread.

On the floor near a stone fireplace, two boys played with sticks. One was tawny and fair-haired, broad of build even at this age, while the other—slighter, darker, more subdued—studied their game with a Corvid-like shrewdness I'd come to recognize over the past few days.

Bjarni and Grim. They were children here, innocent, vulnerable. The house was warm enough, and secluded enough to be safe, but... where was their mother?

I never got the chance to ask. Abruptly Saga pulled me behind him, turning to face the doorway as a shadow slipped through, blackening the golden afternoon.

"Where were you?"

In front of me, Saga straightened, using his frame to partially block my view. Still, I could see the furious creature just beyond him—the man who somehow seemed to dwarf my indomitable mate, if not in height, then in sheer presence. Despite the darkness he cast, he had a glow about him that reminded me of the runes that had flanked the portal, and a strange sort of vagueness to his features that made it difficult for me to focus on any one aspect of him long enough to get a sense of what he looked like.

That thick, pungent odor of bread solidified in my nostrils. I choked. And then another, far worse scent took its place.

It was the scent of rot, of flesh decaying and fluids left to ferment. I raised my free hand to my face, shrouding it against the stench, but that didn't stop my eyes from falling on the tiny corpses decomposing mere feet away, sticks still in hand.

Saga wasn't looking at them. He was only looking at the man before him, ashen, gaze hollow and a million miles away.

"They were *your* responsibility," the man said, pointing at Saga's dead brothers. "You are my eldest. What good are you, if you cannot even protect them in my absence?"

Despite how indistinct his features had seemed

mere moments ago, I now caught a stark and hypersaturated sneer developing like a Polaroid across his face.

"You were always a disappointment. It should have been *you*."

"This never happened," I said, even as the walls of the cottage fell away, crumbling to ash right before my eyes. "Saga, don't listen to him. Your brothers are alive. This isn't real. This is all just—"

"A trial," he rumbled, watching the smoke rise in the distance. "I know. But it's one I don't know how to best." Shaking his head, he looked back to Bjarni and Grim's bug-bloated bodies. "I never have."

I shook my head at him. "But if this never happened, then... then it isn't about *this*. Is it? It's something else. Something I'm not seeing."

"It's something that hasn't yet come to pass," Saga answered, worrying my fingers with his. "But something I've always feared might." Tearing his gaze away from the carnage at last, he added, "It's always been my duty to protect them. To keep my brothers safe. Ever since I can remember, it's been my job to stand in the way of anything that might harm them. One of my greatest fears is failing at that." Tightly, he swallowed. "I've already failed my father in so many other ways."

I opened my mouth to object, but then I could *taste* it—again, that pungent scent filled the air, this time coating my tongue with a rancid film.

"Just... wait," I said, trying to get Saga to focus on me —*only* me. "Let's think about this together. What happened back there? When you were holding that doll?"

Saga winced at the memory, trying to draw away from me and pull me closer all at the same time. "I thought I'd lost you. That who I am... or who I was raised to be... would drive you away from me like so many others. And that ultimately, I would be responsible for your ruin."

"And what drew you out of it?" I asked him, squeezing his hand again the moment his gaze began to stray. "What was it that made you overcome that fear? What made you keep going?"

"You," he said plainly, reaching down to tuck a wayward strand behind my ear. "The moment I saw you, the moment I heard your voice... it was like you stitched my heart back together. Like you put the fire back in my soul. You struck a spark in me. You gave hope a place to burn again. Annabel... it was you."

My heart sang, my bond humming so loudly it threatened to drown out even the darkness that surrounded us. *Fate.* Fate had forced us together, but in Saga's eyes and in his words, I finally saw a glimmer of what could be. If we let it.

"You didn't fail your father," I told him, forcing my mind back to the present, "or your brothers. And you didn't fail me. Nothing of what you've seen or heard here has happened. All of it is a lie meant to make you weak. Something is preying on you, hoping that by the time it's done with you you'll be too broken to fight it. It knows it doesn't have a fair shot otherwise.

"Ragnarök has come. It's true. But you found me, didn't you? And in a way... you saved me." I jutted my chin at Bjarni's and Grim's remains. "And you'll save them, just like you have before. But what's more... you haven't just saved us. You're *going* to save my parents. You're going to keep everyone safe. And I'll be at your side every step of the way."

Saga blinked at me then, head cocked. When we'd retrieved Magni, I'd promised I'd be their mate, so long as I had the opportunity to save my family from the end of the world as well. But what I was offering him now was different, and he must have realized that, because confusion soon replaced the grief writ on his face.

"You... want to do this *with* me?" he asked, taking my other hand in his. "Why?"

"Because I've seen your heart now," I said, looking around at the smoldering ashes of his childhood home. "I've seen the things you fear the most. And I know that one of them is losing me, and the other is losing the rest of those you love. We're not really that different when it comes to family. I didn't see it before now, but we're both selfless. Faithful to a fault—until we bleed. I can feel your heart bleeding right now, in fact, and..."

Cautiously, I laid my hand upon his chest.

"And it's bleeding inside the chest of a man I could love."

Saga cinched my wrist in his grasp suddenly,

pulling me tighter to his body as he leaned down to claim my mouth so rough, yet so sweetly. His warm, callused fingers bracketed the curve of my jaw, sweeping me up into him as if he could devour me, hold me inside him to protect me from the rest of this nightmare we'd embarked upon together.

And we *had* walked in here together. I'd chosen to come after him. I'd needed to. For the first time, he and I were on the same side.

And it felt good. Better than I'd thought it possibly could. As did his arms around me, guarding me, clutching at me, shielding me from the howling wind that had picked up around us and swept the world clean of anything good or living.

Thunder snarled overhead, and I opened my eyes to take in the barren wasteland stretching out around us on all sides. The craggy ground shifted far too easily beneath my feet. I had to hold onto Saga to keep from falling into it and becoming lost between the cracks tearing it asunder.

"How much worse is this going to get?" I asked him. The uncertainty on his face surprised me.

"I'm not sure," he said, holding me to him as he turned his face up to the blackened sky. "I have no idea what this is."

It felt different here. Where before there'd been an almost claustrophobic sense of moving *through* something—crawling through the belly of some ancient and terrible beast—now there was far too much space. If I let go of Saga, I was sure I'd fall up into the sky. Gravity was alien here; uprooted trees drifted by at a lazy pace, some split and smoldering from where lightning had bit them in two.

The mist was still here, rolling and curling around our feet, smelling now of noxious smoke. As it flowed toward the edge of the cliff we were teetering upon, it flowed up, congealing into a parody of a humanoid figure—something altogether *wrong*.

"You're too late," it said, a cacophony of whispers and shrieks trailing behind the thunder. "Ragnarök will tear the universe apart. Your family will die. Your omega will die. You have attempted to meddle in what was meant to be... and you have failed."

"Remember," I told him, "none of this has come to pass. You don't have to set yourself up for disaster by—"

My inspirational speech rose into a cry as a part of the land jutted upward in a stiff and savage arc, slamming right into Saga's face. He just barely managed to push me out of the way before he was sent reeling to the other end of the cliff, nearly toppling over the edge and into the swirling oblivion below.

"Shit!" I yelped, scrambling for him. "What is this?"

"Not a trial," he growled, lifting his face. Twin ruby waterfalls cascaded from his nose, staining his mouth and teeth. "This is not... like the rest. It doesn't feel the same."

As we rose to our feet, he smeared his shimmering blood across his skin like war paint, eyes ablaze. "This thing… whatever it is… I think it's actually trying to kill me."

I hoped my smile was encouraging. "It doesn't know you very well."

Saga smirked, but any begrudging mirth was cut short when the creature that had formed out of the mist reared back, expelling a sonic breath that swept us both off the edge of the world.

The suddenness of it, the utter shock, robbed me of my ability to scream. Soon enough, it was the wind shear doing the same, pulling the breath from my lungs as I hurtled helplessly toward the ground.

It was so far down. I'd never fallen from anything so high before. The tallest thing I'd ever climbed onto was the tree in my old backyard, a tree I'd likely never see again for one reason or another, and—

"Annabel!"

Below—was it below? It was hard to tell with everything spinning end over end—a floating patch of land had broken Saga's fall. I wasn't on the same trajectory and couldn't right myself to align with it, but as I plunged past he reached out and grabbed me, rolling to carry our bodies to the center so the island wouldn't tip.

I wheezed, ribs smarting. Starbursts of pain exploded in front of my eyes. "What the hell is that thing?"

"I don't know," Saga admitted, holding himself over me to shield me from a rain of debris. "But whatever it is, we've got to get away from it. Now."

I looked up at him, still gulping air like it was in short supply. "You're not going to kill it?"

Saga barked a rough laugh. "Annabel, did you *see* it? That thing, whatever it is... it's not a creature in a well. That's on par with the gods."

High above, the beast had clawed its way to the edge of the cliff, gazing at us with only the vaguest suggestion of eyes. From its back, two magnificent, immense wings unfurled, their edges dancing in the wind like torn scraps of paper.

"It's going to come for us again," Saga said, looking back down at me. "We need to be elsewhere when it does."

When he didn't offer up a plan, I pushed up on my elbows. "Well, what do you want me to do about it?"

He wiped his nose again. It was still gushing. "You have to find your magic, or we'll die."

Now it was my turn to laugh. "And how the hell am I supposed to do that?"

"You're not," he said, using his bloodied hand to grasp mine. "*We* are going to do it. Together. Like you said."

Saga's blood trickled into the lines in my palm, sticking there at first, then gradually seeping into my pores. I drew in a startled breath and began to pull away from him, but he held me fast, looking into my eyes.

"Together," he said again. "Trust me, Annabel. Please. And trust yourself too."

This was all so new to me. Could I really do that?

Did I have it in me to not only put my faith in Saga...
but in myself?

There wasn't time to overthink it. If I was even going
to make the attempt, it would have to be now. The creature was gaining lift, taking to the skies in a slow circle,
preparing to swoop.

"Together," I murmured, closing my eyes and fitting
my fingers between his.

I thought it would be slow. I thought I would have
time to find my footing—to adjust to what would
happen next.

But I didn't. Instead, every pathway that had been
closed within me—pathways I hadn't even known
existed—opened all at once.

And out flooded a surge of power so immense my
whole body lit up with it.

Something inside me simply burst, a ripple that
coursed from my core. All along the edge of the tiny
island Saga and I were buoyed on, a familiar set of
glyphs fizzled to life, forming a circle of light that
earned us a terrible roar from the creature so hellbent
on our annihilation.

"You can do this!" Saga yelled over the din of wind
and shrieking. "You can get us home!"

Saga was right. I could. I was certain of it.

Hand in his, commanding the magic that would
spirit us away to safety, I was more certain than I'd been
of anything in my whole life.

24

ANNABEL

The portal swirled around us in a multihued kaleidoscope, until a sharp flash of light tore the dream world away, revealing the grassy patch of land where we'd left Grim, Bjarni, and Magni. I landed on top of Saga, the impact with his hard chest forcing a grunt from my throat.

"You okay?" Saga asked, strong arms closing protectively around my body. Despite the roughness of his voice, there was no mistaking the tender note in it.

"Yeah, I'm...." I stared down at him, the frantic beating of my heart slowly quieting as I took in the unaccustomed softness in his flint-gray eyes. His brothers' voices quieted to a murmur as I finally saw him. My mate. Like I'd seen him in the dream-trial. His deepest fears laid bare, his heart finally open and vulnerable for me. He hadn't claimed me to subjugate me, hadn't forced my surrender because he didn't care about my wants and needs. He'd done it because he was scared of losing his brothers, and he'd tried to dominate me because it was the only way he thought he could keep me from being taken from him.

In his heart, my Saga was scared of nothing more than the thought of failing those he loved and losing them as a consequence.

And one thing I was sure of after this trial? It was that Saga loved me.

It didn't make sense, we hadn't known each other for long—and the instincts that ruled us both had forced a sense of need and belonging so strong it'd been impossible to see how there could ever be anything else. But there was.

Maybe it was the prophecy, maybe Fate had granted us the gift of love in exchange for the complicated weave we found ourselves tangled in. It didn't matter.

"I'm so sorry," Saga whispered, bringing my thoughts back to the present. "I should never have tried to deny your strength. I've seen you now, Annabel. I've seen your power, and I will never make that mistake again." He brought his hand to my face, cupping my cheek gently. "My mate."

The swell of emotion in our bond made me fight back the sting of tears. I breathed deeply and I rested my forehead against his, allowing the devotion in our connection to swallow me whole. I'd seen him now— and he saw me. Saw the strength in me I'd always hoped was there.

"My alpha," I whispered, and he responded by tightening his grip on me.

"If you two can keep your hands off each other for a second, do you mind explaining what the fuck happened in there?" Bjarni's voice cut through. "Is it safe? Because unless you've finally decided to ditch Thor's bastard, we're gonna need to get him through that portal soon."

Magni.

We shared one last, lingering look, silently promising to discuss what'd happened between us further when next we could. Then I climbed off Saga's chest and went to my other mate, who sat on the ground leaning against a rock. Pain drew his face into a frown, and when he caught my eye there was uncertainty in it. He'd felt the emotion in my bond to Saga.

"We completed the trial," Saga said, while I knelt by Magni's side, testing his forehead with the back of my hand. He was burning hot, but closed his eyes with a soft hum of pleasure at my touch.

"But there was... a complication. Something... or someone is trying to block our entry to Asgard. I don't know if the portal is safe. I don't know how much of that trial was a set-up to kill off whoever went through," Saga continued.

"Someone's trying to keep us from Asgard?" Magni asked, forcing his eyes open again to look at Saga, as Grim walked over to the portal to inspect it.

"You did say your bracelet isn't working," Saga said,

rubbing his chin with one hand. "This... entity. He told us he wouldn't let us get in the way. That we couldn't stop Ragnarök."

"We need to discuss this later," I said, because another pained grimace passed over Magni's face. "Grim, the portal. Is it safe?"

"The runes are gone," the dark-haired Lokisson said. "It seems like any other portal now."

"We'll have to risk it," Saga said, a concerned frown pulling down his eyebrows as he looked at Magni. "We need to get Annabel to safety—and our ticket to free passage is about to keel over."

"He's right," I said. "Let's go."

The portal, though no longer adorned with runes, still filled me with trepidation. But Magni needed help, and he needed it stat.

My bond to him hummed out of tune, such a stark contrast to the lightness I felt where I was connected with Saga, filling me with instinctive urgency.

"Come," I said as I went to stand, supporting his big body with my own. I gritted my teeth as he rested heavily on me—the so-called trial Saga and I had endured had drained me more than I'd realized—and Magni was already so much bigger than me. "We need to get you to this Eir-person."

No matter what, I will not fail him. Because failing him... meant the end of everything. I felt it in my core, with a certainty that clutched my lungs and squeezed until it was hard to breathe.

Magni had done many things to me that I had no say in. But he'd also saved me. And I would never forget the look on his face as he lay dying in the wilderness, having given the last of his strength to find me. Because when he claimed me, as haughty and sly as he'd been—he'd bound himself as tightly as he had me.

For better or worse, he was a part of me now. And if I didn't get him to Asgard, he would die. And everything would be lost.

The Norn had spoken the truth about me and the half-gods destined to claim me. It wasn't merely a reluctant omega's yearning to be something more than a broodmare—or a desperate hope that my world could be saved. I'd felt it. When the magic blasted through me, I'd felt the raw strength inside of me well up. It was there—the power to save humans and gods alike. But right now, I didn't have the time to dwell on it, because if my weakened mate died... I would, too.

"Hope Eir is as good a healer as the rumors say," Saga muttered as he slipped around Magni's other side, wrapping the red-head's arm over his shoulders so he could support his weight, shifting the wounded alpha from my frame to his own. "You look like you're halfway to Hel already."

"You should look in a mirror Jotunn," Magni bit out, but there was no venom in his voice. He sagged against the blond alpha, but kept his free arm around my shoulders. He'd never say it out loud, but I knew he needed my closeness as much as he needed Saga's support just then. I pressed in against him, willing him to hold on just a little longer.

Saga caught my eye above Magni's bent head, and in his eyes I saw the same fear churning in my own gut. He'd die too, if Magni went. As much as they may hate each other, the three of us were tied together now. Bound in life as well as death by the marks marring my neck.

I pitied him—and, I was so grateful I had to bite back tears as we dragged Magni to the golden portal. I wasn't alone with my fear—and I wasn't the only one desperate to save my redheaded mate.

I knew Grim and Bjarni were only going along with this because they needed Magni to pass through the gates of Valhalla and find out what they needed to know about me—the mortal they still believed would save their lineage.

Not Saga. Once upon a time, yes, that was all he'd wanted, too. But not anymore. He was right here with me, and I clung to his presence.

The moment we all passed the looming portal, blinding light filled my vision. Instantly, the dreary dampness that had clung to us in Jotunheim evaporated like mist on a warm summer's day, and bright, gentle sunlight caressed my face.

I looked up, surprised at the sudden shift, and blinked several times.

Below me lay the greenest of valleys I'd ever seen, lush forest and swaying meadows intercepted by bands of silvery rivers. In the distance rose a mountain range up so high it seemed to touch the sky. And on its side sprawled a beautiful, golden city. From its edge, a rainbow disappeared in the distance.

"Valhalla," Grim murmured.

"Home," Magni groaned. "You need… to take me home. To Thrudheim."

"His father's house," Saga explained when I raised an eyebrow in question. "Where does Eir live? We need to take you to her. Now." The urgency in his voice was not lost on me—and not on Magni either, apparently. My redheaded mate lifted his head and gave Saga a weak but still undeniably shit-eating grin. "Careful now, or your brothers might think you care about me."

"Oh, I care," Saga gritted. "I care that if you die and we're discovered inside the walls of Asgard, we're gonna end up in a fucking cave with snake venom in our eyes, or whatever the shit your precious family comes up with this time around."

"Deny all you want," Magni said, but it ended on a groan, and he sagged heavily between us as his knees gave out and his consciousness along with them.

"Fuck, we're never getting him all the way to Valhalla on foot," Bjarni muttered as he gently shoved me out of the way and looped Magni's limp arm around his shoulders so Saga didn't carry his full weight alone. "What's plan B?"

"There is no plan B," Saga gritted. "We're in enemy territory, and our guide just passed out."

"Enemy territory?" A melodic female voice asked from behind us. "Are you not godsons, young ones? What is Asgard, if not home?"

I swirled around, but where the portal from Jotunheim should have been was a tall, blonde woman so beautiful I had to do a double take. She was perched in a silvery wagon, which seemed to be pulled by two huge gray cats the size of Shetland ponies. Behind her was nothing but flowering trees and rolling hills.

"Freya," Grim said, and if he felt even an ounce of the sheer shock and awe currently making me gape like a fish, he didn't show it. His mismatched eyes didn't waver from her blue. "If you know we are godsons, you also know whose blood runs in our veins—and why Asgard is no home of ours."

Freya pursed her lips in a small smile, but didn't reply. Then her sapphire gaze turned to Magni. "He doesn't have much time. Put him in my chariot."

Without argument, Bjarni and Saga carried the passed-out alpha to the cat-drawn carriage, seemingly not in the least freaked out by the size or existence of the felines.

Freya motioned to me. "Come, child. You and your other mate need to ride with me. Your two other suitors will need to fly." She threw what looked like two feathery costumes on the ground and pointed to a building in the distance. "Meet us at Folkvangr. Do not let anyone see you."

"Fly?" I mouthed, as Saga grabbed me by the arm

and more or less dragged me into the carriage beside Magni's slumped body. By the wagon's side, Bjarni was inspecting one of the feathery costumes with pure disdain painted across his bearded face, but Grim was already pulling his on, one foot at a time. The second he had his second arm through the sleeve, the feathers ruffled as the fabric seemed to melt into him and suddenly a black raven sat on the ground in his place.

"Home!" Freya's clear voice rang, and the cats set off so instantly, I was jerked backward and into Saga from the sudden motion. He held me tight against his body, shielding me from the wind as the lush landscape tore past us.

I looked up at the golden-haired woman—Freya, as Grim had called her. My grasp of Norse mythology, though scant, was strong enough to recognize that name.

"Freya? You're the goddess of Love, right? Ma'am." I tagged the last bit on when I realized that there was probably some polite way one really ought to address a goddess.

"I am," she said, offering me a small smile. "There is no need for formalities, child. You are the mate of Loki's and Thor's sons. That practically makes us family."

"Oh, uh, okay." I wasn't entirely strong in the Norse gods' family tree, but when I glanced up at Saga for confirmation, he simply shook his head.

"Can you heal him?" I asked, resting a hand on Magni's chest. Our bond was quiet, but not silent. He was still holding on. "There was a... a thing, in Mimir's Well. It bit his arm and... I think, drained his magic."

Freya looked over her shoulder again, but at Saga this time. "Mimir is missing?"

"Well, if he isn't in Valhalla. Whatever that thing was, it sure as fuck wasn't Mimir," Saga said with a shudder. I elbowed him in the ribs for using crass language around a goddess, but all it got me was his arms clamped tight around mine, restraining me.

"That is troubling news," Freya murmured. "Things are worse than I hoped."

"Worse than Ragnarök?" Saga said, voice sardonic.

"Much," she said, a frown drawing down her brow. It somehow made her beautiful profile even more jaw-dropping.

"Does it... does it have something to do with how we had trouble entering Asga—?" my question was cut short when Saga clamped his hand over my mouth, muffling my voice.

Freya whipped her head around, blue eyes piercing me. "Something blocked you from entering Asgard? Or someone?"

I bit down on Saga's palm, and he growled and pulled back his hand. "She's one of them, Annabel. We can't trust her."

"And so is Magni—who's dying. If we can't trust her, you wouldn't have gotten into this wagon, would you?" I said.

"That's different. We don't have a choice when it

comes to Magni's survival," Saga said, dark eyes resting on the goddess. "He's Thor's son—she won't let him die."

"We don't have a choice with the other thing, either," I protested. "We have to find Mimir."

"You went to see the Norns," Freya said.

"Yes, Verdandi. How did you—?" I asked.

"Only they would have told you to seek Mimir's council. And if he's missing... perhaps that means someone doesn't want you to hear his advice."

Saga narrowed his eyes at the goddess. "You know of the prophecy."

"I do."

"Then why would anyone try to stop us?" he asked, pulling me harder to his chest. I might have found it annoying, another display of his alpha dominance, but right then, I was grateful for his strength. I didn't feel particularly like some figure of prophecy—just a scared human in a strange land. I was drained from the trial and worry gnawed in my gut every time I looked at Magni's pale face. My mate. He and I hadn't found each other, like Saga and I had during his trial. We hadn't developed that softness I now felt flutter in my chest where Saga's bond hooked. But he was mine every bit as much as Saga was, and I his—and I'd never forget the way he'd embraced me when we returned for him. Right then, I didn't care for gods or Jotunns, or even Ragnarök. All I cared about was that Magni survived.

Freya seemed to read my thoughts. "We can discuss

that when your brother is safe. Right now, he needs you both," she said.

"He's no brother of mine," Saga muttered, but there was little conviction in his voice. He felt it too, even if he didn't want to admit it. The tie that bound us all together.

The goddess laughed, a pearling sound that filled me with warmth despite my worry. "He is as much your blood as the men you'll risk so much to save, son of Loki. Even now, you feel the bond to him. Don't deny it. Your mate knows the truth."

Saga shot her a glare, but to my surprise he didn't argue again. He merely held me tight and let his gaze flicker back to Magni, and I felt the swell of worry in our bond, even if he was too stubborn to acknowledge out loud what we both knew to be true.

"How much longer?" I asked, letting my hand smooth over Magni's slowly rising and falling chest.

"Not much, little omega," Freya said, holding a hand outstretched in front of her. "Folkvangr is near."

I followed the direction on her arm and bit down on a gasp. What I'd thought was a clump of trees on the horizon was finally close enough that I could see the true nature of the construct.

Slender ash trees, stretching to the sky like columns on a temple, lined a wide path toward what seemed to be a fountain. And behind that, a house wrought from arched timber frames and crowned with silver tiles in the shape of a million leaves rose several stories high.

Beautiful meadows blooming with wildflowers sprawled on either side.

Whoever the architect of Freya's house was, they'd somehow managed to capture her beauty and transform it into real estate.

But as the feline-drawn carriage made its way to the goddess' house, I was struck by how quiet it was. Peaceful, yes, but also... lonely. Not a soul save birds and insects enjoyed the meadows, and no servants came to greet her when we pulled up by the fountain next to stairs leading up to the arched entry to Folkvangr itself.

"Bring him to the great room," Freya said, before she gracefully leapt out of the carriage and climbed the stairs, leaving us to bring Magni in on our own.

Saga heaved a deep sigh, squared his jaw and hauled the passed-out redhead over his shoulder, swearing under his breath when Magni's full weight bore down on him.

"Can I help?" I asked nervously as I tried to help him off the carriage. Saga ignored my outstretched hand, only giving me an arched eyebrow as he climbed off the wagon on his own. "Unless you've suddenly got enough of a grasp of your magic to levitate this fat fuck, then no, sweetling, I've got it."

Despite his complaints, he didn't seem too cumbered down as we made our way up the stairs after Freya. I guessed being a demi-god had its advantages in the strength-department, because I knew from experience that Magni weighed a good bit more than what even your average alpha could carry. He was as massive as the Lokisson brothers, only Bjarni perhaps outweighing them all. If I were to guess, I'd estimate that Magni was somewhere north of four-hundred-pound pure muscle.

The arched entry of Folkvangr led directly into a large open hall with domed ceilings high above. It might have reminded me of a cathedral, because every window lining the walls were open, allowing sunlight and the scent of wildflowers to waft in on a gentle breeze. However, the artwork decorating the ceilings was distinctly more of the erotic nature than you were likely to find in most churches.

Up some steps at the far end of the hall was what I guessed was a throne made of intricately woven silvery branches, and in the center a wide altar rose up. Or, at least I thought it was an altar, until I got close enough to notice the furs and pillows.

"Place him on the bed," Freya said, putting a hand down on the apparently-not-an-altar.

Saga obeyed, and I fluttered after him nervously, as if pulled by a string attached to both men.

"Bare him," the goddess said.

"And that's where I'm tapping out," Saga said, stepping back from the bed. "You're up, sweetling."

"You mean, strip him?" I asked, frowning at the goddess. "He needs medical help—"

"And he will get it," Freya said patiently. "We need to

see the extent of the damages. Free him of his clothes, little one."

Who was I to argue with a goddess? Gingerly, I went about loosening leather cords and pulling on the unfamiliar style clothes. But undressing a passed-out giant was no easy task, not when his leg alone basically weighed the same as me.

After watching me struggle for a while, Saga sighed and stepped in, helping me lift Magni's heavy limbs and torso so I could get rid of the leather and fur covering his body.

I shot Saga a grateful look, but his eyes were glued to Magni's damaged arm, a deep frown marring his face. When I turned to look, I sucked in air between my teeth, my hands finding the dark, writhing markings of their own accord.

They'd spread up along his shoulder and down his side, and I noted with worry that they were starting to span up his wide chest as well.

"What happens if they reach his heart?" I whispered, searching for the goddess.

She stood on his other side, a solemn expression on her beautiful face as she took in the extent of the infection.

"If they reach his heart, he will die," she said.

"What happens when gods die?" I asked, blinking away the stinging in my eyes.

"He would have gone to Valhalla," Saga said from

behind me. "He got his wounds in battle. But with Ragnarök...."

"There will be no Valhalla for Thor's son," Freya said. "The end is here, and the gates are closed for lost souls. There is only one place for the dead to go—and no one returns from Hel. But if we act swiftly, you can save him still, little human."

"Tell me how," I whispered.

"Darkness is devouring his flesh. He needs your light to combat it. Use your connection—use your body to heal his."

"How? How do I do that?" I asked. "The magic, I don't know how to control it."

"Your other mate will guide you," Freya said, and I could have sworn there was a smile in her voice, but I was too focused on Magni to look. "You are an omega, child. There is only one way you can heal your wounded warrior."

Behind me, Saga muttered a low curse, but I still wasn't getting it.

"How—?"

"She means you have to fuck him," Saga said, irritation in his voice.

"What?" I croaked, finally wresting my eyes from Magni to shoot the goddess a startled look. "I can't— he's passed out!"

Freya only looked mildly amused at my confusion and Saga's irritation. "Your connection to both your alphas is anchored in the pleasures of the flesh, omega.

Take him inside of you and let your other mate guide your magic. Thor's son needs you both. Will you save him?"

I drew in a deep breath. In the end it didn't matter if the way to save Magni was to awkwardly sex his passed-out form while Saga and the most beautiful woman—goddess—in the world watched. If I didn't, he'd be lost forever. And so would both Saga and I.

"Yes," I said, slowly sliding my hands up along his chest. "We'll save him."

"Magni. Magni. I need you to wake up now." I'd recognize that voice anywhere, even if the disembodied sound of it seemed to float toward me from blank nothingness. I sighed softly, content in the knowledge that my mate was near.

"Magni."

Tendrils of sensations crawled up along my torso, and my conscience landed inside my body with a near-audible thud.

I groaned, suddenly aware of the ache in my arm and the stiffness in my muscles. And the weakness threading through every molecule in my body.

"There you are," Annabel whispered from somewhere above me, her hand gliding from my chest to my abs, and I realized it was her touch that'd brought me back to my body.

"Are we safe?" I rasped, the effort of speaking nearly tearing my consciousness free again.

"Yes. We're at Freya's house," she said, her hands drawing smooth circles along my body, raising heat in their path. "But you're very sick, Magni. And I... I need to heal you."

'You're not... a healer," I protested.

"She is to you, godson," a familiar voice spoke from further away. Freya. "She's the only one who can bring back what the well dweller stole. She, and your brother."

"Modi?" I rasped, fighting and failing to crack open my eyes.

"No," Annabel said, but instead of elaborating, she ran her palms down to my navel, and a hot flare of need made me groan softly. It seemed even on my deathbed I wanted this omega more than I wanted air to breathe.

Gentle fingers undid my pants, and my cock swelled in anticipation before she'd even touched it.

Of course the goddess of Love would think to heal me with sex magic. Not that I was going to complain, once Annabel's fingers stroked hesitantly up along my dick. It felt like fire and bliss, and I moaned softly into the darkness.

But she was uncertain, my mate. I felt her hesitance and embarrassment in our bond, and knew she was unsure how to proceed.

It was only natural—she was an omega and I her alpha. She was the chalice and I the pitcher. She was born to receive me, not to assert her dominance over my prone body. I yearned to take control, to show her how to enjoy my body as she gasped and writhed underneath me, but my muscles refused to obey my command and I was trapped in my darkness.

"Wrap your hands around him," a low voice grated from somewhere behind Annabel.

Saga. Irritation bubbled in my veins, but my focus returned to my cock when Annabel put both hands around the base of my dick.

"That's it. Move them up and down. Squeeze him like your pussy will," my enemy continued, and I groaned when she obeyed him, his words and the tight pleasure bringing back memories of forcing her cunt open.

"He's so big," Annabel whispered, quiet horror in her voice. "How am I going to—?"

"Nothing you haven't taken before, sweetling. You just focus on bringing him back—and I'll take care of you." His heated words were followed by a small gasp from her and a spark of pleasure rushing through our bond. Her breath came in stutters now, but she kept wanking my dick, squeezing tighter every now and then.

He was rubbing her clit. I knew without looking, could feel it in the sharp pleasure in our bond and hear it in her increasingly labored breathing. He was getting her ready for me.

A confusing mix of arousal, jealousy, and gratitude

rose in my body with the tightness in my loins for every time Annabel brushed her palm over my throbbing cock head. It was my job to prepare my mate, but I couldn't, not from the prison of this darkness. But the man I'd once considered my archenemy could. And he did.

"Put your lips on him," Saga growled, and I had a moment's worth of intense gratitude before wet heat hesitantly closed around my crown.

She tried her best to fit me in her mouth, but she couldn't manage more than the tip.

"Lick him," Saga instructed. "And don't stop until you come."

She breathed in shallowly, her breath hitching in her throat, and I heard the tell-tale slick sounds of Saga's tongue delving into our omega's snatch.

Annabel shuddered, bracing herself against my body for a moment and then obeyed. Her soft little tongue flicked around my crown, lapping up along the head and then down the shaft, teasing and stoking the fires.

The heat in my blood flooded my body, and for the first time since that thing in the well bit me, I felt the spreading infection's slow crawl pause to a halt.

"H-how are you doing that?" I croaked.

"Shh, Thorsson," Freya murmured. "Focus on the pleasure. Trust your mates."

Mates? I wanted to spit out a contest to the goddess' plural usage of that word, but just then Annabel sucked on my frenulum, and my thoughts shattered in a starburst of delight.

I groaned, my hips straining to heed the primal call to thrust, but the darkness bound me too tightly, and all I could do was lay and endure my omega's gentle affections and her own huffs and pants increasing in intensity as Saga drove her closer and closer to the edge. A halting whine and the sting of her teeth, and she was coming, the rich scent of her orgasm filling the air.

"Mount him." Saga's rough order raised my hackles even as my cock spasmed in agreement. I was alpha—I was built to mount my female, not the other way around, but there was nothing I could do as Annabel shifted on the bed, hesitantly placing her hands against my chest for balance.

"You can take him, sweetling. You're dripping wet," Saga growled, the roughness of his voice more than suggesting how hard he was holding back to not shove her face down into my chest and mount her himself. "It'll feel so good when you stretch around his thick cock. C'mon, my love... that's it."

She straddled my thighs and, breathing in deeply, slowly lowered herself. The spike of need burning through my entire body when her lower lips kissed my cock had me gasping. The wet heat of her pussy slowly, reluctantly closed over my cockhead, every millimeter making me ache to thrust up and seat myself completely inside of her. Fevered memories of our first mating thundering in my temples, when my head popped into her tight channel. "I—it hurts," Annabel gasped, and for a second her heat lifted upward as if she were trying to escape our coupling. "He's so thick—"

Saga growled, and her retreat was abruptly halted. "Yes. He is. And you're going to take him. All the way to the root. Your pretty little cunt needs the reminder of who owns her. Who owns you."

Odin's beard. Annabel's reluctant little whimper in response was full of need, and slowly her pussy descended down my shaft. She was so wet, rivulets of slick ran down my length, but her cunt spasmed hard for every inch it was forced to swallow, making it clear she was struggling. It was slow, exquisite torture, and amidst the pleasure of feeling my mate so intimately again, gratitude to the alpha helping her take me twined. He might have been a prick, but there was no denying he knew exactly how to get our omega turned on. She'd mouthed off a lot about having no choice and being forced to mate with us, but she couldn't deny her omega nature. She got off on being dominated.

"That's what happens when you don't take a dick often enough. Your pussy forgets how to open wide. But don't worry, my sweetling—we're gonna remind you," Saga said, and suddenly her wet heat barreled all the way down my length, her ass slapping hard against my thighs as I bottomed out inside her desperately spasming sheath.

Annabel howled, but it was muted in the rush of blood drumming in my ears as white light exploded through my darkness, shattering it until it only plumed at the edges of my vision.

My eyelids fluttered open, and I saw her. My Annabel. Glowing with golden light, head tossed back and back arched, her beautiful face a study in pain and pleasure. Her pussy throbbed around my cock, and the golden aura around her pulsed to the same rhythm.

I'd seen a lot of magic in my life, but never anything like this. Like her magic.

Saga stood behind her, his hands on her hips, keeping her seated on me as he nibbled at the side of her neck, whispering hoarse words in her ear just too low for me to hear. Whatever he said, it made her moan softly, and her slick muscles gripped me tight and deliberately for a moment, despite the flicker of pain passing over her features at the move. The golden light shone brighter in response.

Saga slid one hand from her hips to her breast, the other one delving between her wide-stretched lips to her swollen clit. The second he touched her there, she came undone.

I groaned with my mate as she rocked her hips mindlessly while her tunnel shuddered and pulsed all along my cock, and I felt her orgasm radiate through me, scorching the infection. The black, writhing masses spasmed under my skin in response, dragging a pained growl from my lips despite the ecstasy of feeling my omega come on my dick.

"He needs more," Freya said from somewhere off to the side. "The infection is strong—dig deeper, child."

"She means; fuck him harder," Saga purred, pinching her clit between two fingers. "Ride him, sweetling. Show him your power."

Annabel groaned, biting her lip and for the first time, locked her eyes with me. Slowly, whether to tease me or to ease her pussy into it, she rose halfway up my dick, only to sink back down, sheathing me completely with a shared moan.

I'd never thought I'd enjoy submitting to a female— it went against every fiber of my being, and even now, the deepest of my instincts fought to roll her over and put her on her back underneath me where she belonged. But as Annabel rode my cock, leaning forward to support her hands on my torso, and the pained delight played across her beautiful face, bathed in that golden light... I never wanted her to stop. Soon, her movements became freer, the pain on her face waning for pure bliss and intense concentration as her cunt loosened for me, remembering how to swallow alpha dick like it was born to do. Behind her I was aware of Saga's presence, stroking her body to heighten her pleasure, directing her magic to me with his own, dark touch. The dark marks writhing under my skin singed in response to the onslaught, making me hiss in pain even as I felt my climax steadily approaching, fighting against my omega's light.

"He needs more!" Freya's voice chimed, seeming

oddly distant as the light enveloped the three of us like a golden dome, fading the outside world.

"She hasn't got any more to give!" Saga snarled. "She's already drawing on her life force!"

"No!" I rasped, cold horror seizing my lungs when his words echoed through my pleasure. I stared at my mate, at her still-blooming magic, and found the first frays at the edges. Signs of exhaustion I'd been too rapt up in pleasure to notice. "Stop—Annabel—"

She didn't answer me, but the stubborn flare in her eyes was unmistakable. I growled—why was this woman so fucking stubborn—and turned my attention to Saga, even as my omega kept riding my dick. "Don't let her— It's not worth it. Not her life."

"It's not like we have a fucking choice, is it?" Saga said. "Shit!"

"Help her, young Lokisson," Freya said. "Combine your strength with hers."

Saga frowned. "What do you—?" His brow smoothed, eyebrows reaching his hairline. "Fucking Hel, you can't be fucking serious! She can't!"

"She's an omega," Freya purred. "Your omega. She'll survive."

Saga swore again, gave me a long, hard stare I didn't have the brain power to process, and then put a hand on Annabel's back, pushing her forward.

She obeyed, flattening her breasts against my chest, finally stilling her hips' waves for a moment. It was only then I saw the strain in the corners of her eyes, the sweat on her brow... and the ashen color of her skin that'd previously been hidden by the glow of her magic.

"Annabel," I whispered. "Please. Stop."

"I can't," she said, her voice hoarse and weak. "I can't lose you."

Her words resonated sweetly in my heart and hummed through my veins when she kissed my chest. I knew what she meant—I knew our connection would literally and very physically kill her, should I meet my end, and it tore me apart that I'd doomed her to this fate. And still, those words made my soul sing.

"You're not going to," Saga grunted behind her. His words were followed by a brush of fingers against the root of my cock still buried inside of her, and if I'd had the strength I'd have jerked hard. When a thick finger slid up alongside the length of my dick, stretching Annabel tightly around me, I hissed as she let out a startled grunt.

"What are you—?" she asked, trying to twist her neck around to look at Saga.

"I'm helping you," he said through gritted teeth, forcing her head back around with his free hand. "Focus, my love. No matter what, you can't lose focus."

She obeyed him, though I could see the hesitation in her eyes as she locked her gaze with me. I was right there with her, because Saga started slowly pumping his finger along my cock, inadvertently rubbing it as he stretched our mate.

"The fuck are you doing?" I growled.

"Saving your stupid ass," he snarled back. "You're going to owe me fucking big." Another finger slid in along the first, making Annabel keen and arch her back, the pressure along my length making it hard to focus.

When he pulled his fingers from her sheath with a wet noise, we were both panting hard.

Saga reached for Annabel's shoulders, rising up behind her, teeth gritted with determination, and just then it finally dawned on me what he was going to do.

"Fucking Hell!" I growled, just as the head of my arch-enemy's cock pressed against the base of mine, prodding at Annabel's already stuffed snatch—and then, without hesitation, forced its way in along mine.

Annabel's scream was deafening, nothing but sheer torment and desperation as she fought to get off both our dicks squashed together inside of her. But Saga didn't give her an inch. He kept his hands clamped to her shoulders, forcing her to accept the excruciating invasion.

"You let another claim your cunt before me—this is your price," he snarled into her ear. "Take us—take both of us. Use my magic as I use your cunt!" The savage words were followed by a hard thrust that rubbed against my cock, sending an electricity of bliss along my spine unlike anything I'd felt before. The presence of her other alpha inside of her stirred my aggression and will to claim, but she was so tightly stretched around the both of us that every single nerve in my dick sang with ecstasy.

The golden light flared as Annabel gritted her teeth around another howl of agony and directed her full attention to me. There was so much rage in her eyes, so much fury at being forced to submit like the omega she still hated she was, but also strength like nothing I'd seen before. Everything she was, every raw ounce of power and every painful fear was laid bare between us as she fought against the pain and channeled the magic.

The dark marks screamed in agony as she singed every single one of them in a burst of power that echoed off Folkvangr's domed ceilings, and like a burst dam, I felt my own magic flood my body in a rush of agonized bliss.

I didn't think, couldn't, as my arms closed around her trembling body and I pounded my cock hard and deep up into her spasming cunt, following Saga's ruthless rhythm. My orgasm was on me before I could gasp her name, and I drove in mindlessly, the urge to knot insurmountable.

"Shit! Don't! You'll tear her!" Saga snarled, his own thrust stuttering, but even if I'd been halfway coherent there was nothing I could have done.

He swore loudly, and before I could force my rapidly swelling knot in alongside his throbbing cock, a strong hand clamped tightly around the bulge, squeezing it like a vice.

I came so hard I nearly blacked out. Groaning, teeth buried deep in Annabel's shoulder, I coated her womb with my seed, faintly aware that Saga's semen mixed with my own. I didn't care. Couldn't, because all I sensed was the shocks of spine-shattering pleasure as my knot was milked and my cock massaged by the woman who was fated to be mine from the beginning of time.

I don't know how long I rode the wave of release, but at some point Annabel passed out between us, her own unending climaxes too painful to sustain. A touch of worry finally eased my orgasm into the final shudders, but when I prodded our bond, a peaceful hum resonated back.

"She'll be fine," Freya said, her voice much clearer now, and the note of smugness in it was unmistakable. "She is mortal, after all. Riding two divine studs takes its toll."

It wasn't until then that I remembered Saga. Evidently, he also remembered me. The grip around my knot released instantaneously.

"Did you...?" I was still too groggy to find the right words, but as I stared at the man I shared a mate with, the sensation of his fingers were still brandished in my spine.

"You owe me so fucking big," Saga rasped. A pleasurable shudder made me grit my teeth as he pulled out, bathing my already soaked balls in a rush of semen.

"We're never speaking of this again," I said darkly, turning my attention to my passed-out mate. She looked peaceful in her sleep, and I pressed a kiss to her lips, gratitude welling within me. She'd saved my life. This tiny, human girl had saved my life.

"Well... You may never speak of it again," a voice drawled, and I jerked my head up and caught the sight of fucking Bjarni Lokisson leaning against a pillar, a smug smile across his face even as his legs were still caught in a ridiculously feathery shapeshifter's costume. By his side his dark-haired brother wore an expression of both boredom and disgust. "But I'm definitely going to tell everyone we meet how much you two just love to milk each other's knots."

ANNABEL

"There she is. How are you feeling, pet?"

The relaxed rumble against my back penetrated the hazy fog of sleep. Both bonds hummed contentedly in my chest, but I knew the speaker was Magni. Only he called me "pet."

"Like a bulldozer ran me over. And then had sex with my flattened corpse," I croaked, wincing as I cracked my eyes open.

A rough hand cupped my cheek. "I'm sorry," Saga murmured. "It was the only way."

"Sure it was," Bjarni's voice rumbled from somewhere off the side, amusement lancing it.

"Shut. Up," Magni snarled.

I rolled over, wincing at my protesting abdominal muscles, and met Saga's soft gray eyes. Worry marked the corners, but his gaze was still light and brimming with happiness.

"It's okay," I whispered, because I knew he spoke the truth. Magni would have died if he didn't. I'd needed Saga's strength and magic inside of me to funnel the golden light into Magni.

"Your strength... I never knew a mere mortal could possess such magic," Magni said from behind me, and despite the respect in his voice, I swallowed down an annoyed sigh. At least he realized I was more than just a walking womb—even if it was obvious the only reason for that was that he'd seen the magic I only barely knew of myself. If I hadn't had it, the respect I heard in his voice now wouldn't have been there. Saga and I had found each other when I found my magic, but it wasn't quite the same. He'd seen my strength, my compassion... and his heart opened because of that, not for some freaky power I possessed.

"So now what?" I asked, instead of giving in to the irritation with my redheaded mate. This, right now? This was so much better than anything I could have hoped for before. There was peace between the three of us, contentedness. Even if it wasn't going to last, I didn't want to be the one to ruin it.

Silence spread, and I felt just a flutter of unease in my chest from both bonds hooked there.

"What?"

"I told your alphas that I believe someone within Asgard is trying to bring about Ragnarök," Freya said, stepping into my field of vision next to the altar-bed.

"What—what do you mean? Like a god?" I asked,

frowning as I struggled to sit up. When I did, I spotted Grim and Bjarni standing by the foot-end. I covered myself with my hands and shot the blond bear of a man a glare for his obvious stare at my breasts.

"Yes. Like a god," she said. "Only someone with a lot of power could interfere with Magni's bracelet and the portal."

"But why would a god end the world?" I asked. "Aren't they—you—the good guys?"

By my side Saga snorted derisively.

"I don't know," Freya said, a frown drawing down her brow. "But whoever they are, they know about your prophecy, and they will try to stop you. You have to be very careful."

"We have to find Mimir," I said. Mostly because it was the only direction still left for us. If even the home of the gods wasn't safe, then there was nowhere else for us to go to search for answers.

"Is he in Asgard?" Grim asked. "He and the Allfather supposedly meet on occasion."

"If he is, he will be in Valhalla," Magni said. "But first, we must go to Trudheim. If there's a traitor in Asgard, my family must be alerted. And Modi will want to meet Annabel as soon as possible."

"Great. Another alpha," I muttered, scrubbing my hand not covering my chest across my face. I remembered the five glowing threads Verdandi had woven around mine, and judging from what'd happened since I stepped foot in Jotunheim so far, Fate wasn't going to let me get out of any of those bonds. But that didn't mean I had to like the prospect of yet another man trying to bend me to his will.

"He will be an honorable mate," Magni said, his tone defensive. "Unlike some of your other choices."

I shot him a glare, some of my warm contentment from our sex fizzing into irritation. "If you remember, I didn't exactly choose any of you. Some Norns on a power trip did. Let's just get this over with, can we?"

The bloom of hurt through the bond I shared with the redheaded alpha surprised me, but he only shot me a dark look before he rolled off the bed, bending for his clothes we'd discarded. "As you wish."

"Godlings, I need a moment alone with your mate," Freya said, seemingly ignoring the suddenly frosty temperature in the hall.

Saga frowned. "Why?"

She chuckled, a pearling sound, and ruffled his mushy hair. An unexpected shot of anger rose in my gut at her touch, but it vanished again when she removed her hand from him. Saga shot me an amused smirk, and I flushed hotly, realizing he'd felt the bolt of jealousy in our bond. And liked it.

"To prepare her for her travels through the kingdom of the gods, alpha. She is mortal—there are things she will want to know. Things overprotective men won't understand. Now, out of my hall, young ones. Shoo!"

I bit back my amusement at the goddess' hand movements that followed the shooing, and even more so when all four big, burly alpha males obeyed her with nothing but a grumpy mutter.

"You've got to teach me how to do that," I said when we were alone in the hall, stretching my sore body and testing the muscles in my abdomen.

"Perhaps one day I will," she said, a smile dancing at the corner of her mouth. "But not before you learn a few things on your own."

"Such as?" I asked, arching an eyebrow at her.

She only smiled gently at me. "If I simply told you, dear child, you wouldn't learn it. You will need to understand much about what you are before you are ready to learn all the secrets of Asgard."

"You mean my magic," I said, biting my lip. "It still feels so... alien."

"Your magic is a great weapon, Annabel, but it's not all you must learn to wield. You are an omega, my blessed child, and yet you fight against your very nature. It is not a weakness to overcome—it is your strength, and you will need to learn to harness it to fulfill your destiny."

I grimaced. "I don't see what good there is about being an omega, or how it'll help me stop Ragnarök. All discovering I'm an omega has done so far is—"

"Is bind two enemies in unity, and heal Thor's son when few others could have saved his life," she interrupted me. "Had you not been an omega, you would not wield the power over your mates that you do. And without them—all five of them, working together—the worlds will end. This prophecy is about you, Annabel, but it is also about them. You must learn that there is power in submission, little one, or we are all doomed."

I frowned, trying to take in what she'd said. Everything in me rebelled at the thought that submitting to five domineering men was any form of power, but... after what had happened when Saga forced me to accept both he and Magni at the same time, it was hard to deny that my magic somehow responded to it.

"Don't be sad, Annabel," Freya said softly, brushing my hair from my face. "If you learn to accept your nature, you will find happiness. And, perhaps, love."

"You have to say that—you're the goddess of love," I muttered.

She laughed. "I am. But I am also the patron of omegas. And I see how you and your blond mate look at each other. You already love him. Perhaps Magni as well—even if you haven't yet acknowledged it, hmm?"

I didn't answer, and she merely chuckled.

"You should get dressed, child. Your alphas grow restless, and you have a job to do."

TRUDHEIM TURNED out to be much different from Folkvangr. Where Freya's house was a tranquil temple set in natural splendor and solitude, Magni's dad's house was... quirky.

It towered up multiple stories, and had a number of

outbuildings surrounding it. Even from a distance we saw what Magni told me were servants scurrying to and fro. Those same servants, once we entered through the gates, stopped to greet Magni and throw long looks at the three Lokissons. I passed pretty much unnoticed between the four giant alphas.

Magni led us to the main house, which despite its towering nature didn't look particularly like something you'd imagine the thundergod himself would live in. It was slightly uneven and had many cute windows. I honestly wouldn't have been too surprised if a wizard on a broomstick burst out the door when Magni opened it, but only a cat scurried past our legs and into the courtyard.

"I'm home!" Magni bellowed into the kitchen, stepping through ahead of us. I followed him in the door and arched my brows at the old-fashioned but very large kitchen. It was warm and inviting, but also empty.

Thudding sounded from upstairs, followed by footsteps on the wooden stairs leading into the kitchen, and then a pretty, young, blonde woman flung herself into Magni's arms, burying her head in his chest. "Magni!"

White hot jealousy spiked like a lance up my spine. I wasn't aware of the warning snarl that ripped from my throat or my bared teeth before the girl pulled her head from my mate and gave me a startled look.

"Trud, I want you to meet—"

"His *mate*," I snapped, fighting back the urge to punch the blond girl in the nose.

Trud stared at me with her mouth open for a second. Then she broke into a huge smile and shoved away from Magni, only to gather me up in an embrace that cracked my back. "Magni's mate! Is it true? Oh, how wonderful!"

"Annabel, this is Trud. My sister," Magni continued, without so much as attempting to hide his wide and infuriatingly smug smile.

"Sister?" I croaked, attempting and failing to free myself from her bone-breakingly tight hug.

"Half-sister," Grim said, the pointed note to his voice suggesting he was having a dig.

"Magni," Trud said, finally releasing me though she kept a hand on my shoulder. "Three Jotunns appear to have followed you home."

"It's a long story," Magni said, placing his hand on my lower back. "A very long story. Is Modi here? I need to speak with him. Urgently."

"He's out back—training," Trud said, frowning. "What is it?"

"Come with me. We don't have time for me to explain it twice," the redhead sighed, clasping me closer to his body. Saga's lip curled up at the overtly display of ownership—and really, I was kind of amazed he'd taken it quietly so far. He pushed Trud out of the way and wrapped his arm around my now free side, glaring at Magni.

"Magni. That Jotunn is pawing at your mate," Trud said, arching an eyebrow at the three of us.

Magni sighed. "As I said: It's a very long story. Now, come on."

He walked us through the house, which didn't ease up on the quirkiness with its wooden arches and cozy nooks and crannies, leading us to a backdoor and out into what I half expected to be a cozy cottage garden. Instead, what greeted us was a large patch of dirt with what appeared to be wooden training dummies and a large, topless man with long red hair pulled back in a ponytail, much like Magni's. He was currently attacking one of the dummies with a sword, his big body moving like a panther's.

"Modi," Trud called. "Magni's home. And he's got a surprise with him. Or four."

Modi stopped a fluid attack on the dummy, twisting around toward us with a wide grin. "Broth… er." His eyes narrowed as he took us in, lingering on the three Lokissons. "I see you brought me fresh meat to practice on. It has been a while since I had a good fight."

Bjarni rolled his shoulders, a vicious grin spreading on his lips as he grabbed for his own weapon, but Saga's hand on his stilled him.

"We're not here to fight, son of Thor," my blond mate said, almost managing to keep his voice neutral, void of the venom I knew simmered just below the surface. "We're here for a… business proposition."

"Really? A business proposition?" I hissed under my breath.

"I found the answer. I found her," Magni said. "I know how to save us all from Ragnarök."

Modi jerked his head from his staring-contest with Bjarni, eyebrows reaching his hairline. "Truly? You truly found a way?" He looked so much like Magni with his red hair and strong jaw, yet the differences between them spoke of the half-blooded relationship they apparently shared. Where Magni's eyes were forest green, Modi's were sky blue, his features every inch as handsome but not as sharply cut. He looked like a clean-cut superhero—exactly what you'd imagine a Norse god to look like except for the red hair and lack of beard.

"I did," Magni said, gently pushing me a step forward. "Do you know of Mimir's prophecy about the woman who can unify the sons of gods in the face of Ragnarök?"

Modi raised an eyebrow, looking me over for the first time. "Tell me you didn't mate a human omega on one of Mimir's crackpot prophecies, brother."

"It's not a crackpot prophecy, Modi. It's real. She's real. She's got magic... strong magic," Magni bristled. "She can save all of us."

"But?" Modi said, his blue eyes flickering from me to Magni. "There's a catch, isn't there?"

"We have to share her. With them." Magni tilted his head to the side, where Saga still had a hold of me.

Modi stared at Magni for two long seconds. Then he burst into a rumbling laughter. "If you think I will ever share a woman, let alone a mate, with the scum of Loki's loins, you must have hit your head."

"You may laugh, brother, but I know you," Magni said through gritted teeth, and in our bond his frustration flared hotly. Frustration—and hurt. "You will do what you have to to save your family. And dad will be safe with my bond to her, but Trud and Sif? Will you let them die because you're too proud to do what must be done?"

These two really understood how to make a girl feel special.

"I'm sorry, Magni. But you show up here with a human woman and three of Loki's sons and spew off some wild plan to stop the inevitable. You must know how crazy this sounds." He shook his head and aimed a finger at Saga. "The last time I saw you, Lokisson, I promised you an ass-kicking if you ever showed your face in Asgard again. And here you are, waltzing into my father's home, asking for what? Mercy?"

A snarl rumbled through Saga's chest, his muscles tensing as if ready for battle, but it was Magni who answered.

"He isn't asking, Modi. I am. Your brother. And not for mercy. I am offering you a chance at survival. *We* are offering it. Please—my blood. Take it."

"Magni—" Modi sighed.

"Modi," Trud interrupted, her voice sharp enough to gain the arguing brothers' attention. "The very fact that he shows up in our father's house dragging along those three should be enough to at least consider he could be right. Can we at least greet our new sister before you deny the very reason for her presence?"

Modi made a flapping gesture with one hand. "Sure. If you want to entertain this lunacy for a bit longer, by all means. Greet our brother's mate—who's also the mate of these three trolls, if I am to understand this plan correctly? Why not ask Mom to prepare a wedding feast while we're at it? Invite all of Asgard to celebrate the scum of the betrayer!"

"Watch who you call troll, lightning boy," Bjarni growled.

"Stop being so dramatic." Trud sighed with an eye roll. She stepped in front on me, blocking my view of the agitated god and offered me a small smile. "Welcome to Trudheim, my sister. May I?" She held out her hands, palms up.

Hesitantly, I put my hands in hers. The gentle buzz I was slowly starting to recognize as the presence of magic enveloped my fingers.

"Don't be startled, I'm just having a little peek," Trud said, closing her eyes. She was silent for a moment, then gasped softly. "Oh, my."

"What?" Modi asked, impatience coloring his voice. "Is she singlehandedly going to stop Ragnarök then?"

"That I can't say." Trud opened her eyes again, studying my face with her brilliant blue eyes. Curiosity sparkled in them. "But she has been touched by Fate, that much is certain. Be wise, brother mine. Don't let hatred cloud your judgment."

Modi huffed, throwing the sword he'd been using to practice on the ground. "Fine. They can stay until Father returns. He will know what to do."

I didn't miss how Grim rolled his mismatched eyes at that statement, nor Saga's derisive snort, but thankfully no one said anything. The situation was already so tense, the air practically sparked against my scalp.

"Come, you must be hungry from your journey. Midgard is so far," Trud said, gesturing toward the door we'd just exited. "Eat and rest while we wait for our parents to return. They will be excited to see my brother's new mate—even if she does come with three Jotunns."

"So long as Thor arrives first," Magni muttered under his breath. When I arched an eyebrow in question, he ignored me, using his hand on my lower back to guide me back into the house

ONE THING I couldn't complain about in Thor's house was the food. Trud had servants bring a vast array of breads, cheeses, fruits, and meats, and every single bite tasted like heaven. I hadn't eaten anything but spit-roasted game for what felt like an eternity, and the novelty had quickly worn off.

I was halfway into a solid food coma by the time the kitchen door swung open.

I jerked upright, my heart slamming into overdrive at the thought of finally getting to see the god of thunder himself, but the person entering was most definitely not him.

It was a tall woman with hair that looked like pure, spun gold, and in her features I recognized much of Trud. Her mother, then. And Modi's, but not Magni's, if I'd understood their family relations correctly.

"Mom," Trud said, getting up from the wooden table we'd eaten around. "We have company. Magni brought home a mate. And... friends."

Sif looked up, her eyes widening slightly as she took in our little group. But surprise soon vanished in the face of anger.

"You bring Jotunn scum into my house?" she hissed, rounding on Magni.

Seemed Modi didn't get his attitude from strangers.

"It's a long story, Sif, but it is with a purpose," Magni said, and despite his calm voice I felt something flicker in our bond. Dread? Or was it... fear? "They are here because they can help me protect this family from Ragnarök."

"Stop Ragnarök?" she asked, voice pitching high with incredulity. "Have you lost your mind, boy? I don't care what harebrained scheme you've cooked up to win Thor's favor this time. I want them out of my house —now!"

"Mother," Modi intervened, glancing at his brother once before he gave her his full attention. "There is more to the story. Trud finds it wise to wait until Father is home to decide what to do with these... house guests."

Sif didn't move her glare from Magni. Her nostrils flared as she stared him down, and it dawned on me that this woman hated my mate.

Instincts to protect flared unexpectedly in my gut, but instead of saying a word she turned around and walked out the door, slamming it after her.

"Well... that was awkward," Saga said happily. "Still not the favorite son around here, huh?"

Magni gave him a dark look, but much to my astonishment, didn't bite his head off. Instead, he kicked the chair he'd been sitting on back under the table and turned silently, heading for the backdoor.

I glanced around the room, hoping someone else would step in, but no one did. Sighing, I turned toward the back door and made a small hand motion toward it. "I'll just...."

No one stopped me when I crossed the room, not even Saga.

I found Magni by the training dummies, Modi's discarded sword in hand. He was chopping angrily at the dummy, more brute force than finesse in his swings.

"Hey," I said, stopping by a nearby fence post. "Wanna talk about it?"

He gave the dummy two more whacks with the

sword before he looked at me over his shoulder. "There's nothing to talk about."

"Your stepmom is kind of a bitch," I said, frowning as he went back to butchering the defenseless block of wood and straw. "I get that it's a lot to hear the whole destined-to-save-the-world-by-gangbang thing. Trust me on that one. But... there was something really personal about the way she snapped at you. Why does she hate you?"

Magni didn't answer, except from rough grunts of exertion as he kept attacking the dummy.

I hesitated for a moment, but the flare of agony in my chest from where his bond was hooked made me step forward until I could wrap my arms around his torso from the back and rest my forehead against his spine. Finally he stilled, but instead of turning around, he simply stood. Sword hanging limply in his hand.

"I don't know why I thought it'd be different this time," he murmured. "You don't know how long I've tried... I crossed to fucking Midgard to save her and her family, claimed a mate, and brought her back, and still, it's the same stupid shit."

"I'm sorry," I murmured, because that was all I could say in response to the hurt throbbing in our bond.

Magni breathed in deeply. "My father was married to Sif when he fucked my mom. I'm a constant reminder of his betrayal. I get it. But this... this is bigger than any petty wounds from the past. Why can't they see that? Even Modi...."

"Because they're not insane," I said, pulling back from our embrace now that he seemed to be calming down again. "You basically just told your brother to get in line, because he's mating this stranger you just dragged home whether he likes it or not, and also, he gets to share her with what's quite clearly not his favorite people in the world."

Magni snorted, finally turning to look at me. There was still darkness in his eyes, but a small smile played on his lips. "You think my delivery needs work?"

"Maybe a little," I said.

Softness touched the corners of his eyes, and he raised his hand to my cheek, but before either of us could speak, a loud bang from inside the house shattered the moment's calm.

More crashing and the unmistakable roar of Bjarni's battle shout followed. Magni was moving before I could, rushing to the commotion. I followed hot on his heels, my heart throbbing with equal parts worry for Saga and adrenaline readying me for what sounded like a violent fight.

But when we entered the kitchen, Magni stopped abruptly, making me smack into his back with a grunt.

"Magni Thorsson," a booming but distinctly feminine voice sounded. "You stand accused of bringing the traitor's sons into Asgard."

I glanced over Magni's arm and blinked several times. The speaker was a leather- and plate-clad female, nearly seven feet tall with magnificently white wings sprouting from her back. Seven other creatures of equal stature stood around the kitchen, six of them paired off with a subdued Lokisson between them. My heart skipped a beat at the sight of Saga in their clutches.

"Accused?" Magni spat. "These men are here as my guests, under my patronage! Release them at once!"

"So you admit it?" what I assumed was the leader said. "Then you will come, and you will face judgment. Submit."

"What?" I squeaked, as she and the only other winged being without a prisoner stepped menacingly toward Magni. "Magni, what's happening?"

"These Valkyries seem to think they are going to pass judgment on me for following the laws," Magni growled, his muscles bunching as he prepared for a fight.

"Brother, please. Don't." It was Trud. Her voice was urgent. "Don't fight them. You'll only scare your omega. Go—we'll follow."

Magni hesitated, glancing from her to me over his shoulder. He was clearly calculating his chances at overcoming them, and as our eyes met, I saw the realization in them. He couldn't guarantee I wouldn't get hurt in the fray.

Grinding his teeth together, he stepped forward, hands held out. "I will come willingly, Valkyrie."

"Magni! No! Where are you taking them?" I lunged

at him, for what purpose I hadn't yet decided, but a large hand on my shoulder held me back. Modi.

"They're taking them to Valhalla to stand trial for Loki's crimes," he said, his voice dark but void of emotion. "My mother must have alerted them to the Lokissons' presence. And Magni's involvement."

"This is bullshit!" I hissed, fighting to get out of his grip. I stared wildly at Saga and Magni and naked panic threatened to take over. "They haven't done anything! Let them go!"

"Their crimes are in their blood," the head Valkyrie said, not even sparing me a contemptuous look as she guided her prisoners toward the door. "By daybreak, they will pay for what Loki did—with the same traitorous blood that flows through their veins."

WEAVING FATE
THE OMEGA PROPHECY II

THE STORY CONTINUES IN *WEAVING FATE*

Ragnarök is here. The end of the world is eating away at

Asgard as well as the human realm until there is nothing left but ice and darkness.

I'm supposed to stop it—it's my literal fate, thanks to a meddling Norn and an MIA prophet. Me, and the five alpha gods destined to claim me as theirs.

Only now, three of my would-be mates are captured, held in Valhalla until I and their brothers present Loki in chains to stand trial for treason. He's the God of Mischief, the Betrayer who sold out gods and humans alike for his own, twisted goals... And if we want a chance to save our loved ones, we will have to out-trick the trickster.

But magic or no, I am just a human. And I am an omega. My two companions are my only hope of defeating Loki, but their rivalry threatens to tear us apart.

They are both fated to claim me. Neither wants to share me with the other.

∼

READ WEAVING FATE

∼

Go to www.nora-ash.com to get your copy of *The Omega Prophecy II*

CONNECT WITH NORA

Want to chat all things alpha? (and ruthlessly sexy book-boyfriends in general?)

~

Join Nora's Reader's Group:

EMAIL:
www.nora-ash.com/newsletter

FACEBOOK:
https://www.facebook.com/groups/Yayromance/

ALSO BY NORA ASH

THE OMEGA PROPHECY

Ragnarök Rising

Weaving Fate

Betraying Destiny

DEMON'S MARK

Branded

Demon's Mark

Prince of Demons*

ALPHA TIES

Alpha

Feral

ANCIENT BLOOD

Origin

Wicked Soul

Debt of Bones*

DARKNESS

Into the Darkness

Hidden in Darkness

Shades of Darkness

Fires in the Darkness

MADE & BROKEN

Dangerous

Monster

Trouble